VENOM
HOUSE

Arthur W. Upfield

VENOM HOUSE

A Scribner Crime Classic

COLLIER BOOKS

MACMILLAN PUBLISHING COMPANY

New York

Collier Books
Macmillan Publishing Company
866 Third Avenue, New York, NY 10022
Collier Macmillan Canada, Inc.

Library of Congress Cataloging-in-Publication Data
Upfield, Arthur William, 1888–1964.
Venom house.
I. Title.
PR9619.3.U6V4   1988   823   88-16191
ISBN 0-02-025901-8

First Collier Books Edition 1988

10 9 8 7 6 5 4 3 2 1

Printed in the United States of America

CONTENTS

VENOM
HOUSE

Chapter One

INTRODUCTION TO DROWNING

LIKE the hotels, Australian trains are not what they ought to be, and Detective-Inspector Napoleon Bonaparte was glad to leave the bone-shaker at the four-pub town called Manton where he was to take the service car to Edison— Edison being a one-pub town on the coast south of Brisbane.

The youth guarding the station exit accepted his ticket with native indifference, and languidly informed him that the service car would be parked outside the Post Office.

The one point in favour of the service car was that it did have four wheels. It must have come from somewhere, and could be expected to go, if only for a yard or two. The driver was tall and lanky and young. He wore an English cloth cap back to front, hung a burnt-out fag to the corner of his mouth, and evidently preferred his shirt tails outside his drill trousers. The single redeeming feature was a pair of grey eyes which actually laughed.

"She's all right," he assured the prospective passenger. "Get you anywhere any time."

"I want to go to Edison."

"Then you gets to Edison when she gets there. You Inspector Bonaparte?"

"I am Inspector Bonaparte."

The grey eyes took in the carefully-groomed passenger: his smart grey suit, light grey felt, brilliantly polished shoes. They also noted the dark complexion, the straight nose, the firm mouth, the eyes which recalled the blue of the sea.

"Well, we're all set," the driver asserted, tossing Bony's suit-case upon the back seat already crowded with parcels, spare tubes and tools. "Hop in the front gallery, Inspector. No other passengers this trip. Old Mawson said to look out for you. Sorta busy, and couldn't come himself."

Bony almost committed Mr. Pickwick's injudicious error of asking the age of the cab horse. The alleged automobile complained when accepting his weight, and it shuddered when the driver started the engine by tickling something under the rusty bonnet and then leaping to the steering-wheel before the effect of the tickling could die in a convulsion. The gate-change gears were slammed into first and the journey begun with flying-saucer acceleration.

"Twenty-one miles to Edison, isn't it?" questioned Bony.

"And a bit," replied the driver. "Could do it in thirty minutes, but the road's crook and we gotta coupler places to call. You gonna go into them drownings at Answerth's Folly?"

"Yes. What is your name?"

"Mike Falla. Me old man's got a farm two miles outa Edison, but I couldn't stick the cows and feedin' pigs. Cars is more in my line."

"You have other cars?"

"One more. Not as good, though. Can't beat the old stagers, y'know. Cars we're getting now falls to bits as soon as you take 'em on the road. They're all spit and polish and no guts."

2

The town road became a track, and abruptly the track dipped to take a narrow bridge spanning a chasm of a gully. The driver changed down to first and braked the contraption with the engine. Beyond the bridge Bony asked:

"Saving your brake linings?"

"Ain't got none. They turned it up beginning of last winter."

"You manage all right without brakes?"

"Yair. Nothing wrong with the ruddy engine to ease her up." The cigarette butt danced a jig across the wide mouth. "Funny about them drownings, isn't it? Beats me. Ed Carlow wasn't exactly a sissy, y'know. Six feet something, and sixteen stone if an ounce. Fight sooner than spit. Don't get it at all. And old Mrs. Answerth was harmless enough, and she had nothing to be killed for. Sorta reminds me of Ginger, them drownings do."

"Ginger!" murmured Bony.

"Yair."

The track was like a snake on the rampage, twisting to avoid the larger trees of the scrub hemming both sides. Being mid-September in Southern Queensland, there were teeth in the air meeting Bony's face. The yellow track, the grey-green tree-trunk and the dark green foliage of massed shrubs were painted with the vivid veneer of spring. The service car fought its way to a rise, gasped at the top and sang with relief when nosing down the opposite slope. Speed increased. Each successive bend was taken by the complaining tyres, and at each bend Bony anticipated disaster.

"One day you will meet an oncoming vehicle," he remarked.

"Yair."

3

The cigarette butt continued its dance. Like a lion springing from its lair, the car spun on to the floor of a wide valley, and followed a rule-straight yellow ribbon edged with wire fences. Beyond the fences flat paddocks were tiled with ploughed chocolate clods. Here and there were small neat farmsteads about which waved fast-growing maize. The time now being favourable to ask the driver for attention, Bony reminded him of Ginger.

"Dog," replied Mike. "Greatest fightin' dog I ever had. Red Irish terrier. Tackle anything from rats to the old man's prize bull. Any stray dogs come around our place, Ginger got going. Usta tremble all over with a sorta joy. Always the same tactics, too. He'd kid the stray down towards the dam, sooling him to fight by pretendin' he was scared. Then down by the dam he'd hop into him, and when the stray had had enough, Ginger would drag him into the water and drown him. Always drowned 'em, he did. D'you know what?"

"Well?"

"The bloke what done our drownings musta seen Ginger doing his stuff, and got the idea off Ginger. Ed Carlow had been in a fight and the bloke held him under Answerth's Folly till he drowned. And old Ma Answerth was held under, too. Same way as Ginger held his strays under."

"There may be something in what you infer," agreed Bony. "Many people know of Ginger's methods?"

"Hundreds. I usta breed kelpies. Good many town dogs would come out to visit, and Ginger would attend to 'em. Then the owners would arrive and start an argument, but not before I'd buried the bodies. The old man's no sap, and I can always pull my weight, but one day Mary Answerth came out looking for her heeler,

4

and it so happens that Ginger was just getting her heeler into the dam. She outs with a shot-gun and shoots Ginger cold, and she called us plenty. We sorta objected, and she slaps the old man down and passed me a coupler jolts what snapped me off at the knees. Nothin' worse, Inspector, than a woman with the wrong sorta punch."

"Mary Answerth . . . she is the daughter of the late Mrs. Answerth?"

"One. T'other is Janet. All lolly stick and lisp. Not bad-lookin', though. There's a son, too, but I've never seen him. A bit wonky, y'know. They keep him chained up. See this gate ahead? You hop out and open her while I circles."

Having acceded to similar requests in the far outback, Bony knew what was expected of him. The driver changed to low gear and braked with the engine, and as they passed a gate in the right-hand fence, the passenger jumped from the vehicle and ran to open it. Meanwhile, the car proceeded past the gateway, circled and so came to it again, to pass through. Then, having slammed the gate shut, the passenger ran after the still moving car and boarded it. The driver's judgment was excellent. So was that of the passenger.

A mile off the main track, they came to a farmhouse where the car was finally stopped by being run mid-way up a steep bank. There it was held by a block of wood thrust behind a rear wheel by a small girl. A woman appeared from the house, and Mike Falla gave her several parcels and a sheaf of mail. She regarded Bony with undisguised curiosity, and the driver said:

"Inspector Bonaparte. Gonna find out all about the drownings."

Silently groaning at the publicity, Bony acknowledged

5

the introduction. The woman raised her brows, and the little girl stared up at him whilst chewing the end of her beribboned pig-tail.

"Terrible, those murders," exclaimed the woman. "We hope you stop them, Inspector. Always knew something awful would come out of Venom House."

"Venom House?" encouraged Bony.

"That's what us locals call the Answerth place. You'll be seeing it, Inspector. And Answerth's Folly what's all round it. Unnatural place, and queer people, the Answerths. And don't you go and say anything about what I said. That Mary Answerth's a real terror, and we don't want her over here abusing us."

"I wouldn't mention it," Bony assured her. "As you say, I shall be calling on the Misses Answerth."

Mike Falla dropped his cigarette butt into the dust and retrieved it as though a treasure. He chuckled dryly, saying they would have to be going, and motioned the passenger to take his seat. He climbed in behind the enormous wheel, and then leaned far out to supervise the little girl who juggled with the chock. Expertly she dragged it free without being run over when the car slid down the bank. There was a violent jerk when the engine crashed into power. Bony waved good-bye to the woman and child, and prepared for his act when the car reached the road gate. They said nothing, prior to the perform-ance, and afterwards, when Bony, winded by exertion, settled again, he asked:

"How long have you had this run?"

"Nine monse. Started the first of January. No one else put in for the contract, so I got it. She pays good, too."

"It should do . . . on the capital outlay."

"Aw! Fair go, Inspector. Bloke gotta start sometime,

6

some'ow. The old man went crook 'cos I left the farm, but he came good when I got the contract. Gimme his car."

"Did it have any brakes?"

"Too right, she did. But a front wheel came off her and she ended up against a tree and caught fire. Had to buy this one, and it put me back, but I'm coming good slow-like. One day I'll have enough dough to buy a bus. Y'see, once the electric power comes to Edison the town's bound to grow. People will want to come to our beach. What with the electric power and a good road, well, I'll be on the up and up and able to run a fleet of buses."

The cigarette which had accompanied the wide mouth all the way from Manton danced again. Bony watched it with interest, and this time he studied Falla's face and found character.

"Edward Carlow," he prompted. "Been long in the district?"

"Yair, born there . . . near Edison. His old man had a farm. Never did no good. When he died, the farm was took off the Carlows. Mrs. Carlow had nothing but what she stood up in, and Ed was sick of working for his old man what usta booze all they made. There's young Alf, too. Him and me went to school same time.

"When old Carlow pegged out, Ed started a butcherin' business in Edison. Got helped, they say, by Miss Janet Answerth. As there wasn't no butcher's shop before, Ed came good. Some say he come good too fast for proper tradin'. Might be something to it. In no time Ed bought a new delivery van. Used it to bring the carcases from the slaughter yard they built out of town. Got more'n a bit flash as time went on. Bought a nice house in Edison and

7

give it to his mother. Me old man said he wasn't surprised when Ed ended up in Answerth's Folly."

Abruptly the track turned away from the valley and snaked upward among the hills. The service car roared along the defile created by the jealous forest, and Mike concentrated on his work. Presently he said:

"Me old man usta tell me: if ever you robs a bank, Mike, be sure to plant the dough and don't spend none of it for five years. People is terrible suspicious these days. If you buys a new shirt, they wonders where you got the money. You keep your eyes on our stock, Mike. A butcher who don't have to pay for a carcase of meat makes a hell of a good profit in his shop."

"Did Edward Carlow ever fall into trouble?" asked Bony.

"Not him. Ed was too wise to slip up on anything."

"And yet he was found drowned in Answerth's Folly."

"That's where he ended up. Still, old Mrs. Answerth wasn't flash. She ended up the same way. Anyhow, it seems that Ed ending up like that was a good thing for his mother and young Alfie. Mrs. Carlow now manages the shop, and Alfie helps her. A farmer close by does the slaughterin' for 'em."

The track became steep, rounding bend after sharp bend, beyond ten yards each bend a blind one. Rounding a bend, they found a horse standing squarely on the track. The animal made to leap into the forest, slipped and sat down. Mike yelled and barely managed to steer his vehicle past the horse's tail. And then when rounding the hundred and first bend they saw standing squarely on the track a giant of a man wearing skin-tight moleskin trousers tucked into short leggings and a blue shirt. Just off the track was his saddled horse.

8

So steep was the rise that the engine was not over-strained to brake the car to a stop. Mike clambered out, and the big man joined him.

"Gud-dee, Henery!" shouted the driver.

"Gud-dee!" responded the giant. "You bring out that cross-cut, Mike?"

"Yair. Roberts said they had them wedges you ordered, so I fetched 'em, too. Meet Inspector Bonaparte, come down from Bris to find who done the drownings."

"Gud-dee, Inspector!" rumbled the giant. "Hope you has more luck than the d-s what come down on the Carlow murder."

"Thanks," Bony returned, now thinking that on arrival at Edison he would surely be given a public reception.

Cross-cut and wedges, parcels of bread and meat, one letter and several newspapers were placed on the road. Mike accepted payment, having to raise the hem of his shirt to thrust it into a hip pocket. There were further 'gud-dees', and the horseman was left standing by his horse and cutting tobacco from a black plug with a knife like a cutlass.

"Bit of a character, Henery Foster," Mike remarked. "Got his camp in the bush a mile and a bit off the track. Terrible good axeman. Cuts fence posts and sleepers for the railway. Does pretty well."

The track began to fall away round the bends until it came to flat country where grew bigger trees and the scrub was thick and verdant.

"A bit further on is where they found Ed Carlow's van," Mike said. "It's where three tracks junction at an old logging stage."

Bony recalled the details of the sketch map attached to the Official Summary of the Carlow Murder Investigation,

9

but to pursue the subject taken up by this nonchalant young man, he asked:

"About a mile from Answerth's Folly, isn't it?"

"Yair. Three mile to Edison. Seventeen and a bit to Manton. Can't get what Ed Carlow was doing with his van at the logging stage. There was nothing on it when old Mawson found it."

"You have been to Answerth's Folly, I suppose?"

"Usta sneak a bit of fishin' in it with the other kids," replied Mike. After a prolonged chuckle, he added: "Had to keep wide of Miss Mary Answerth, though. She wouldn't have no one inside their fences."

"Ever go to the house?"

"No, never. Water all round it. Leastways, water all round the sorta island it's built on. There's a causeway to the island, but the water covers it now. You can wade over the causeway if you know where the holes in it are."

"The Answerth's use a boat, of course?"

"Yair. But they keeps it locked to a tree stump this side, and don't never use it unless specially. They wades over the causeway. Funny lot, them Answerths."

Shortly after giving that information, Mike Falla drove his service car into a large clearing. On the far side was a car and a station wagon. Beside the car stood a man and a woman. Compared with the woman, the man was puny.

Chapter Two

THE MISSES ANSWERTH

THE man was of average height, raw-boned, of sandy colouring. His mouth was large, his nose prominently bridged. The steady eyes were granite-grey. The manner of his walk, as he advanced, and not the clothes he wore, betrayed the policeman. The woman was not noticeably tall, due to her cubic proportions. She was watchful, suspicious, her pose having something of the explosiveness of the rhinoceros and something of the ponderability of the elephant. With her fists punched against the belt about her cord breeches, she epitomised leashed force. Bony's gaze merely flickered about the policeman: it was held by this woman with the brick-red complexion, the light grey eyes, the Roman nose, the great mop of black hair.

"Inspector Bonaparte?" the advancing man queried, and Bony's attention reverted to him. "I'm First Constable Mawson. Hope you understand, sir, not being able to meet you."

Bony acknowledged the salute and nodded. Mike Falla called from his car:

"You coming on to Edison with me, Inspector? Can't wait . . . long."

Mawson accepted Bony's cue and told Mike to go on. He moved stiffly, and the tint of his face wasn't wholly due to wind and sun. Then the woman was confronting Bony, and her greeting reminded him of the horseman who had met the service car.

"Gud-dee, Mister . . ."

"Bonaparte . . . Inspector Bonaparte," Bony returned suavely.

"I'm Mary Answerth," she said, and would have edged Mawson behind her had he not stood his ground. Again the hands were clenched hard to the leather belt. The feet encased by riding boots were planted wide apart and like century-old trees, giving the impression that nothing human could topple her over. "I take it you've come from Brisbane to investigate my mother's death?"

"That is why I am here, Miss Answerth," Bony agreed, still suavely.

"Then I hope you do better than those fools who came down to find Carlow's murderer," she said challengingly. "No one here expects anything from Mawson. As he says himself, he's a policeman, not a detective. I shall expect better from you. These killings must be stopped."

The dark brows were met above the eyes no larger than farthings. The constable intervened:

"Now, Miss Answerth . . ."

"I tell you . . ."

What she intended to add was blanketed by the roar of Mike's engine, and when speech was again possible, Mawson was ready to employ further placation.

"Naturally, sir, Miss Answerth is much upset by last night's tragedy. She insists that Mrs. Answerth be buried tomorrow, and I have explained that the formalities may not be completed to permit that."

"Now, look here, Inspector," the woman snarled, for her large square teeth were bared. "They took the body to Edison early this morning, and Doc Lofty's had it all day. There's no sense in keeping it after the post mortem."

"Please accept my assurance that the delay will not be protracted one minute longer than is necessary," Bony said. "I have yet to examine the known facts governing the lamentable tragedy, receive the post mortem report and confer with the coroner."

"Leave the coroner to me," commanded Mary Answerth. Constable Mawson opened his mouth to speak, but was cut out by Bony's voice, now low and yet metallic. The words were icily distinct.

"I have been assigned to investigate the circumstances surrounding the death of the late Mrs. Answerth. I will leave nothing, or anyone, to you, Miss Answerth. You will be notified by the coroner in due course. The matter is entirely in the hands of the police. I am the police. If you wish to make a statement concerning the death of Mrs. Answerth, Constable Mawson will take it down in writing, when you can sign it."

"I've already told Mawson what I know about that. Now look here . . ."

"Pardon me, Miss Answerth."

The flat stomach sank inward as the vast bust expanded. The woman's square chin jutted like a doorstep and her eyes flashed. She stared into the blue eyes of the slight man she confronted, tried to stare him out, slowly realised that in this she would never succeed. Abruptly she turned away and strode to the station wagon. It rocked when she entered it, and silently the two men watched it being driven swiftly away. Sighing with relief, Constable Mawson said:

"Quite a tartar, sir. Lives too late, in my opinion. Should have lived a couple of hundred years ago when the scum knuckled to their betters."

"The body is at Edison?"

"Yes, sir. I had it conveyed to the morgue at 8.50 this morning. The doctor hadn't completed the post mortem when I left the town at three o'clock this afternoon."

"Then we had better run along and hurry him." A minute later, when they were on the track, Bony said: "What accommodation does the local hotel offer?"

"Not so good, sir. I was thinking that perhaps you'd like to put up with my sister, who sometimes takes paying guests. She's a good cook."

"I'll try her cooking. We must pick up my case from the service car. However, first things first, Mawson. Relate to me the happenings of today."

"At 7.57 this morning I was called to the telephone by Miss Mary Answerth. She said that on her way to give her men their orders for the day she had found the body of her mother floating on the lake we call Answerth's Folly. With one of the men, she had gone in the station boat and retrieved the body. There was no doubt that Mrs. Answerth was dead.

"As Miss Answerth proceeded to give me orders, I cut her short by saying I would leave at once with Dr. Lofty. I had to wait ten minutes for the doctor, but we reached Answerth's Folly at 8.35. While the doctor was examining the body, I got Miss Answerth to tell me about her discovery of it.

"It appears that every work-day morning Miss Answerth leaves the house and wades over the causeway to the men's quarters on the shore end. There's a long story behind how the house came to be surrounded by water, and the rest. Anyway, Miss Answerth was nearly over the causeway when she saw something unusual floating on the Folly, and presently she saw it was her mother's body. It was about twenty yards off-shore and half that distance from the causeway.

"The men were at breakfast when she reached the quarters, and she ordered the cook to fetch the boat and went with him to bring the body to land. She then went back to the house and telephoned me. The cook . . . feller by the name of Blaze . . . substantiated her story in part.

"This being the second drowning in Answerth's Folly, and the first being medically proved to have been homicide, we thought that Mrs. Answerth had been murdered the same way, that is, by being held under the surface and drowned, like Edward Carlow was murdered. On examining the body, Dr. Lofty found a red mark about the neck indicating that the woman had been strangled with a light rope or a cord having distinctly bulging strands. However, he would not be definite about this until he had done the post mortem."

"Was the body clothed?"

"Yes, fully dressed. The air imprisoned by the clothes kept the body floating. When subsequently I visited the house to interview the inmates, I learned that Mrs. Answerth was last seen alive when going up to bed. There was no suggestion of suicide."

"What was the reaction of Mary Answerth when you arrived with the doctor?"

"Nothing out of the ordinary, sir. I didn't expect to find any difference in her front. She was very angry . . . and most times she's angry . . . and demanded that I get going and arrest the murderer. You know, like being annoyed at having a steer lifted. She roared when we insisted on having the body brought to the morgue, but made no bones about bringing the body to the morgue in her station wagon, she herself driving it. At the morgue she bullied Dr. Lofty to get on with his examination so's she could hand the body over to the undertaker, and I'm thinking that Lofty has purposely delayed his report just to get his own back for what she said to him."

"She seems unusually masculine," Bony observed.

"I'll be candid, sir," Mawson said, grimly. "There's no one in this district I'm afraid to handle if he has to be handled. Excepting that he-woman. She's ruddy dynamite. I'm more than glad that Headquarters sent you down here at once."

"I was not sent, Mawson. I chose to come. The case promised interest, in view of the other murder. We'll discuss that tonight. Tomorrow we'll visit the scene and pay our respects to the Misses Answerth. May I hope for your co-operation?"

Mawson made no effort to hide his eagerness.

"Certainly, sir. Only too pleased to give a hand. Inspector Stanley didn't want any co-operation when he came down on the Carlow drowning."

"And failed to finalise it, Mawson," Bony reminded. "I understand you have been stationed here eight years, and therefore would know the district and the people as well as your own quarters and your family. I am familiar with Inspector Stanley's attitude to the uniformed men. He cross-examined you, and you felt he was trying to trap you into making an error. Naturally, you were unable to give of your best. He wanted only the bald facts, I'm sure. In addition to facts, Mawson, I shall want from you opinions, suppositions, ideas. I shall want you to treat me as a colleague, and eventually as a friend. Thus we shall succeed."

16

"Glad to hear it, sir. It's like breathing fresh air to listen to you."

"Good! Take your first breath by omitting the 'sir' when there isn't a third party present. I am Bony to all my friends. Even the Chief Commissioner calls me Bony to my face. Did you ever meet him?"

"Only on Passing-Out Parade."

"Choleric, Mawson. Horrible blood pressure. I am sometimes concerned that he will drop dead before me . . . when damning and blasting me for declining to obey orders at the double. But at heart a kindly man, Mawson. Like myself, Colonel Spendor is unable to suffer fools gladly or otherwise. So this is Edison."

"This is Edison," repeated Mawson. "Situation very healthy. People just like people of other towns, having the same virtues and vices. One pub, two churches, three banks. The bank managers don't associate with the publican, who could buy up the banks, and the publican don't associate with the parsons. Usual women's leagues and such-like. Average number of drunks, till-ticklers, scandal-mongers and snobs."

And yet, Bony found Edison in advance of 'other towns'. When the track became a macadamised road, the policeman's car began to work up a long slope. The road entered the town, and Main Street continued the slope upward. They passed a bank, some shops and the Shire Hall. They stopped beside the service car halted outside a dilapidated tin shed, from which Mike Falla emerged to transfer Bony's case. They proceeded up Main Street, passing the police station on one side and the home of *The Edison News* on the other. Bony caught a glimpse of the butcher's shop, other banks, a church either side the street.

The hotel was of red brick, a modern monstrosity and a travesty in this street of weatherboard and cement sheet and corrugated iron. Then Bony was looking at a neat little villa at the very top end of the street, guarded by two poplars and a white-painted picket fence. He was given a momentary vision of wide spaces in which lay folds of tree-covered hills, long white sand dunes, a wide arc of vivid blue sea. The light abruptly dimmed, and he found himself in a small hall furnished with a hat-stand, two chairs and a telephone on a small table. He heard Constable Mawson say:

"My sister, Mrs. Nash. Inspector Bonaparte, Jean. Like to put up here for a bit."

He bowed to a gaunt, grey-haired woman in her early forties. He was not charmed, for her face was wrecked by recent illness, and her dark eyes were without expression. One second that impression lasted. The next second she was smiling at him. The dark eyes were alive. The lips were parted in a smile of welcome, and swiftly-drawn lines brushed away all the hardness.

He was introduced to a large front bedroom exceptionally well furnished, and then to the lounge, colourful and inviting, which he could consider his own. Having showered and dressed, he was introduced to the dining-room, where he ate a first-class meal with his hostess and her daughter.

When the light was almost gone from the inverted celestial bowl resting upon the world at a lower altitude than the town, he entered the office of the police station to find Constable Mawson at his desk.

"Now, now, Mawson, don't get up. Smoke if you wish. Both of us will probably do a lot of hard smoking before we're through."

"Thank you, sir . . . Bony."

Bony drew a second chair to the side of the constable's desk, and proceeded to manufacture an alleged cigarette.

"The P.M. report come in yet?" he asked.

"Doctor said he'd like to bring it himself. Suggests I ring him when convenient to you."

"Oh! Considerate. Better call him now."

Mawson's hand was beginning to reach for the instrument when its alternating buzzer demanded attention. Mawson lifted the instrument. Bony could hear the distant voice. The policeman looked at him beneath quizzing sandy brows. He spoke with grave politeness.

"Yes, the Inspector is here now. Yes, very well."

The large sandy-haired hand was cupped about the mouth-piece.

"Miss Answerth wants to speak to you," he said. "Miss Janet Answerth."

"Oh! Oh, how d'you do, Inspector Bonaparte. I'm Janet Answerth. I'm so glad you are available. You can spare me a few minutes?"

The voice was soft and the enunciation clear save for a slight lisp. What could have been nervousness in the caller Bony at once unchivalrously attributed to woman's paving the way to the naming of a want. He was right, too.

"Yes, Miss Answerth. What can I do for you?" he purred.

"I've been wondering, Inspector, if we can come in the morning for poor Mother's body. I do hope . . . I hope, indeed . . . that Doctor Lofty didn't think it necessary to mutilate it. Mary, my sister, has been most upset. You will forgive her for being a trifle brusque, won't you?"

"Naturally, Miss Answerth."

19

"You see, Inspector, we often read of these dreadful things in the newspapers, and then when we are ourselves involved in such a tragedy we are horrified that anything of the kind could enter our lives. You will understand, I'm sure. We hate to think of poor Mother lying cut up on a cold slab or something. It's just too grim. You will let us come for her in the morning?"

"Regretfully, Miss Answerth, I am unable to make a decision," Bony told her. "However, I shall be calling on you at nine tomorrow morning, and may be able to advise you."

"Oh!" There was a distinct pause. "You wish to come here?"

"To make a few enquiries. Formality, you understand."

"Yes, of course, Inspector. How silly of me to be shocked by the idea of a visit from a detective-inspector. I will arrange that the boat is ready to bring you. You see, the causeway is dangerous to anyone who doesn't know just where the deep holes are. It's under water. We can easily wade over it, but as the water is often coloured, strangers cannot see it and would step into a deep hole for sure."

"Very well, Miss Answerth. At nine in the morning."

"You really could not decide to let us have the body . . . in the morning?"

"No."

The negative reply was softly but stressfully given, and the voice from the Answerth house betrayed nothing of disappointment when the conversation terminated.

"Your opinion of Janet Answerth?" Bony asked Mawson.

"Very nice little woman," replied the constable.

"Much younger than the other, more civilised. Reminds me somehow of a little moorhen. Quite a good type, I think."

"Are you married?" Bony blandly asked.

"I'm a widower," replied Mawson, openly wondering. "Another sister keeps house for me. Why?"

"I wished to assess the value of your opinion."

Chapter Three

DR. LOFTY'S VIEWS

"Before we contact your Dr. Lofty, tell me about the first murder," requested Bony. "Take your time. Begin with the victim's early background, his history. More often than not, homicide is the climax of a story beginning years prior to the act."

"When I came here eight years ago," Mawson said after thought, "Edward Carlow was nineteen years of age and worked for his father, a farmer. The old man was never much good, and when I'd been here two years his drinking habit reached a climax and he left the family dead broke. Beside Edward, there was his mother and his young brother, Alfred, still at school.

"When the old man dropped out, the owners of the farm decided to find another tenant. The rent hadn't been paid for years. The owners were these Answerths, who were influenced by their local business agent named Harston. Harston, by the way, is our deputy coroner.

"I never got to the real rights of that farm matter, but it seems that Miss Mary was with the business agent all the way, Miss Janet being against throwing the Carlows out and all for giving Edward Carlow the chance to succeed. I'm still not certain, mind you, but it seems that Miss Janet put Edward Carlow into a butcher's shop here in Edison and found a house for the family close by.

"In those days, Edward Carlow was big and dark and handsome. Although he'd worked on the land he wasn't dumb, and it's been said that his mother gave him a better education than he'd have had at the local school. Anyway, Miss Janet took the wheel and started him off in the butchering line. Edison badly needed a good butcher, and Carlow never looked back. Began deliveries with an old truck and within a year was delivering with a smart new van.

"They left the house Miss Janet found for them for a better one Edward Carlow bought. There was new furniture, too, and Alfred was sent to finish his schooling in Brisbane. The business certainly flourished."

Constable Mawson paused to light his pipe and hesitated to proceed. Receiving no comment from Bony, he went on:

"A little more than three years ago, a farmer reported the loss of steers. Then another man reported that the number of his sheep was down by thirty. While I was making enquiries about the sheep, they were found on virgin country, and there's a lot of it in spots. Finding these sheep sort of put a question to the loss of the steers, for they also could have taken to the scrub and remained lost.

"One day I was over towards Manton delivering a summons when I chanced to meet the Forest Ranger. As it was near midday, we boiled the billy and had lunch

22

together, and during the yabber he mentioned that several farmers and one or two sheepmen had asked him about stock which had got away.

"That made me think a bit. You know how it is in a district like this. The local butcher is always suspect when stock goes missing, and more often than not isn't to blame. I began to look at Edward Carlow. By now he was softer than when he'd been on the farm. He was drinking at the pub, and doing a bit of betting.

"So we come to June of this winter. The Forest Ranger reported that he'd found evidence of possums having been trapped. As you know, this year's fur prices have been very high. Also, possums are protected. The Ranger had his eye on a timber cutter named Henry Foster, and we agreed that Henry Foster could be the illegal trapper and that Edward Carlow could be the skin buyer from Foster. Could be, mind you. We had no proof.

"My ideas about Carlow's prosperity were firmed a lot when his empty van was found parked in the scrub near that old logging stage where you met me and Miss Answerth this afternoon. How come that that van was concealed by the scrub when Carlow's body was a mile away in Answerth's Folly?

"Carlow was last seen about five p.m. on August 1st. He was then driving out of town, Mrs. Carlow saying that he was going to Manton, where he was courtin' a woman. She couldn't tell us the name of this woman, and we couldn't locate her. I believe she was truthful about it, that Edward told her a yarn about courting a girl.

"The next day, shortly after eleven in the morning, Carlow's body was discovered by a feller named Blaze, the men's cook out there. It was by the merest chance, too. The cook shot a duck and when wading out to get the bird actually kicked against the submerged body.

"The van wasn't found until the following day when we began examining every off track from the track to Manton. It was well concealed by the scrub, and finding the van was chancy because, during the night Carlow was murdered, it rained heavily and tyre tracks were scarce. That afternoon, Inspector Stanley and Detective Jones arrived from Brisbane and took over."

"You had then questioned the cook and the Answerth stockmen?" Bony probed.

"Blaze, the cook, yes. There were no men in camp the night Carlow was murdered. Excepting the cook, the only man employed at that time was the head stockman. The shearing was over and the sheep put into the spring pastures, and so work was slack. The head stockman was on the booze here in Edison. Feller by the name of Robin Foster."

"Same name as the wood cutter."

"Yes. Henry Foster's brother."

"How did the cook come out of it?"

"Seemed to me he came out square. Only a weed of a man, and elderly into the bargain. Carlow was a big man and could have defended himself easily against a man like Blaze. According to medical evidence. . . ."

"We will leave that to Dr. Lofty," Bony interposed. "Contact him now, and ask him to come and yabber . . . the word being yours." Lofty was telephoned, and Bony then asked:

"Is the man Blaze still cooking for the Answerth men?"

"Yes. Been there a very long time. Used to be head stockman. Turned to cooking when age fastened on to him."

"You examined the van belonging to Edward Carlow?"

"Too right. There were several cut-open sacks in it and a light tarpaulin. Obviously last used to transport meat. Remembering the possum query, I examined the inside of the van pretty thoroughly. Not a single possum hair in it. I did find evidence that coke had been loaded, and subsequently established that Carlow had brought a load of coke from Manton for use at his home."

"Did you mention the Forest Ranger's suspicions concerning the possum-trapping to Inspector Stanley?"

"No . . . o."

"Why not?"

"What we thought about that possum angle was just surmise," replied Mawson before giving the correct reason. "Beside, the Inspector didn't want co-operation."

"Still, had you mentioned the matter, Stanley would have had experts sent down from Headquarters to examine the van with meticulous thoroughness. The possum point is important, and I thank you for drawing my attention to it. Where's the van now?"

"With Mrs. Carlow. She took over the butchering business. Alfred does most of the shop work and uses the van to transport carcases to the shop from the slaughter yard. As I said, they employ a man to slaughter for them. Ed Carlow used to do his own slaughtering."

"The slaughter-man . . . character?"

"Local farmer. Good character. Has an alibi no one could bust."

"What about the timber cutter . . . Foster?"

"Said he was in camp all that night. Couldn't shake him. But . . . His camp is within three miles of the logging stage."

Bony made another of his cigarettes. Years of practice had not brought skill to his fingers, and his fingers

25

remained careless if tenacious in following one pattern. Every cigarette bulged in the middle and dwindled to a point at either end.

"You have given your facts, Mawson," he said presently. "Now give your opinions. First, why was Carlow murdered?"

"Personal opinions, mind. Because he owed money for carcases to a cattle or sheep lifter, or owed money for skins to a possum trapper. He tried to put it over a man who would not stand for it."

"Sound," Bony murmured. "Who murdered Edward Carlow?" Mawson slowly shook his head, saying:

"Wouldn't care to guess."

"We'll find out. Sounds like the doctor arriving. How d'you get along with him?"

"All right. Good man with babies, they say. Co-operative with us. Done a lot to get the local hospital on its feet."

Mawson rose and crossed to open the door. He was there a half-minute before welcoming Dr. Lofty, and when the doctor entered Bony was ready to receive him. Lofty had the physical appearance of a jockey, the eyes of a hypnotist, the voice of seduction. Mawson's introduction of Bony produced momentary shock, followed by keen interest.

"A privilege, Inspector!" he drawled, and produced a foolscap envelope which he dropped upon the desk.

"Good of you to come round," murmured Bony, and they all sat. "Your P.M. report? Thank you. Before we discuss it, I would be obliged did you concentrate on your post mortem on the body of Edward Carlow. I've had small opportunity to study that case as presented by my Department's Official Summary and other data.

The scene at least is common with this last crime."

"As you say, Inspector, the scene is the same in both murders," agreed Lofty. "One was drowned, the other strangled. One had put up a fight for life, the other hadn't been given even that chance."

"We begin, Doctor," Bony said. "You knew Edward Carlow when alive, of course?"

"Yes."

"Was he ever your patient?"

"On several occasions. For minor causes. Accidents. The man was a perfect specimen . . . until he took to drink. At the time of his death the liver was spotted, one kidney was diseased, and he was unhealthily fat. Still, he would have lived for years. My grandfather drank three bottles of whisky every day during the last four years of his life, which ended at a hundred and two. I wanted to look inside him, but the relations wouldn't have it. Most interesting old chap."

"You like post mortem work?"

"Love it."

The little man's black eyes were bright with laughter. He made himself comfortable on the straight-backed kitchen chair and smoked a cheroot with enjoyment.

"Edward Carlow, I understand, was forcibly drowned. Taking into account his diseased kidney and spotted liver, what kind of man, physically, must the murderer be?"

"A man who could take either you or me between his forefinger and thumb and pinch us in two separate parts, and then sit on each part and flatten it to mere parchment."

Bony was not amused by being thus associated with the wispy, skinny little doctor. He said:

"Carlow's body bore evidence of a fierce struggle?"

27

"It surely did. There were patches of ecchymosis all over him. He fought for his life in the shallow water of Answerth's Folly, or he was first struck unconscious and then dragged into the water. Mud and weed from the bottom of the Folly were embedded under the fingernails, and weed and organisms were found in the water taken into the lungs and stomach. There were, of course, all the other appearances of drowning."

"D'you know if he could swim?"

"For years he was the beach guard at our annual aquatic sports," Dr. Lofty said slowly. "There's no possible doubt that Carlow was forcibly held under water until he was dead."

"How long, in your opinion, was the body submerged?"

"Eight to twelve hours."

"Assuming that the body had not been found until it rose to the surface normally, do you think a superficial examination would have disclosed the fact that the dead man had fought desperately before drowning?"

"Are you thinking that the murderer, being unaware of his victim's injuries, calculated that the superficial injuries would not be evident after the body had been submerged for several days? That he hoped the coroner's verdict would be death by misadventure?"

"Yes, along that line, Doctor. It's possible, is it not?"

"Quite."

"Therefore, the murderer knew something of pathology?"

"He could have learned that much from a medical textbook, but more likely from a published report of an inquest. I've read in the newspapers two such reports this last twelve-month. There's no proof, though, that the murderer intended this."

28

"But he drowned the man when he could have killed him with his hands about his throat, or with a stick or a stone."

"If he wasn't himself played out by the struggle and had strength only to hold his victim under water."

"Let us pass to the death of Mrs. Answerth. How old was she?"

"Sixty-nine."

"Therefore, frail?"

"Yes and no, Inspector. Mrs. Answerth had always led a very active life. Up to the time of death, she grew the vegetables in the garden about the house, and attended to the fowls and ducks. She suffered slightly from lumbago, but her heart and lungs were sound. When I last saw her, and that was two years ago, she walked upright and her mind was unimpaired."

"She was not drowned, I think."

"She was strangled with rough cord or light rope. The mark of the ligature was quite plain. She was dead when her body entered the water. I believe death was very rapid, and that death was due to asphyxia rather than to shock. There was but little mucus froth and no water in the lungs.

"The body was fully clothed," the doctor proceeded. "I found more weed adhering to the back of the head than to any other part of it. There was a quantity of weed pressed into the cavity between the neck and the back of the blouse, and there was much weed adhering to the calves of the worsted stockings. All that provides me with a picture. I can see the body being dragged through shallow water by the cord or rope with which the woman was strangled, and then, when the ligature had been removed, pushed out into deep water."

29

"Where, it was thought, it would sink," added Bony. "Assuming that the body had not floated, that it remained submerged till putrefaction brought it to the surface to be found and at once examined by you, what might have been the result?"

"It would be probable that the mark of the ligature had faded into the general slough of the skin, and also the internal appearance would be such as to indicate drowning. Assumption would point strongly to death by drowning, but in view of the Carlow drowning, assumption would not have been accepted."

"H'm!" Bony smiled his thanks. "Do you remember, Doctor, or you, Mawson, whether during the inquest on Carlow anything was said of the specific gravity of the body?"

"Yes," promptly replied Lofty. "Old Harston . . . he's the coroner, you know . . . asked me if it wasn't a fact that the specific gravity of a fat man, like Carlow, was much lighter than that of the body of a lean man."

"He wanted to know if the body was weighted with anything which submerged it," added Mawson.

"And I had to give a lecture on the subject," Lofty continued.

"Mrs. Answerth was not a fat woman, was she?" inquired Bony.

"No, she was tall and gaunt. She had no more fat than I have," answered the doctor.

"And therefore her murderer possibly thought it certain that her body would sink and remain submerged for days." Bony stood. "The body of the next victim disposed of in Answerth's Folly will be efficiently weighted."

Dr. Lofty stubbed the butt of his cheroot and rose from his chair.

"Pleasant prospect," he drawled, and Bony decided that the accent had been cultivated. "You know, Inspector, another asphyxia case will bore me. Arrange that the next one is by bullet or bludgeon. Good night! Anything you want of me, don't hesitate."

Mawson accompanied him to the street gate. Bony studied the doctor's excellent photographs of the cord mark round the dead woman's neck. Voices drifted inward through the open doorway, and he looked up to see a tall, prosperous-looking man precede the constable into the office.

Chapter Four

VENOM HOUSE

MR. HARSTON was imposing and emphatically solid. To observe him was to regret that he wasn't wearing morning clothes, complete with top hat and spats. Instead, he wore a pair of beautifully cut gabardine trousers and a sports jacket of extremely conservative hues. The hazel eyes were alive and friendly. The tint of the grey hair from which rose the bald dome, the crow's-feet and the mouth combined to place his age in the late fifties.

"Sit down, Mr. Harston," Bony said affably. "I understand you are the deputy coroner. Happy to make your acquaintance. I am, of course, looking into the circumstances surrounding the death of Mrs. Answerth."

"So I've been given to understand by Miss Answerth

31

. . . Miss Mary Answerth, Inspector." Mr. Harston carefully arranged the creases of his trousers. "Er, I can assure you that everyone here wishes you success in your investigations. It's very late to call on you, but I was prevailed on to do so by Miss Answerth, who telephoned me half an hour ago with reference to her mother's body. They'd like to have it as soon as it can possibly be released."

"That will depend now on you as coroner," Bony stated. "I have the report of the post mortem conducted by Dr. Lofty, and from it you will agree that an inquest is called for. The report definitely favours homicide. Perhaps you would glance through it."

Mr. Harston accepted the document with a faint: "Ha! Just too bad!" He produced black-rimmed spectacles attached to a thin black ribbon, and took his time to read the report.

"Yes, an inquest is certainly indicated, Inspector. Have you thought of a date convenient to you?"

"Well, no, Mr. Harston. It would, I think, be best to defer the date . . . say for a week or ten days. I arrived only late this afternoon, and haven't yet visited Answerth's Folly. I intend doing so early tomorrow."

"Oh! Yes, very well, Inspector. The body . . ."

"There's no reason why the family cannot take charge of it tomorrow . . . tomorrow afternoon . . . after I have interviewed the members of the family and staff. You could, I think, decide to sign the release at one o'clock. You have known the family for some time, I understand."

"For many years, Inspector. When I came to Edison I was but a youth, and old Jacob Answerth was almost my first client and became my most valued one. He was a strange man, full of inhibitions, and sometimes violent, in order, I think, to triumph temporarily over fear. There's

32

a name for it which I cannot recall. Anyway, he was generous to me, making me a beneficiary under his will, and in his will he commanded his daughters to have me continue as their business agent, general adviser and friend." Mr. Harston chuckled. "They obeyed the command to the extent that I have, since the old man's death, been a sort of Grand Vizier."

"He suicided, did he not?"

"Yes. Shot himself. No apparent reason. Financial position was pleasing and secure."

"I understand there is a son. What of him?"

"By the second wife . . . the late Mrs. Answerth. Mary and Janet are the children of the first wife. Morris Answerth would be about twenty-six or seven. Not quite normal. Harmless, of course, but needs supervision. He doesn't enter the picture so far as I am concerned. I haven't seen him for years. After old Jacob blew out his brains, the younger daughter, Janet, returned home and slipped into authority over the family. A quiet girl, artistic, universally liked. Mary manages the station and the stock and the employees. An Amazon. She offends my sense of what is right in a woman."

"I met her," Bony smilingly admitted.

"Rude, ignorant, violent and almost always objectionable," Mr. Harston proceeded. "Mary Answerth has shouted me down in my own office. She has called me every name used by rough working men. She has openly insulted me in the street. Because now and then I feel that her attitude is less deliberately intended than natural to her, and in view of her forebears, I've put up with it, and eventually found it best to give back as much as she gives. I have to admire her for her business acumen. Peculiarly enough, I get along better with her than with

33

her sister. Yes, old Jacob Answerth didn't leave behind him easy clients."

"May I assume that Miss Mary Answerth is equally objectionable to other people?"

"That is so."

"Would the Answerths, as a family, be likely to have enemies?"

"It's likely that Mary Answerth has a hundred enemies. But Mrs. Answerth, no. Mrs. Answerth was entirely negative. From the time her husband died, she was never seen in Edison but once, and on that occasion she came to town to consult Dr. Lofty."

"Did you know the first wife?"

"Oh, yes! The first wife was a kind of hanger-on to a gang of travelling shearers. If you think of the last woman on earth to snare into marriage a wealthy pastoralist, you will see that woman. Mary is her very flesh and bone and mind. Janet takes after her father, or rather her father would have been more like her had he been more balanced. The second Mrs. Answerth was the daughter of respectable and affluent pastoralists. She wasn't happy with her husband."

"Was she happy with her stepdaughters?"

Mr. Harston blinked. His eyes hardened. Yet he spoke with seeming frankness.

"I cannot honestly say that she was particularly unhappy, Inspector. She was not a normally happy woman. Her only son, Morris, was ever a sore disappointment, and her husband never forgave her for that boy."

"Who now benefits by her demise?"

"No one. Old Jacob left his entire fortune, save for the few bequests, to his daughters in equal shares. He didn't leave a penny to his wife or son, and Mrs. Answerth never took legal action. To murder Mrs. Answerth doesn't add up, does it?"

Bony rose to his feet and the coroner-business-agent followed suit.

"It will, Mr. Harston. We'll talk again, if you will spare me your time. Meanwhile, there's no hurry for the inquest. I dislike adjourned inquests, you know. Much more interesting when the coroner is able to charge a person with murder, don't you think?"

"Yes, I suppose it would be, Inspector. We'll hold the inquest when you are ready."

This time Bony accompanied the caller to the front gate, and there he asked his final question for the night.

"I heard someone refer to the Answerth house as Venom House. Is it widely known by that name?"

"I'm afraid it is. And by no other," replied the business agent. "The Answerths have a wretched history. It's quite a long story. The family began in evil times and evil has clung to it all the way down the years. When you are ready, I can give you the history of it."

"Thank you. Good night, Mr. Harston."

Assuring Bony that he would delay signing the release of the body till one o'clock the next day, the deputy coroner crossed the street to his house and, pensively, Bony returned to the station office.

"Your opinion of Harston?" he asked, and Mawson smiled faintly.

"He thinks he's a cut above the bank managers and the parsons," replied the constable. "He's chairman of the Bench and a stickler for court procedure. Makes quite a good coroner. Very well off, I believe. Owns property and a couple of farms. Has one son an officer in the Navy and another in business down in Melbourne.

Wife's president or secretary of women's organisations."

"H'm! We'll call it a day, Mawson. You could take me to Venom House in the morning . . . be there about nine?"

"Certainly. Should leave at eight-thirty."

"Make it eight o'clock. I shall want to examine the locality where Carlow's van was parked. Good night!"

At half-past eight the following morning, Bony alighted from Mawson's car and surveyed the large natural clearing amid the jumble of hills where the van had been parked in the scrub. Mawson led the way into the scrub on the side opposite the old logging stage and pointed out the place where the van had been found. It was impossible for anyone in the clearing to have seen it, such was the massing of semi-tropical vegetation.

"What exactly did Inspector Stanley do about the van?" Bony asked.

"Had it dusted for finger-prints," replied Mawson. "Steering-wheel gave only Carlow's prints. Examined the sacking and the tarp inside it. Had the vehicle driven over soft ground and photographs taken of the tyre imprints. Tyre tracks gave nothing. It rained somewhat more than two inches that night Carlow was killed."

All this Bony knew from the Official Summary, and copies of the finger-prints and the tyre-prints were in his suitcase. He was confident that had he been assigned to the Carlow murder investigation he would have discovered much more from this page of The Book of the Bush than Stanley and his assistants had done. And that despite the hindering rain.

Mawson took a track little better than a green-grey tunnel, for the early morning mist percolated thickly into the massing scrub and hid the upper portion of the trees rising from it. Emerging from the far end of the tunnel, they came to a wide slope of cleared land ending at the base of an opaque wall surmounted by the faintly blue sky and tinted light gold by the still invisible sun.

As the car was driven down the slope, to the left appeared the dark shape of many buildings. These buildings became identifiable; a wool shed, a small shearing shed, the men's quarters, and other out-houses. Within an open-fronted shed stood the station wagon which Mary Answerth had driven and a smart single-seater coupé.

Mawson stopped the car almost on the edge of the Folly and cut the engine. Immediately there came to them the call of ducks and far-away hooting of swans. The silvered water was like glass, and upon the glass stood, here and there, the grey trunks of long-dead trees.

Somewhere near the men's quarters dogs barked. Along the shallow shore of the Folly came a duck followed by five ducklings. The old lady deviated to avoid the car and, having steered her brood past it, veered again to follow closely the grass-edged shore.

The tinting of gold sank downward to claim the mist to the glassy surface. The air was cool and pleasurably breathed, and it brought the scents of luscious growth, of cattle, of gum-wood burning in a stove. A distant shadow materialised in the mist, became a featureless oblong based on nothing, and both men silently watched as the shadow solidified to a large flat-roofed house. The tips of the taller of the dead trees standing in the Folly were gilded by the sun, and the mist magically thinned to reveal the windows and the great arched porch to the front entrance of the distant house.

"Must be very damp," commented Bony.

"Stands on a sort of island made by a levee all round it," Mawson said. "Once there was no water here at all. A river used to pass the house on the far side, but one of the Answerths interfered with its exit to the sea and despite all their efforts the outlet was permanently blocked. Water couldn't get away and so formed this lake. It's why it's called Answerth's Folly."

"I would say that the artificial island on which the house stands is one-third of a mile from us. What is your guess?"

"Bit more, I think. From here to there is the causeway, covered by about a foot of water."

Colour was brushed upon the house. It was built of grey stone and comprised two storeys. Facing them were six windows on the ground floor and seven on the upper floor. All the windows were of a past era, tall and narrow. The house stood upon a green base.

"What does that house remind you of?" inquired Bony, and Mawson was prompt to make answer.

"Buckingham Palace. Very small edition, of course."

"The green is grass growing on the levee?"

"Must be. I understand that the levee encloses about two acres of land."

"I'd like to own that house. Unusual. Its history will be interesting. Slip up to the men's quarters and ask that cook to come here. Meanwhile, I'll indulge in the wishful spending of a hundred thousand pounds lottery prize."

"I wouldn't even get that far," grumbled Mawson, and departed.

Venom House! Strange name to give a house . . . behind its back. What had Harston said? The Answerths have a wretched history. They began in evil times and evil has clung to them down through the years. Yes. . . .

Voices recalled him to the approach of Mawson and another man, and Bony left the car to survey the station cook. He was about the same size as Dr. Lofty, but his legs were like twin bows bent to speed an arrow to right and left. He wore white moleskin trousers, a white cotton shirt, and slippers. His age? Anything between fifty and ninety. His eyes were dark and screwed to the size of small marbles, and this mannerism, together with the burned and lined face, was a finger-post to his origin . . . the sun-burned plains of the Interior.

"The men's cook, sir," Mawson said, stiffly. "Name is Albert Blaze."

"Come and sit down, Blaze, and talk," Bony invited and himself sat on the running-board of the car.

"Good-dayee, Inspector. I'll sit and yap any time, but I don't know much."

The long tail to the 'day' was further proof that Albert Blaze had been bred somewhere near the heart of the continent. There was music in the way he drawled the greeting.

Chapter Five

SISTERS AT HOME

"How long have you been cooking for the Answerths?" was Bony's first question. The reply wasn't delayed.

"I told Inspector Stanley that."

"Did you? Now tell me."

Bony's expression was bland when regarding the little man seated beside him. Despite his age, Blaze hadn't forgotten how real men sum up each other. Calmly, unhurriedly, he examined Bony's face feature by feature, and so came to discard his first impression for another more accurate. Here was no bashful half-caste, no slinking half-caste, no simple half-caste. Here was a half-caste never to be found in the vicinity of such places as Darwin, where the riff-raff of both races congregate. Here was a half-caste who could have come from the Tablelands, the Diamintina, the Murchison.

"I began working here in '24," Blaze said, easily but coldly.

"Before then you were, of course, riding the stock routes with cattle. How many years were you on the cattle roads?"

"All my life before I came here. If you want to know why I left the cattle country to work on a place no bigger than a cattle station's backyard, I won't be telling you. That happened a long time ago."

"I'm not prying, Blaze. I was wondering if you and I know the same places. I believe we do, and we will swap yarns later, if you care to. At the moment we'll concentrate on the death of Mrs. Answerth. You have been cooking for the men . . . how long?"

"Nine years. I was head stockman before that," answered the ex-cattleman. "Got too old and stiff for the work. I'm near eighty, you know."

"Don't believe it."

"All right . . . bet-cher. No good, though. Can't prove it. But I'm eighty this year accordin' to the bloke what brought me up."

"All right! You win. You were having breakfast when

Miss Mary Answerth called you all to rescue the body of Mrs. Answerth, were you not?"

"The men were at breakfast. I never eat none. I was in the kitchen when she came in with the news, and I went with the others down to this causeway. She sung out to us to take the boat. Boat's always locked up, and I keep the key."

"Why is that?"

"Been locked up since young Morris Answerth got out one night and went for a row on the Folly. Anyone wanting to leave the house, or go over to it, has to wade, and if they falls in a hole they has to swim. And if they can't swim they has to drown. Only time boat's used is to take over rations, tow over wood, and carry Miss Janet, who won't always wade. I got orders to take you and Mr. Mawson over, if he wants to go with you."

"How often did Mrs. Answerth leave the house?"

"Oh, pretty seldom. She'd always wade, night or day. She wasn't over this side the night she was murdered, if that's what you're after."

"How d'you know?" flashed Bony.

"No one seen her, anyway."

"That night two men were employed here in addition to yourself. Are they as sure, as you seem to be, that Mrs. Answerth was not here that night she was drowned?"

"Sounded as though they were. You ask 'em. Robin Foster, he's head stockman now, is up at the pub on a bender. Young Tolly had to ride out, but he'll be home come lunch time."

"When did Foster leave to go on a bender?"

"Yesterdee mornin'. Went to town with Miss Mary drivin' the body, and stopped in town. Wave a feather dipped in whisky across his nose, and Foster would leave

41

a job for the nearest pub if he was a thousand miles away."

"Oh, that kind of man."

"That kind of man. You would know 'em."

"Of course. When Edward Carlow was drowned, Robin Foster was on a bender in town, wasn't he?"

"Yes. Seems to know when to go."

"There was no one with you in camp?"

"No. I was cooking for myself."

"And you had a fancy for roast duck?"

"Teal. Just a couple. I don't eat overmuch."

"And you shot a couple. Where . . . from here?"

Blaze stood, and Bony stood with him. The cook pointed a steady finger.

"See that tree what looks like Billy Hughes in a temper," he asked, indicating a dead trunk having two threateningly poised arms. It was a hundred yards off-shore and about half a mile distant. "Well, I shot me teal about opposite that tree, and I had to wade for 'em. I'd picked up one, and was going after the other, when I kicked against something soft and giving-like. I stirs it around with me foot, and up comes Ed Carlow."

"How deep was the water at that place?"

"To me waist. It's pretty shallow out from there. Course, I was a bit surprised. Ed Carlow hadn't no right being there. He wasn't workin' on the place. I said to him: 'What in 'ell's the game, Ed?' He looked crook, too. Anyway, I wades after me second duck, and then I comes back and tows Ed ashore, the yabbies dropping off him all the time. What with the excitement of reporting him to Miss Janet, who had to telephone to Mr. Mawson, I forgot to put me teal into the safe and the dratted flies ruined 'em. Couple of plump birds they was, too."

"Pity, about the birds," agreed Bony. "Take us over to the house now, please."

"All right." The cook stared at Bony with a hint of anger in his screwed-in eyes. "Well, ain't you goin' to ask if I had it in for Ed Carlow, and that it's funny I happened to kick him up from the bottom?"

"No. Why?"

"'Cos Inspector Stanley did. You're a policeman, too."

Bony smiled, and said softly:

"Ah! But you see, Blaze, you and I know the same places, and therefore, I am not so dull."

Mawson thought that all this back-chat was a waste of time. He was unaware of Bony's purpose decided upon when he and the cook were coming from the kitchen. Blaze walked to the boat tethered to a stump, walked to it mincingly, despite his years and the slippers on his feet. When he was pulling at the oars, Mawson asked if there were as many ducks as in other years, and Blaze said there were not.

They were midway to the house, when the front door was opened and Mary Answerth came out to stand on the levee, and watch their progress.

"Gud-dee!" she said to Mawson, who was first to leave the boat. "Gud-dee!" she said to Bony when his turn came. "Bert, you camp in the boat until Inspector Bonaparte wants to go back." And without further speech she led the way to the house.

The distance from the levee to the house front was something like fifty yards. Greensward stretched away upon either side, swung away round the flanks of the building. Six ewes were as lawn mowers always in action. The house porch was arched and deeply inset, there being one broad step to reach the studded door. Either side the porch was a tall side-light of frosted glass, and above the porch was a stained-glass window reaching almost to the wide cornice. To the right were three upper-storey windows, and movement at the second attracted Bony's attention.

The second and third windows were guarded by steel lattice in a diamond pattern, and from one of the openings a hand was thrust and appeared to be beckoning. The house front being in the morning shadow, Bony paused to watch the hand, and then made out the line to which a weight was attached. On the porch, Mary Answerth turned about and, seeing what interested him, said impatiently:

"My brother. Spends most of his time dropping things out of his window and getting them up with a magnet. Does nobody any harm."

Saying nothing, Bony walked to the descending magnet. It was within a foot of the ground when he reached the line. Gently he tugged at the line, waited, and the magnet proceeded to descend. On reaching the ground, the 'fisherman' jogged it about and almost at once the bait caught a metal pencil case and a screw. There were other metal articles, and Bony manœuvred the bait to catch additional 'fish', when he stood away and watched the catch being drawn up. He was smiling on rejoining Mawson and Mary Answerth.

Mawson looked his interest, the woman scowled. She entered the house, followed by the men, who found themselves in a spacious hall. The furniture was unimportant, for the staircase mounting to the upper floor was another kind of magnet. Bony had never seen anything comparable. It rose like the stem of a flower to bloom at the gallery serving both wings. The banisters

44

and the treads, where uncovered by the once royal-blue carpet, were the colour of honey, the hue undoubtedly warmed by the stained-glass window above the door. Bony thought of the coach placed at Cinderella's service, and he was conscious of effort to revert his gaze to the walls of this vast hall, to note the rich panelling, aged and aloof.

Mary Answerth was crossing the hall to a rear passage, and he could not delay following her. He hoped that his shoes were clean when stepping off the strip of royal-blue to uncovered parquet.

Then he was at the back of the hall, with the distracting staircase behind him. The passage ahead was dim and seemingly filled by the huge woman. Her boots and his shoes ought to have sounded upon the bare floor, but the featureless dark walls and bare ceiling swallowed all sound. He became conscious of cold, the cold of frost on grass rather than the dank cold of the freezing chamber.

Their guide turned left, and he saw the entrance to a large and heavily raftered kitchen. The metallic eyes of polished kitchenware stared soullessly at him. Friendly warmth touched him as he, too, turned left into another passage. He passed opened doors, noticed the sunlight pouring through tall windows into rooms reminding him of the illustrations of the *Pickwick Papers*.

A moment later, he stepped into a different house.

The room was long and lighted by a single huge pane of glass framed with velvet curtains of dove-grey. The walls were of primrose-yellow, the ceiling of palest aqua. The furniture was of modern design in silver ash and silk brocade. Hand-woven blue-grey rugs graced the polished flooring.

Turning from the window, a woman came forward to

45

meet them. She was of medium height and slight of figure.

"Inspector Bonaparte! And Constable Mawson!" she said, with the merest trace of a lisp. "I am Janet Answerth. Please sit down."

Bony honoured her with his inimitable bow, and no cavalier ever bettered it. Janet Answerth's grey-green eyes widened, brightened. He said:

"I regret the circumstances compelling me to force myself into your presence, Miss Answerth. It's generous of you to receive us so early."

"Oh, we quite understand, Inspector Bonaparte. Do we not, Mary?"

"Damned if I do," growled her sister. "We could have answered questions in the kitchen . . . or at the police station."

"Oh, dear!" murmured Janet, seating herself. Mary wedged herself into a long-armed, low-backed chair, and thrust forward her leather-encased legs. Bony sat with Mawson on a divan, and glanced at a smoker's stand.

"If you care to smoke, Inspector . . ." Janet said, and nodded her sanction.

"Thank you. I'll not keep you longer than necessary. By the way, I think it probable that the coroner will comply with your request made last night. He hopes to reach a decision by midday."

"We're most grateful, Inspector," Janet cried. "It's all been such a nightmare."

This was a rare occasion on which Bony felt he could not roll a smoke. Producing his case of 'real' cigarettes, he crossed to offer it to Janet. He was conscious of Mary Answerth leaving the room, and he had but just regained his seat when she re-entered carrying a china

46

spittoon. This she placed on the floor, and proceeded to thrust herself down into her chair, and then began cutting chips from a tobacco plug, an old pipe dangling from between her large and square teeth.

"I want to know something of the last hours of your mother's life," said Bony, hoping that if Mary Answerth spat her aim would be straight. "The circumstances call for patient enquiry. You know, of course, that Mrs. Answerth did not die by drowning."

"I knew it, but Janet wouldn't believe me," muttered Mary, the pipe still between her teeth. "When I saw the mark round her neck, I knew she'd been throttled."

"How horrible, Inspector," Janet whispered as though remarking on the picture of a traffic accident. "What reason . . . who . . ."

"We must try to uncover the motive," Bony smoothly cut in. "Miss Janet Answerth . . . tell me when did you last see Mrs. Answerth alive?"

"Oh! I think I told Mr. Mawson about that. It was yesterday morning. No, it wasn't. It was the afternoon of the day before yesterday. In the kitchen. I had reason to go to the kitchen to instruct Mrs. Leeper. She's our housekeeper-cook, you know. Mother was there. Doing something. I don't remember what."

"You did not see Mrs. Answerth afterwards . . . at any time during the remainder of the day or evening?"

"No, Inspector."

"You're a liar," interposed Mary, and having lit her pipe she tossed the spent match into the spittoon.

Her sister flushed and grimaced with disgust.

"You always were a liar, Janet," proceeded Mary. "A natural born liar. You were talking to Mother just after dinner that evening. In the hall. You had just come down

47

with Morris's dinner-tray, and I heard you tell Mother she wasn't to visit him as he was poorly."

"Mary, how can you!" flamed Janet.

"When you last saw Mrs. Answerth, she was not upset, or different in her manner?" interposed Bony, regarding the younger sister.

"I don't know. I didn't speak to her. I saw nothing about her that was different to what she usually was. She'd been ailing for years, you know. Sometimes she was very depressed about poor Morris. He is . . . well, he's always been childish."

"Your mother . . . she was able to get about without aid of any kind?"

"Oh, yes. She liked digging the garden and looking after the hens."

Bony turned to Mary.

"When did you last see Mrs. Answerth alive?"

"Round about ten o'clock that night. When she was going to bed."

"She seemed her normal self?"

"No different."

"Really, Mary, you mustn't tell the Inspector such fibs," cooed Janet, and stubbing out her cigarette, she crossed her slim legs and leaned back with her hands clasped behind her small head. The grey-green eyes were smoky. The sunlight gleamed upon her red-gold hair. The expression on her triangular face was of triumph. "At eleven o'clock that night, I heard you and Mother arguing below my bedroom window. I heard you ask Mother what the hell she was doing out of doors at that time of night. I saw you both come inside and I heard the front door close. So I wasn't dreaming."

Mary spat, and Bony was relieved that her aim was

true. Holding the mouthpiece of the old pipe away from her face, she permitted a sneer to grow.

"You're always dreaming this and that," she said. "If you weren't always dreaming and mooning about Morris, you'd have let his mother go up and see him that night. You haven't let her see him for weeks. You wouldn't let me see him, either, if you knew how to stop me."

"Really, Mary, you are vulgar and mean," Janet said quickly.

"Vulgar, eh? You're telling me. I'll be bloody vulgar if you insinuate I murdered Mother. I told her to come into the house. She'd been standing under Morris's window to call good night to him, because you'd refused to let her go to his room to say good night. I sent her up to bed, and I followed her upstairs and heard her shut her door before I closed mine."

Janet Answerth began to cry. To Mary, Bony said:

"How was your mother dressed . . . when you brought her into the house?"

"Same as when I found her dead in the water next morning."

"How d'you know that, Mary?" sobbed Janet. "There's never any light in the hall."

"I'm not saying there was a light in the hall," snapped Mary. "I'm not blind, and the stars were out. Mother was wearing her usual day clothes, and she was dressed in them same clothes when I found her. And you keep your gob shut when the Inspector is asking me questions. If you don't, I'll slap it shut that hard you won't open it again for a month."

With astonishing alacrity, Mary Answerth left her chair and advanced towards her sister. Janet's sobs were cut. She stood. The sunlight falling upon her red-gold hair

49

appeared to create a scarlet dye seeping downwards to stain her face. Her eyes were abruptly large, and bright green. Her nostrils were thin and white. She was about to speak . . . and Mawson was between them.

"Now, now," he soothed. "No fireworks, please. Sit down and just answer the Inspector's questions."

Bony helped himself to one of his own 'tailor-mades' and touched its tip with a match. Above the lighted match, he regarded the tableau, his face calm although inwardly he was delighted. The tension waned, and Bony spoke:

"I would like to visit Morris Answerth."

Mawson was too late to hinder them. They slipped by him to confront Bony, anger replaced by dismay, and in unison exclaimed:

"You can't see Morris!"

Chapter Six

THE FISHERMAN

OLD MAN MEMORY produced from his card index a picture for Bony, and whilst regarding these two women so did he gaze on the picture of a small Australian terrier standing beside a bulldog. Janet stood before him in an attitude of entreaty: Mary stood with lordly and contemptuous indifference.

"Morris isn't normal," Janet Answerth said. "He's never been out of his room for years."

"Which is why I will go to him and not order Constable Mawson to bring him down here."

"But, Inspector . . ." Mary began.

"His room?" interrupted Bony.

"I will take you," Janet said, sadly resigned, and walked to the door.

On leaving this modern architectural creation for the original building, Bony felt as though he passed, in two steps, from summer to winter. He caught a glimpse of a large woman in white within the kitchen, and then the darkness of the passage was like smoke until they entered the hall. Treading the royal-blue carpet, he resisted the impulse to touch the gleaming honey-hued balustrades, and, on arriving at the gallery at the head of the staircase, was shocked to observe that the carpet running both ways from it was threadbare and colourless. Still following Janet Answerth, his gaze clung to that hall of extra-ordinary beauty.

And then he was walking along another dark passage till Janet stopped before a confronting door at the angle. From a wall hook she took down a key, with which she unlocked a padlock securing a stout door-bolt. As she drew back the bolt, Bony placed a hand on her arm.

"I will go in alone, Miss Answerth."

"Oh, no! You must not. Morris mightn't be friendly towards you."

"Constable Mawson will come at my call. Miss Answerth will not enter with me, Mawson."

"Very well, sir."

Bony opened the door, entered, closed the door and paused with his back to it.

No one was within the room. It was spacious . . . long and narrow. It was lighted by two windows in the front

51

wall of the house and one at the end wall. All were guarded by steel lattice fixed to the outside. In the centre stood a large magohany table on which was a mechanical train set, a Ferris wheel, a contraption of some kind, and a litter of what small boys call their junk. There was a magnificent stone fireplace and on the wide mantel one object only, a tall cloisonné vase. Two common kitchen chairs, a dilapidated leather arm-chair, a throne chair of cedarwood, a large glass-fronted bookcase having two panes broken, and a faded chintz-covered couch completed the furniture. The floor was covered with modern but worn linoleum. The walls were black-panelled to the smoky ceiling.

The room was tidy and the air clean. It was almost a pleasant room. The application of furniture oil and wax would have made it bright and wholesome. Following the first swift survey, Bony's gaze returned to the throne chair. Once it had been painted or varnished black. Now the seat was worn to natural tan, and the tops of the massive and carved side posts were equally worn. The oddity was interesting, but Bony hadn't the time to cogitate upon it, for through a doorway opposite the fireplace there appeared a boy.

He was cleanly dressed in the uniform of Eton. The dark-grey trousers needed pressing. The short Eton jacket needed to be brushed, but the wide Eton collar was spotless, as were the white shirt-cuffs. He came forward with measured tread, to look down upon his visitor with eyes, either blue or grey, expressive of astonishment. His hair and trimmed beard were the colour of Janet's hair the hair being combed low on the left side and smelling strongly of the oil making it gleam. His voice was soft and well accented.

"I saw you . . . coming in the little boat. Does Janet know you are here?"

"Yes. You are Morris Answerth, aren't you?"

The man in the schoolboy's clothes gravely nodded, saying:

"I think I oughtn't to speak to you. Janet mightn't like it."

"But I have her permission." Bony failed to read the effect of this statement. The face was pale like all faces of the imprisoned, but the physical wellbeing was undoubted. With a slight shock, Bony realised that his training in the art of defence, plus his natural ability to counter violence, might serve him little should this man go into action. He said: "Surely you do not mind me coming up to talk with you?"

"Talk with me?" came the puzzled voice.

"Yes. About your train. About your magnet. About you. About anything you would like to talk about."

Morris Answerth smiled, slowly, shyly, and it was the most pathetic smile Bony had ever seen on a grown man's face.

"My magnet!" he exclaimed. "I fish with that, you know. Did you see me catching fish?"

Bony chuckled with creditable realism.

"Yes. You did splendidly."

"Do you like my room?" The voice was eager.

"Very much. Will you show me your things . . . your fishing-line and magnet?"

The eagerness seeped away. The eyes were troubled. Then uneasiness was banished by cunning, and the scrawny red beard heightened the effect. A large hand gripped Bony's arm below the elbow, and Bony determinedly refrained from wincing.

"You would tell Janet."

53

"I would not," asserted Bony, indignantly.

"Yes, you would."

"No fear, I wouldn't," came the ungrammatical assurance. "I never tell Janet anything. Doesn't do, you know, to tell her anything."

The cunning vanished. The smile returned. The painful grip was removed. Morris said:

"Janet would scold me if you told her things. She makes me cry when she scolds. She's very nice, but when she scolds she has a dreadful look on her face. She never beats me like Mary did once. Mary is very strong. Stronger than I am. At least she thinks she is. But she doesn't know. Three times a day I do my exercises. Would you like to see me at my exercises?"

"Of course. You are training to become very strong?"

"Stronger than Mary. You won't tell Janet I told you, will you?"

"Certainly not. Haven't I said so?"

"That's right. Mother made me promise not to tell about the exercises. The idea is that I become much stronger than Mary, and then when Mary wants to beat me again, I am to resist."

"Think you will be able to?" asked Bony. "Your sister is very, very strong."

"I know. But some day I'll be stronger than she is, and then I'll snap her neck like a carrot."

"You don't like Mary, I can tell."

"Oh, I don't think I dislike her," protested Morris. "It's Janet who hates Mary. Janet doesn't know about my exercises. You mustn't ever tell her. If you do she will scold me and have that look on her face. Mary is very kind. She gave me the train set and the magnet to play with. But it's fun training to be strong."

"How old are you, Mr. Answerth?"

"Mister! Oh, I say! I'm not old enough for Mister, you know. Let me think. My forgetary *is* bad. Janet says it is, and she's always right. Oh yes . . . I'm just fourteen. Janet says I am, and she must know. Mary says so, too. Who's outside the door?"

"Friend of mine. Just waiting for me."

"Oh! Then it won't matter if he hears me doing the exercises." Morris smiled delightedly and laughed with studied restraint. "If your friend stays quiet, I can hear if Janet or Mary comes up. They don't know I can hear them. I've never told them, but I can hear them in time to stop them finding me out doing something wrong."

"How was it you didn't hear me, and my friend, coming up?"

"Oh! That was because I happened to be in the bathroom. Shall I do the exercises now?"

"I would certainly like to watch."

With the conceit of a boy much younger than fourteen, Morris Answerth removed the absurd collar and the well-fitting Eton jacket, and rolled up his shirt-sleeves, revealing the arms of a wrestler. When slowly he opened his arms and angled them, the biceps rose to small mountains, and the forearms became great ropes. Turning away, he performed cart-wheels round the centre table. From the far end of the room, he ran to leap cleanly over the table. He placed one of the kitchen chairs on the table and cleared that. Crawling under the table, there on his knees he made his head and hands the three points of a triangle, and slowly straightened his legs till he stood with the massive table balanced on him. As slowly, he sank again to his knees, grounded the table and crawled from

55

under, not a crane upset, the toy train still upon its rails.

Smiling proudly at his audience, he turned to the fire-place and took up the heavy poker. This he bent to a U, with no muscular strain evinced on his face. He chuckled as he straightened the poker. Replacing it, he walked on his hands to Bony and retreated to the nearer window. Standing, he proceeded to bend forward to touch the floor with finger-tips keeping his legs straight. He kept this going for five minutes, and might have continued indefinitely with the next exercise had not Bony motioned him to stop.

How many hours a day, and for how many years, had this boy-man thus whiled away in this room from which he had escaped but once? Coming to stand before Bony, he asked, hopefully:

"Well? What do you think?"

"Remarkable," replied Bony.

"One day I shall be stronger than Mary."

"And you will snap her neck like a carrot?"

"If Janet tells me to. She won't, of course. She doesn't mean me to. She was only joking. She said so."

"Of course. Have you been here long?" asked Bony.

"Yes. I've always been here. Excepting once. It was glorious."

"Tell me about it."

"You would really like me to? Then I will. One night, Janet forgot to bolt the door, and I crept down-stairs and went out. It was dark, but the stars were bright, and I could see. I went to the water, and I boarded the boat and pushed it about with an oar. Then I didn't want to do any pushing, so I sat and watched the water and the stars lying down in it. After a long time I pushed to land, and I walked in the grass and found a little lamb. I had a little nurse of the lamb, and then I found another one and a lot of mother sheep.

"It was growing light then, and I ran about on my hands and knees and baa-ed like the little lambs, and the lambs came running to me, so I nursed them again. They liked it, too. It was good fun. Then I saw Mary coming, and she was vexed with me, and she brought me home and then she beat me until I went to sleep. When I woke up, I was very sore, and Janet was here. She was crying and she said I had been a very wicked boy, and that I must never do that again."

"And you never did?" Bony asked, softly.

Solemnly, Morris Answerth shook his head.

"No. I never dared. And Janet didn't leave the door unbolted. If she had done, I might have dared, you know. It was such fun playing with those little lambs." The wistful smile vanished. The cunning returned, and the mouth was twisted into a leer. "Some day I'll be stronger than Mary, and then I'll go over the water again and play with the lambs. And if Mary tries to beat me, I'll snap her neck like a carrot."

"How do you know carrots snap?"

"Oh, Mother told me. Mother cried when Mary beat me. It was Mother who told me to do the exercises. She showed me how to. Mother told me that if I kept on with the exercises I'd grow so strong that if I wanted to go over the water and play with the little lambs Mary would not be able to stop me."

"Does Janet know your mother told you to do the exercises?"

"Oh, no, and you mustn't tell Janet."

"But Janet knows you are strong and becoming stronger?"

57

"Yes, she knows that. She watches me take my bath twice a week. She can't trust me to wash my neck properly."

"Your mother, of course, comes to see you every day?"

"She used to come, and then one day Janet told her she was a bad influence over me, and after that she came only now and then, and Janet always came with her." Morris chuckled, and the leer returned. "But Mother thought of a way to talk to me. She'd come and lie down outside the door, and I'd lie down inside and we'd talk in whispers under the door. Mother hates Mary and Janet, and they hate her. And Janet hates Mary. All of them tell me so, but I never tell what they tell me. You won't, will you?"

"Of course, I won't. By the way, where did you obtain the fishing-line?"

"Oh! Oh, I don't know. It just came here with some pieces of string Janet brought when I wanted to mend something. I have great fun with it when I don't use it for a fishing-line. I got it from the books Mary brought me to read. I can read and do sums. Mother showed me how to read and do sums, you know."

"Good!" encouraged Bony. "Tell me about the fun you have."

"You would really like to see?" Again the pathetic smile. "I'll find the books and show you."

Morris Answerth crossed to the bookcase, Bony following. There were piles of children's adventure stories and comics, and Morris chose one pile dealing with the adventures of 'Clarry, the Cowboy of Bar-O-One'.

"Clarry never misses with his lasso," he explained, flicking open a number to find a picture of the redoubtable Clarry. "When he draws his six-gun, you know, he always shoots the villain. They won't let me have a six-gun, but I made a lasso, and I'm as good as Clarry. Like to see me?"

"You won't lasso me, will you?" Bony protested, and Morris laughingly promised to refrain.

From an old sandalwood chest Morris Answerth brought forth a long length of electric wiring flex, one end of which was attached to his large magnet. Removing the magnet, he shook the flex loosely over the floor revealing that the other end had been bound into a small loop. Running the now free end through the loop Morris had his lasso.

Standing away from the mantel, he lassoed the cloisonné vase, and, the woodwork about the vase being discoloured, Bony approached to observe that it was actually caused by the incessant blows of the lasso.

The tops of the side posts of the throne chair had also lost their veneer and the carved wood worn was worn by the continuous thrashing they had been given by the lasso before the thrower had become proficient.

With extraordinary and apparent carelessness, Morris lassoed the chair from every angle, including backward over his head.

There was a plaster bust of George Washington on top of the bookcase. This he lassoed about the neck and flicked it towards him, catching it that it might not smash on the floor. He set his train in motion on its circular track and lassoed the engine. Did it twice to prove the first cast was not a fluke. And as he worked, his face was lit by enthusiasm as though he were, indeed, the great Clarry himself.

Bony applauded, one hand behind him grasping the door handle. Morris Answerth recoiled his lasso and came forward. Now he was smiling.

"You try," he urged.

Softly laughing, Bony told him he would have to go.

"Another time I'd like to very much," he said. "You will have to teach me. Now I must be going, but I'll come again. Would you like me to?"

"Oh, indeed, I would. I'm sorry you have to go. What is your name?" Bony told him, and he smiled happily. "Well, good-bye, Bony. You won't forget to come and see me again, will you?"

"No, I will not forget, Morris."

The man-boy held out his hand, and Bony accepted it. He expected a crippling grip: he was given a gentle pressure. Morris stepped back. They both smiled. Bony opened the door and backed out . . . slowly . . . still smiling at the smiling Morris Answerth, who stood leaning against the great table, with the coiled lasso of flex dangling from one great hand.

Chapter Seven

KEEPER OF THE RAT HOUSE

JANET ANSWERTH was waiting for him in the hall, and the golden light from the stained-glass window added to the lustre of her hair and tinted her face with gold dust.

"Morris was all right, Inspector? Not violent?"

"Your brother was rational, Miss Answerth," he assured her.

"I'm so glad. What did he say? Did he say anything about poor Mother?"

"He interested me with his train, and his fishing-line with a magnetic hook."

"Oh, that! He amuses himself for hours dropping things from his window and drawing them up again." Her gaze was centred steadily at his eyes, and she went on: "He didn't talk about me, or Mary? You see, he's very troublesome at times. Nothing we do for him pleases him, when he has a bad turn."

"You haven't told him about Mrs. Answerth?"

"No, Inspector. We thought it best not to, not for a little while."

"How long has he been like that?"

"Oh, for years. We first noticed he was peculiar when he was very young, and then as he grew older he suffered from periods of depression which always ended with an outburst of frightful temper. We have had to be very firm with him."

"He was examined by a doctor?"

"Of course! Old Doctor Mundy used to see him, and finally said he would never really grow up."

"I'm sorry. Is Doctor Mundy still living in Edison?"

Janet shook her head, saying that Dr. Mundy had died shortly after her father's death.

"Who attends your brother?"

"We all do . . . that is, Mary and I, and his poor mother when she was well." There was a distinct pause, when Janet added: "Lately, though, we had to dissuade her from being with him too much. I'm afraid Mother wasn't good for him. She had become very difficult, you know."

"His door is invariably bolted?"

"Yes, ever since somebody forgot to turn the key," Janet replied. "It's so easy to do that, isn't it? We had the bolt fixed because that requires mental effort, you understand. Not just turning a key. . . . That time the key wasn't turned, Morris escaped from the house late one night, and next morning we found the boat had vanished. He was eventually found in one of the paddocks, and fortunately he was quiet and returned to his room without any fuss."

"Is there a particular reason . . . forgive the question . . . a reason for him being dressed like a schoolboy?"

"Of course there is, Inspector. Mentally, Morris has never grown up. You've seen that for yourself. We decided that the best way to manage him was to treat him as a child all the time, and so when his second Eton suit wore out, we had another made for him, and so on." Her eyes brightened with golden tears. "To see him in schoolboy's uniform is easier for us, too. We'd had such great hopes for little Morris, and it has all been disappointments."

"He seems contented with his lot, and this is something achieved for one in his tragic state," Bony said, sympathetically. "Tell me, how many are there on your domestic staff?"

"Only the cook. Mrs. Leeper. We manage quite well with just Mrs. Leeper, and a man who comes over now and then to cut the wood and do the outside work we cannot do."

"Then after I've had a few words with your cook Constable Mawson and I will keep Blaze waiting no longer."

"Very well, Inspector. Mrs. Leeper will be in the kitchen, I expect. Please come this way."

"Perhaps you would permit me to interview her here."

"Yes, if you wish. I'll send her along."

"I thank you." Bony waited till Janet Answerth left

them before saying to Mawson: "I will talk to the cook outside."

Passing to the porch, he lingered to appreciate the sun-lit expanse of Answerth's Folly. The light wind touched the surface with its brush of gold, and the great grey trunks of the trees, which sprang to life when the world was young, were pillars supporting the gentian sky. They stood but here and there upon the water which had killed but could not bring them down, and about them swam the ducks and the pelicans and the swans. The distant land lured the eye to regard with fleeting interest the row of station buildings, to pass on up the long grassy slope to the green forest.

A rustle of starched garments caused him to turn and see a stout and nimble woman regarding him with wide dark eyes. Her hands were slim, and her feet appeared to be too small for her bodily weight. She was wearing a nurse's white linen cap, and it was the voluminous white apron which had rustled when she moved. She epitomised saintly cleanliness.

"Ah! Mrs. Leeper?"

"I am Mrs. Leeper," she replied, her voice clear and precise. "You wanted to see me?"

"Yes. Kindly accompany me for a few minutes." Bony stood aside to permit her to go ahead down the porch step, and as they walked on the close-cropped grass, he put his opening question. "Just what is your position in this household, Mrs. Leeper?"

"I am keeper-in-general of the rat house," was the answer, and he stopped to look at her, his brows lifted. Her button of a nose crinkled with humour, but grim mockery lurked deep in her eyes. "I hope you won't make my position here more difficult than it is by telling tales."

"You have my word, Mrs. Leeper, that I never gossip. Tell me, who is the real head of this household?"

"I am."

"Indeed!"

"They don't know it, Inspector."

"The Misses Answerth are not particularly courteous to each other."

"They have forgotten how to be."

"Meaning that they are normal when insulting each other?"

"They're never normal," Mrs. Leeper replied with emphasis. "And there's nothing abnormal about that because only one per cent of humanity is normal. These people have their idiosyncrasies, if that's the word, which are a little out of the ordinary. They have lots of money, but they walk round the house at night without a light. Never collide with anything in the dark. They stick to oil lamps when they could easily have their own electric generating plant. And sometimes they are out of speaks for weeks."

"H'm! How long have you been here?"

"Ten years almost."

"D'you like being here?"

"Certainly not. I dislike the place, and the people. I don't like darkness and silence, and rooms and passages which are always cold. I like sunshine and fresh air, and plenty of carbolic. I like laughter and joy, not studied politeness with an undercurrent of hatred which seems to have seeped into the very stones of the place. As I just told you, I'm here for a purpose. I'm here to save money to buy a hospital of my own. I've been matron of a large mental hospital, but I could never save money."

"Then you must be capable of managing these . . . Answerths?"

"Yes, I can manage them easily enough, but I never let them know it. It's an art, Inspector, managing the mentally sick."

"It must be," agreed Bony. "They are then, mentally ill?"

"Yes, but not quite nuts. Don't mistake my words. The two women are fully capable. Miss Mary runs the station and the men. Miss Janet thinks she runs the house and everyone in it. She paints beautifully, and plays the piano. Keep them apart, and they're tractable."

"And how long do you expect to stay here to have enough to buy a hospital of your own?"

"Oh! Oh, perhaps two more years. These people pay very well. They have to, you know. There's no entertainment. I don't leave this place except once a year for three weeks' holiday in Brisbane."

"Almost a prisoner, eh?"

"Almost . . . due to myself, of course. I needn't stay. I want money, and the less one spends the more one saves."

"There is horse sense in that, Mrs. Leeper. When did you last see Mrs. Answerth alive?"

"See her! It was just after nine that night she was drowned. She came to the kitchen as usual for her cocoa and biscuit. The last time I heard her was about eleven when Miss Mary brought her into the house and sent her up to bed. I heard Miss Mary scolding her and then I heard their room doors being closed. Mrs. Answerth must have waited and gone out again when she thought everyone was asleep."

"D'you know why she went out?"

"Yes, I think I do." The wind teased the woman's

white cap and rustled the starched skirts. Her unadorned face shone in the sunlight, as though continuously she scrubbed it with the carbolic soap she appeared to like so much.

"She was a walking tragedy," Mrs. Leeper continued. "Poor thing! I felt very sorry for her. She had no place here, and all she thought about was her son. Sometimes she would cry because they wouldn't allow her to visit him, and when she seemed happier recently, I wondered what was behind it and watched her."

"When was that?" interjected Bony.

"About two weeks ago. I found out that she'd steal downstairs in the middle of the night, and go outside and talk to Morris, who came to his bedroom window. She'd stay talking to him for half an hour or more."

"Turn casually towards the house and tell me who occupies which room. Avoid letting anyone see we are interested in the house."

"Very well. Take the top floor rooms left of the coloured window. The first one is Miss Janet's. The next two windows are in the room occupied by Morris. There's another window to that room round the corner, the window Morris would talk to his mother from. On the other side of the hall, the first room is Miss Mary's. The next was Mrs. Answerth's room. The next one is empty. There are other rooms up there which haven't been occupied for a hundred years, by the cobwebs and dust in them. If they gave me all that unused furniture . . . all antique . . . I'd be able to invest in a hospital as big as the Brisbane Town Hall."

"Your room . . . is where?"

"On the ground floor next to the kitchen."

"Much experience in mental hospitals?"

"Sixteen years," replied the cook.

"Your opinion of the mental condition of Morris Answerth?"

"I haven't an opinion because I've never seen him but once. The women look after him. From what they tell me, though, it seems he stopped growing mentally when he was about seven."

"Were you not curious about him?"

"Yes. But I'm not here in my professional capacity. I accept everything as being in order. Mr. Harston, the agent, manages their affairs. It was he who obtained the position for me. He told me all about Morris, and said I wasn't to interfere."

"Were you here when he escaped from his room?"

"Yes."

Bony felt the hardening towards his questioning.

"Tell me what happened on that occasion," he said, quietly.

"Well, Miss Mary was eating her breakfast when Miss Janet ran into the dining-room to tell her that Morris wasn't in his rooms. Miss Mary swore at Miss Janet, and called her a so-and-so fool for not locking the door the night before. They went out to find the boat gone. There used to be a boat tied to a stake this side of the causeway. Miss Mary raved at Miss Janet, and Miss Janet cried and kept saying she had locked Morris's door.

"I stood on the porch and watched Miss Mary wading over the causeway. Miss Janet ran about like a dog trying to find its kennel, and I called to her. It was 'Poor little Morris', and 'What can have happened to my little boy?', until I was fed up and shouted at her to behave. Then Mrs. Answerth appeared on the scene, and when I told her what had happened she flew into a temper and told Janet that Mary must have let him out to get the chance to beat him. Accusations flew about, the old lady screaming that she hoped Morris would snap Miss Mary's neck like a carrot.

"Several hours after I pacified them, Miss Janet came down from the roof, where she'd been on the look-out with binoculars, to say that the boat was returning. She told me not to bother any more, and to return to the kitchen. When she thought I was out of the way, she went to the levee and waited. From the dining-room window I saw the boat being rowed round the house by Miss Mary, and Morris sitting in the stern.

"Miss Mary rowed the boat to the levee at the causeway, and Miss Janet fastened the chain to the stake and said something to Miss Mary or Morris. Then Morris left the boat and Miss Mary held him by the arm and marched him into the house and upstairs."

"Where was Mrs. Answerth when all this was going on?"

"I didn't know till some time later," replied Mrs. Leeper. "According to the old lady, Miss Janet locked her into an upstairs room, and that must have been just after Miss Janet saw the boat coming back. Now where was I?

"I stood in the hall listening, and had to scoot back to the kitchen when Miss Janet came down. She was crying again about 'poor little Morris'. She stayed in the kitchen, still crying, but louder. I think she did it on purpose to stop me hearing yells coming from Morris's room. The next day, the old man who comes to saw the wood fixed a bolt to Morris's door, and there was a padlock to the bolt so that it couldn't be slipped free until the padlock was removed."

"D'you think the yells you heard coming from Morris's

room meant that Morris was being beaten?" asked Bony.

"Sounded much like it to me," replied Mrs. Leeper, and, regarding her, Bony found in her face nothing of disapproval. Shading her eyes with a hand, the woman gazed over the Folly. Although her hands were small, her forearms were large and firm. About her was still the authority of the hospital matron.

"Was it from that time that Mrs. Answerth was never allowed to visit her son?" he enquired.

"No. I don't think so, Inspector. That came later . . . much later."

"When?"

"I don't remember exactly when. I do remember Mrs. Answerth complaining to me that Miss Janet said she wasn't to visit Morris any more because she was a bad influence over him."

"It was after Mrs. Answerth had been stopped from visiting her son that she left the house very late at night to speak to him from below his window?"

"It could have been. I'm not sure."

Chapter Eight

OLD HANDS GOSSIP

NOTHING was said during the return trip from Venom House, and then before leaving Blaze, Bony said he would call on him again just to talk of places known to both. Blaze sucked at his pipe, nodded, his mind reviewing pictures of long ago.

When their car was a quarter-mile in from the edge of the forest, Bony asked Mawson to stop.

"I'll leave you here and go back for a word or two with Blaze," he said. "I want to talk to Robin Foster, the head stockman, who appears to be on a bender just when he is required to give information. Might be as well to arrest him for something and lock him up so that he will be sober later today."

"All right!" agreed Mawson. "How will you get to town?"

"Walk . . . if I cannot beg a lift. Ring Doctor Lofty and ask him to let us have another print of the pictures he took of the body of Mrs. Answerth."

The constable having departed townward, Bony entered the scrub and emerged immediately above the cluster of station buildings. From this point he was able to walk to the men's kitchen and dining-room without being observed by anyone on the roof or at an upper window of the distant house, anyone armed with binoculars. Several chained dogs gave warning to Blaze, but he ignored the barking and was therefore surprised by Bony entering the kitchen by the rear door.

"Said I would return soon," Bony reminded the cook. "Are you boiling the billy for a mug of tea?"

"Yes. What are you after?"

"Bit of a gossip. Information. A mug of tea." Bony sat on a packing-case at the kitchen table and proceeded to roll a cigarette. "Suppose you often think of the old days and wish you were back on the stock-routes and in the outback townships?"

"Often wish I was young again and could ride and drink like a man." Blaze sighed loudly. "What part of Australia d'you come from?"

"North Queensland . . . south of the Gulf."

"H'm! Thought so. Or over west by Halls Creek. Detective-Inspector, eh! You've got on well."

"Political influence," murmured Bony.

"Don't think," Blaze scoffed. "When was you in Cloncurry last?"

They talked of Cloncurry, of Halls Creek, of Broken Hill. Talked of the pubs, and the progress, if any, in these famous settlements. And then they spoke of the cities, and of this coastal district where Blaze had been working for many years, and the reason for this great change in the cattleman's life did not emerge.

Bony chose his moment.

"Do you know much about this place and the Answerths?"

"Most all there's to be known," replied Blaze. "I was head stockman here before Mrs. Answerth was married to the boss. His brother, Morris, was alive when I came here. Morris died by a gun: Jacob by a horse pistol."

"Of late years did you see much of Mrs. Answerth?"

"Not often," replied Blaze, stroking a withered cheek with the mouthpiece of his pipe. "She'd wade over sometimes for a yarn. Usta like talking about the old days when she came here as a bride. She never had no happiness at Venom House. She called it Venom House, you know, and now no one don't know it by any other name."

"Tell me the history of it," Bony urged.

"All right, if you're interested." Blaze seated himself on a rickety chair. "Back in the Year One there was great doings in these parts. That there lake wasn't there. There used to be a river what came down from the hills to west'ard and ran in and out among the giant gums on them flats, and so to the sea. The country was lousy with

71

kangaroos, and kangaroo rats, possums and the rest. It was a sort of Paradise for the blacks, who never went short of tucker.

"The first white man who come into this country was a Morris Answerth, the present mob's great-grandfather. Over in the house is a diary what he kept. Mrs. Answerth brought it one day and let me read it.

"Seems that the first Morris came down from Brisbane driving a bullock team and wagon. On the way he collected a dozen runaway convicts, and a woman he bought with two gallons of rum from her parents, who had settled just out of the city. She was only fourteen, and didn't have no say in anything. He'd picked up a Chinaman, too, and made him his offsider.

"Proper hard doer he must have been. He claimed all the land he wanted. The abos argued the point, and he shot 'em down. Then others rattled him by spearing his cattle, so he and his gang rode out hunting and shot more of 'em. Then it appears that one of the men was a stone-mason by trade, and Morris Answerth, being something of an architect, decided to build himself a house.

"You could write a book about how that house was put up. When his men went on strike, him and the Chow flogged 'em after he'd shot a couple of 'em. He knocked his wife about until she turned up her toes after bearing him a son. When the son grew up, he started to argue with his old man, and the old man planned to shoot him.

"Accordin' to the diary, the original Answerth got no further than planning. Seems that the son, also called Morris, got in first. The second Morris went on with the house-building, finished her, built up the cattle herd and imported sheep. He and his men finished off the blacks, too. Then he married, and by this woman had two sons,

72

the first one being called Morris and the other Jacob. They was almost grown-up when their mother had her throat cut by a bushranger, and their father got the same knife between his ribs 'cos he paused a bit with his horse pistol."

There flashed a humorous twinkle in the old cattleman's brown eyes, and the stem of his pipe caressed his long whisky-riddled nose.

"They was real doers, them first two Answerths," he went on. "And this Morris and his brother Jacob wasn't so far behind 'em. They had been left the station in equal shares. Neither of 'em would sell his share to the other, and they snarled like dingoes over a bone. In the end, Morris . . . that's the third Morris . . . was found against a wire fence with most of his head blown off by the shot-gun beside him. By this time the Law had come to these parts, and the Law said it musta been an accident.

"As I told you, I was head stockman then. Jacob was like his old man, full of roars and spit, and fight sooner than say good day-ee. He tried it out on me, but I'd been reared tough, and after he come to, we had a coupla drinks.

"One year, a gang of shearers come to work, and with 'em was a woman who did their cooking and washing. Didn't belong to any particular man, and Jacob married her. She thought she could fix Jacob, but she had six more thinks coming. He tamed her in less'n three days, so he told me, and he was sore 'cos it took him that long.

"By her he got Miss Mary and Miss Janet. Miss Mary's the dead spit of her mother. Miss Janet's always been a mystery to me . . . taking after her uncle more'n anyone I know. When their mother . . . the one-time shearers' slut . . . fell off a horse and broke her neck, Jacob hunts

73

around and takes up with the daughter of a near-by squatter. Respectable squatter, too, and from him he gets the idea of being social. So he sends young Janet up to Brisbane for a first-class education. Mary's that hopeless, he lets her be.

"The second Mrs. Jacob Answerth had a son what's called Morris, the present Morris. Seems that the boy was always wonky so that he has to be kept shut up. Anyway, when the boy was six, Jacob sort of lost interest in things and decides to push off . . . using his father's old horse pistol. Why that horse pistol I don't know. It made a terrible-looking bloke of him.

"Anyway he left the place in equal shares to Miss Mary and Miss Janet, and nothing at all to Mrs. Answerth and young Morris. Miss Janet came home from college and started to manage the house. Didn't get far 'cos Miss Mary soon spoke her little piece.

"And that's the way with these Answerths, Inspector." Blaze looked at Bony pensively. "You know what I think? I think that them blacks what was flogged and burned and shot and clubbed by the first Answerths and their convict cobbers, pointed the bone at them and their descendants. I wouldn't say this to no one else because they wouldn't understand. You understand, I'm game to bet."

"Yes, I understand, Blaze. A tale of woe, to be sure, but we must now confine our thoughts to the tragic demise of the second Mrs. Jacob Answerth. Someone strangled her with a cord, and removed the cord. Then pushed the body off the causeway, or out from the shore. I would like to establish just where she was murdered. You know this sheet of water, currents, depths and shallows. Tell me about this Answerth's Folly."

74

"From the beginning?"

"Please."

"When I first come here, this Folly wasn't set. As I told you, the bit of a river came down from them western hills and snaked over the valley, passing just beyond the house, and so on to the sea that's a full three miles away. All the land had been cleared exceptin' for the big trees what was left to give shade to the stock. And some years, in summer, there was a flood or two what submerged part of the valley in spots.

"Old Jacob's brother, Morris, got the idea of widening the outlet to the sea, and snagging the river, so that the flood water would get away quick and not widen out over the flats. Seemed a sound idea, and Jacob fell for it. They hired teamsters with horses and bullocks, and they widened and deepened the outlet.

"The following summer there was a cyclone or two come down from Cooktown, and these cyclones played hell in general to the work done on the outlet. For every ton of sand and mullock shifted by the teamsters, the sea piled in a hundred tons. And stopped the river getting out at all."

Blaze steadily regarded his guest, saying:

"That's when I knew them old blacks had boned the Answerths. There was that river outlet doing its job for hundreds of thousands of years, keeping back enough water for the ducks and other birds to be snared by the abos. Then the abos gets wiped out. Then the Answerths what wiped 'em out mucked about with the river, and down on 'em comes the boning in full blast.

"The river not being able to get away gradually overflowed out on the low-lying flats, and then the paddocks, and then creeps round the house and surrounds it. Jacob . . . by that time Morris had blown his head off . . . got

75

the teamsters to work making the causeway from the house to higher ground, shifting the outbuildings and the stockyards, building a levee round the house to stop the water going in through the front door. Coupler years after that, Jacob had to put 'em on again raising the causeway and the levee. Another five years goes by and they wants raising again . . . and Jacob goes on strike. Musta begun thinking about that old horse pistol at that time. Extra to the Gov'ment taking bits and pieces of land off them Answerths, the blacks took eight thousand acres off 'em by blocking the river outlet."

"The present Answerths did nothing about it?" asked Bony.

"Not a thing. They put it to the local council to open the outlet, and the council said they was short of about three million quid for the job. Then they puts it to the Gov'ment, and the Gov'ment sent men down who did nothing but scratch their backsides."

"Now the causeway is covered with more than twelve inches of water and many holes gouged in it," Bony mused. "How many, other than the Misses Answerth, know the way across by wading?"

"Only me. The old lady knew the way, as I said."

"Would Morris Answerth know?"

"Don't think. How could he? He's never broke loose exceptin' once, and that time he took the boat."

"Are there any dangerous currents?"

"Only when the wind blows hard. Then you'd think you was on the beach up round Broome."

"Was the wind blowing that night?"

"No, she was fairly quiet."

"After such a blow, after the wind drops, how long do the currents keep moving?"

"Might be eight to a dozen hours," was the answer. "I remember once. . . ."

A telephone bell shrilled in another building.

"That'll be the house," Blaze said, standing. "Phone's in the men's hut."

He was gone three minutes, and Bony drank more tea and rolled a cigarette.

"Want me to take the boat over for Miss Janet and Miss Mary," the cook said on his return. "They're going to the funeral this after at four o'clock, and they're all dolled up. Says I could go with 'em. Think I will. The old lady was all right, you know."

"I didn't observe any telephone poles crossing to the house," Bony said, and was told that the line went east to join the poles from the Edison Post Office. Also that it was not possible to communicate with Edison by this station line.

"Go back in your mind to the Carlow drowning," Bony requested. "It rained hard that night. Did the wind blow?"

"Oh, a bit. Not enough to rouse the currents, though. Or the day before and the day before that."

"You were the only man here at the time. Had the night been quiet, with no noise of the rain on the iron roof, could you have heard sounds of a struggle on the land opposite where you found Carlow's body?"

"Don't think. Unless one of 'em shouted out. Don't think they made any noise. There was four dogs chained up close by here, and none of 'em so much as yelped."

"Well . . . thanks for talking," Bony said, rising to his feet. "I'll be getting back to Edison. Don't mention the fact that I called for a yabber. By the way, when was the shearing finished this year?"

77

"End of July. July 27th it was."

"Shearing began . . . ?"

"Last day in June."

"How many shearers?"

"Two. There was a picker-up. And Robin Foster's brother done the wool pressing. Bloke from over Manton way came to do the classing."

"Local men, the shearers?"

"No. The picker-up was a lad from Edison. And Henry Foster works most time timber cutting round about."

Bony walked to the door, where he turned, to say:.

"I'll come again sometime, for another yabber."

Chapter Nine

THE NEANDERTHAL

IT was a few minutes before three o'clock when Bony entered the police station, to find Mawson in full uniform. Automatically the constable stood, and remembered in time not to salute.

"Going to the funeral," he explained, noting Bony's interest in the uniform. "Timed to leave the undertaker's parlour at four."

"You enjoy funerals," Bony said matter-of-factly, and Mawson flushed.

"Best to go along," he said. "These Answerths are influential."

"And influential people require police attendance at

their funerals. Anything I ought to know in this instance?"

The question worried Mawson, for he was still unsure of this Inspector, this remarkable half-caste who had nothing of the policeman in his outward appearance. He recalled the iron stiffness of Detective-Inspector Stanley, and the same mental stiffness of the officer in charge of his own Division. With them it was impossible to compare this man unfavourably.

"Perhaps you've never come up against what's like a blast of cold air coming down from somewhere up top," he said, diffidently. "I've never felt it, and don't want to, but the feller before me did. He had a disagreement with Miss Mary Answerth and she told him she'd have him shifted from Edison. He came back by telling her he had a job to do and would go on doing it, and that no one could shift him. In two months, he was shifted to a one-pub township so far west that he could throw a stone into the Northern Territory. He had nothing to do there but look at the sand."

"How d'you think Miss Mary managed that transfer, Mawson?"

"Through the local Member of Parliament who has the ear of the Chief Secretary who has the ear of the Chief Commissioner. Same bloke is still our M.P. So I does my duty, and I dips me lid to the Answerths. The bloke before me had a wife and three kids to educate, too."

"And was lacking in tact, I expect. Anyway, I'll hold the fort while you are absent. Did I hear someone swearing in the back yard?"

Mawson smiled, and found that it hurt. Bony noted the livid mark on the left cheek.

"In pursuance of your directive," Mawson said. "I parked Robin Foster in one of the cells."

79

"Strife?"

"Plenty. He wasn't really drunk enough to arrest easily. Had to borrow Mrs. Carlow's wheel-barrow and call on bystanders to assist in the name of the King. Took four of 'em and me to get Foster in the wheel-barrow to the lock-up. Wheel-barrow's damaged. Three assistants damaged, and I'm going to have a black eye. But he'll be ripe for questioning any time you want him."

"You charged him with . . . ?"

"Drunk in a public place, to wit the sidewalk outside the Edison Hotel, using obscene language, resisting the police . . . and one or two more items. It was before I put on me uniform for the funeral."

"Your day will not be without interest," Bony said, smilingly. He fingered the cloth-covered cord of the telephone instrument. "Did you obtain prints of Lofty's photographs?"

"Yes. Here they are."

Accepting the large envelope, Bony withdrew the pictures to arrange them in an arc on the desk.

"I suppose I ought to be armed with a large magnifying glass," he said. "I decline to carry one, however, because it tends to sag the coat pocket. Peculiar mark round the neck, isn't it? The cord which strangled the unfortunate woman comprised two wires each covered with cotton materials over rubber and twisted into a rope . . . like this telephone cord."

"By gum, that's true," agreed Mawson. "Telephone flex."

"Or electric light flex. Is electric power being brought to Edison?"

"No. Been hoping for it, but it seems we can go on hoping."

"Are any of the houses or offices here wired for electricity?"

"No, not to my knowledge."

"There isn't an electrician living here?"

"No."

"Get me Dr. Lofty." A minute later the doctor was on the phone. "Thank you for your prints, Doctor. Yes, just what I required. I am wondering if the mark about the neck suggested to you the type of cord employed?"

"Yes, light packing-case rope," replied Lofty.

"What is your reaction to my suggestion that it might be telephone or power flex?"

"Entirely favourable, Inspector. Damn it! I should have thought of telephone cord. Why, it's looking at me now."

"Thanks. I'm glad we agree. You might . . . er keep that up your sleeve. Going to the funeral?"

"Oh yes. Are you? Everyone will be going."

"I have work to do, Doctor."

"So have I, blast it. But . . . can't get out of going."

"Well, enjoy yourself. Good-bye and thank you." Bony replaced the receiver on its cradle. "Telephone flex, Mawson. Electric power flex. Did you observe that Morris Answerth was fishing from his window with power flex?"

The constable's eyes narrowed, and, leaning over the desk towards his superior, he drawled:

"No. Now you're telling me. Funny sort of cord to have in Venom House. It's not wired for power. I . . ."

"Is there a telephone mechanic stationed here?"

"No. Repairs done by Manton people."

Bony glanced at the wall clock, rose and passed to the front window. A hearse was drawn up before the mortician's parlour across the street, and many cars parked along the kerb behind it. The sidewalk was crowded.

"What is your opinion of the Answerths, and the cook, based on our visit there this morning?" he asked without turning round.

"They seemed edgy to me," replied Mawson. "But then there was a murder in the family. Those two women weren't exactly full of mutual love. They sort of gleefully bowled each other out, and both of 'em were upset when you insisted on seeing Morris. You don't think . . ."

"Why dress a grown man in a schoolboy's clothes, Mawson? Why keep him confined to his rooms? Why prevent his mother visiting him of late? I found him rational, if childish. I found him tidy in person, clean, and meticulous in keeping his books in order. His room was clean and fairly tidy. There was no evidence that a person of unsound mind inhabited that room. Now you be off to your funeral. They are bringing out the casket."

Continuing to stand at the window, Bony watched the policeman cross the silent street. All about Bony was silence, but from a distance came the sound of a man's muffled shouting.

The casket was placed inside the motor hearse. There was a vision of masses of flowers. People appeared to dwindle in number, and the cars became prominent. The undertaker walked down the street before the hearse, and car by car moved away in procession.

Following the hearse was a utility almost buried beneath flowers. Following that was a smart sedan in which were two ministers and Janet Answerth, in black. Behind the sedan was the station wagon driven by Mary Answerth

82

and without a passenger. Car after car passed the police station, and Bony recognised Mr. Harston in one and a woman in a van driven by a youth and having on the panel the words 'E. Carlow, Butcher'. When the last car had glided down the street, there was not one person to be seen. The town wore its Sunday clothes.

Bony found the key of the lock-up and passed out to the rear yard. At the back of the yard were three cells under the one roof, with a face behind the grille in the centre door. The shouting stopped as he approached the prisoner.

"What's to do?" he enquired, mildly. "You seem to be making a fuss at a most inopportune time."

The prisoner's faded blue eyes glared from behind the bars, and fair hair almost met the eyes, so low was the forehead.

"Let me bloody well outer here," he roared. "I bloody well done nothin' agin the bloody law."

"Drunk in a public place. Resisting the police. Assaulting the police. Using obscene language. Damaging property, to wit a wheel-barrow. Creating a public nuisance. Obstructing the footpath. And . . . oh well, that will do to go on with. Let us say a month."

"A bloody month," shouted the prisoner. "Caw!" He was abruptly awed by the enormous wickedness of the coppers. "And who the bloody hell are you?"

"I," began Bony, pretentiously, "I am Inspector Napoleon Bonaparte. I am fate. I am doom. And you are facing a month." Leaning against the wall of the lock-up, he gazed round the angle of the grid to watch the prisoner's expression change to swift uneasiness, and then to bewilderment. "Care to answer a few questions, Foster?"

"I don't bloody well know nothin',"

"You know how old you are, surely?"

" 'Course I bloody well know how old I am."

"Then you know something. Answer my questions to the best of your knowledge and ability, and I'll unlock the door that you may return to the hotel and continue your bender. It's not in order, but then I am not an ordinary policeman. Do we trade?"

As Foster was completely sober, as he suffered a poisonous hangover, as the pub was within three hundred yards of his thirsting throat, what could he do but trade?

"All bloody right," he snarled. "But I bloody well tell you I bloody well know nothin'."

"You were in Edison on a bender that night Edward Carlow was drowned in Answerth's Folly, weren't you?"

"I bloody well was . . . thank Gawd."

"Why are you thankful?"

"Why! And you a bloody demon? If I hadn't been on a snorter of a binge that night you bloody (twice) demons would of said I drowned Ed Carlow, that's what you'd have bloody well done."

"And immediately after Mrs. Answerth's body was found you came to Edison with Miss Answerth and started on another bender," Bony persisted. "When the inquest was held into the death of Edward Carlow, you were still on that bender and were incapable as a witness."

"I wasn't bloody well wanted for a bloody witness," shouted Foster.

"You thought you might be required to give evidence, and so kept yourself full of booze."

"I'm telling youse . . . I bloody well didn't."

"You are, it is obvious, a person erroneously called a real Australian," murmured Bony. "Your employment

84

of the national adjective proves it. However when I want you as a witness, Foster, I take steps to have you sober. Do we understand each other?"

"Caw! Strike me bloody blue!" The prisoner grabbed at the bars, and tugged and pushed and shouted: "Let me outer this bloody joint. When do I bloody well get out?"

"Perhaps next month if you don't pipe down. You are the head stockman employed by the Misses Answerth. How many acres do they own?"

"Acres! Sixty bloody thousand acres, and nine outer ten bloody houses and shops in Edison . . . that's what them Answerths own."

"How long have you been employed by them?"

"Six years."

"You forgot the adjective that time. How many sheep did the Answerths shear this year?"

"How . . ." The small blue eyes winked. "How many sheep?"

"You heard me. Come on."

"Three thousand, four hundred and eighty-two, including the bloody lambs, was the tally."

"Any shortage from the previous muster?"

In the faded blue eyes a shutter fluttered as quickly as that before the camera lens.

"Don't think," was the reply.

"Better try. You were and are the head stockman."

"They's was a few down at the bloody shearing."

"How many down?"

"Caw! What am I supposed to bloody well be? Gettin' on for a bloody hundred, we reckon. Every place is losing a few sheep these bloody days."

"Did you work in the shearing shed?"

"Course not. I had me bloody time cut out drafting the bloody woollies into the bloody sheds, and taking the cleaners out again to the bloody paddocks."

"Did you help shift the wool after it was baled?"

"Only once I helped Miss Mary with the bloody bales in the wool shed."

"How many bales were there?"

"Cor bloody blimey! What d'you bloody well take me for? A bloody tally clerk?"

The next question was sharply spoken.

"When did you last see Mrs. Answerth alive?"

Foster swallowed. Sweat glistened on his ribbon of a forehead.

"Not for bloody monse. Long time afore the bloody shearing any'ow."

"You had nothing against her, did you?"

"What, against old Mrs. A! Talk bloody sense."

"What did you have against Edward Carlow?"

"A bloody lot. He was flash, for one bloody thing. About as straight as a porker's tail. I wasn't the only one hereabouts what had no bloody time for Ed Carlow, the big, fat, bloody . . ."

"The other national adjective isn't permissible, Foster," Bony hastily interposed. "Your brother didn't have any time for Ed Carlow either, did he?"

"No, he bloody well didn't. But he was drinking with me that night Ed Carlow got bloody wet."

"Well . . ." Bony slipped the key into the padlock barring the door. "That will be all for now, Foster. I may want to ask further questions, and when I do you will be sober."

The door was flung open, and the prisoner came forth. Save for straightness of back, he was Neanderthal. He confronted Bony with bared teeth and clenching hands reaching down to his knees.

"Thanks for bloody well nothin'," he shouted.

"That'll be enough," Bony told him, airily. "By the way, return the wheel-barrow over there to Mrs. Carlow. Apologise to her for damaging it."

Foster rocked on the heels of his riding-boots.

"Caw! The bloody nerve. Why, you bloody . . ." Stepping close to Bony, he glared at him, in his eyes the Neanderthal's contempt of restraint and for consequences. A huge fist shot upward to contact Bony's jaw.

It was, of course, not fair to Foster. He was still full of dead whisky and beer, he had never been scientifically trained, and had nothing with which to think. A battering-ram pounded into his stomach . . . so full of dead beer and dead whisky . . . that made him bend forward to receive the toe of a shoe smack against his Adam's apple. As he had very little neck, the shoe work was a credit to the expert. He proceeded to gasp for air, as he rocked on his feet. And then he appeared to lie down flat on his back, the back of his head being the first to contact the greater solid.

On regaining composure, he discovered himself to be kneeling, his left arm held by a vice having ten separate jaws. He was ordered to stand, and stood. He was ordered to march, and marched. He was ordered to gaze upon the broken wheel-barrow, and gazed.

"You will return the wheel-barrow to Mrs. Carlow's shop," said the soft voice from somewhere behind him.

Then he was free. He whipped about and crouched. The man he saw appeared to fade away behind a pair of brilliant blue eyes which magically grew large and larger. He felt for the handles of the barrow and, finding them, pushed the barrow out of the yard and to the street.

"I'm behind you," softly spoke the voice.

What was the 'bloody' use? The butcher's shop was closed, so he left the barrow outside the 'bloody' door.

Chapter Ten

THE BOSS OF EDISON

MAWSON had returned from the funeral, and Bony was writing notes, when heavy feet pounded on the floor of the outer office.

"Here comes a customer," Bony murmured, adding data to matter headed: 'The Wool Clip.'

Mawson stood, and Bony secretly commended him for this respect for superior rank, this refusal to take a yard when given a foot. Abruptly, the room appeared to be full of Mary Answerth, and Bony stood.

"Good afternoon, Miss Answerth."

"Gud-dee, Inspector. I've come to pick a bone with Constable Mawson. They tell me, Mawson, you've locked up my head stockman."

The window light was full upon her, and Bony noted the whiteness about the woman's nostrils and the smallness of the black eyes with the peculiar uniform of the irises. She was wearing gabardine trousers into which was tucked a khaki blouse having a high and close-fitting collar. Mawson admitted his crime.

"Yes, marm. Drunk in a public place."

"Drunk my back . . . my foot, Mawson. Foster was sitting on the bench outside the hotel, reading the *Sporting News*, when you arrested him. Just like that." She accepted the chair offered by Bony, and the chair was no longer visible. "I want Foster on the job. We got to dip cattle in the morning. I'm taking him back to the quarters."

"It was necessary, Miss Answerth," Bony interposed. "It was necessary for Foster to answer certain questions I wished to put to him. As he had been drinking, and was not sober, I ordered his incarceration."

The black brows shot upward.

"You did?"

"I did."

The silence was brittle until Bony rested his elbows on his papers, which crinkled like breaking glass. Mawson saw his superior join his hands and rest his chin on the finger-tips, but his mind was engaged with the picture of the wrecked office as it would surely be.

"I ordered Foster's arrest because he was present when the body of Mrs. Answerth was removed from the water, because it was necessary to question him, because he was not sober, and, Miss Answerth, because a witness must be sober when questioned."

"Have you finished with him?"

"I have questioned him. And I have considered charging him with several additional counts which should result in a month in gaol."

The hard mouth widened and the chin jutted. The black eyes almost met above the bridge of the beak nose. The face, the personality, was so masculine that Bony was repelled. Her gaze clashed with his, and he felt her mental strength. She said, slowly and almost hesitantly, as though the situation beat her and she could not believe defeat:

"Well, if that's how it is, Inspector." Swiftly she recovered. "My cattle's got to be dipped in the morning and I want Robin Foster out of gaol."

"Then, Miss Answerth, you can have him and welcome," Bony told her. "Doubtless he is well soused again. Should you have any trouble in persuading him to return to his job, tell him that if he's in town at six tonight, he'll be taken inside again."

Mary Answerth's face broke into pieces and was refashioned by a smile in which there was much of anticipatory triumph. "You can bet a couple of deaners that Robin Foster won't be in town at six tonight. Can I have a word or two in your ear?"

Bony glanced at Mawson, and the constable withdrew to the outer office. The visitor produced her pipe and tobacco and proceeded to load it from a paper bag. Bony thoughtfully rolled a cigarette.

" 'Spect you think I'm pretty wild and woolly," remarked Miss Answerth whilst puffing the pipe into action. "I am. There ain't a horse I can't master, nor a man." She paused to add a rider: "Exceptin' p'raps you. With you I has me doubts."

Bony smiled and, like Brer Rabbit, 'said nuffin.'

"You see, Mr. Bonaparte, I'm the eldest of this generation of Answerths, being forty-four and Janet forty-one. I was dragged up by me back hair. You could say I never had no schoolin', but I had the sort of schoolin' to fight life and all them what lives it with me. I'm no weakling, I'm not going to blow my head off like my father did.

"You take Janet. Janet's a lying little bitch. She was always a crawler, always clinging and lith-ping, always a liar. Time after time I've seen her putting it over men, watched 'em go all soft-like and moo at her like poddy calves when she looked 'em over, and wanted something. She got at Father, too. He gave her all she asked for: sent her up to Bris for an education, to learn the piano and paint pictures and gabble out poetry like a baby that's wet itself. And me rounding up cattle, and brandin' them, and throwing young stallions in the yards, and helping with the shearing, and driving loafers of men, and knocking 'em down, too, if they tried to tell me my business. I've slept more times under a tree than a roof. And the roof Janet sleeps under every night I've kept over her and Morris.

"If I wasn't able to master men like Robin Foster and old Harston, Janet would now be on the streets and Morris put away in a lunatic asylum. And strangers would be living on all that us Answerths bent our backs to build up.

"Don't you go and fall for Janet, Inspector. There's nothin' weak about Janet. She can talk polite, and she can read novels and spout poetry, and she can use her brain better'n most. If anything happens to me, she gets all the estate . . . gets the ruddy lot."

"Surely you haven't reason to think that anything will happen to you?" enquired Bony.

"Well, something happened to my stepmother, didn't it?" She waited for agreement, then insisted, "Didn't it?"

"Yes, Miss Answerth, something certainly happened to Mrs. Answerth."

Now Bony waited. The huge woman knocked out her pipe against the heel of her riding-boot and stood. She was regardless of the smouldering tobacco strewing the floor. Bony would have risen, but with the weight of one hand upon his shoulder, she kept him to his seat.

"You took a bird's-eye view of our Morris," she said grimly. "As you don't go round with your eyes shut, you saw that he's like me, pretty hefty. You know, there's something about him what reminds me of a tame bear that came to this town. The man with the bear whispered into its ear to sit down, and it sat down. He told it to stand on its hind feet, and it did. Janet is like the man with the bear, telling Morris that some day he'll be strong enough to break my neck like a carrot, and mindful of telling him to have a go when she's sure he'll manage it. Now I'll be going after that Foster. Gud-dee, Inspector!"

"Good afternoon, Miss Answerth!" he gave her when her hand was lifted and he was able to rise. He accompanied her through the outer office and along the short path to the gate in the wicket fence, and there she said, seriously:

"Be careful you don't tell anyone what I've said. And don't you go getting notions that Jane or Morris strangled Mother. Janet hasn't got the guts, and Morris wasn't out of his room that night. 'Sides, he liked his mother. Gud-dee!"

"Does your brother know that Mrs. Answerth is dead?"

"Yes. I told him before leaving for the funeral."

"What did he say, do?"

"Nothing. He went on playing with his train. Be seein' you."

Standing just within the gateway, Bony watched Mary Answerth climb into the station wagon, which she drove up the street to park outside the hotel. The attitude of a lounger on the sidewalk betrayed the fact that she asked him a question, and also the fact that she received his respect, for he 'dipped his lid'.

She reappeared, to walk to the back of the vehicle and

92

throw open the two doors. Leaving them open, she strode into the hotel. Bony waited, laying odds with a sparrow in favour of the head stockman. He lost. The stockman appeared. He emerged like a rabbit from its burrow, a rabbit that never paused to look about before leaving its sanctuary. Behind him appeared Mary Answerth. One of her great hands was gripping the Neanderthal's collar, and the other had gathered the slack of his trousers' seat. The unfortunate was propelled to the back of the station wagon, lifted and tossed within. The doors were slammed and locked, and Miss Mary Answerth climbed in behind the wheel.

Slowly the vehicle was turned, to be driven down the incline past the police station. The woman waved her hand. Hatless, Bony bowed acknowledgment.

Bony sauntered up the street. The sun was red and the shadows were long and dark. It wanted but nine minutes to six, and within the hotel the disgraceful National Swill was in full flow, men pouring as much liquor down their throats as possible before the fatal hour of drought arrived. Across the street, a woman dressed in black and a youth smoking a cigarette were regarding the broken wheel-barrow outside their shop, and near them Mr. Harston was conversing with a minister. Women loaded with parcels were entering cars and gigs drawn by horses, and men were impatient to be out of town.

Before entering his lodging at the very top of the street, he stood to survey the world of hill and dale and dune and sea lorded by this small cut-off township of Edison. To the northward he could see Answerth's Folly, and the grey roof of Venom House above the tree tops. He could see the stark dead trees standing in water over near the blocked outlet to the sea.

The sins of the fathers visited upon the children. There was no escape from what is an irrevocable law of nature. But little more than a century ago, those dead trees were alive, that water wasn't there, and the camps of the inhabitants dotted the river-side, the smokes rising high into this still air. With but little trouble, game and fish were to be had to keep stomachs full and maintain the laughter of women and children. In those far-away days, morality was of iron. Laws, customs, beliefs, in which fear played no small part in gaining compliance, ruled benignly a people who, satisfied with little, wanted for nothing.

All had vanished before the human offal tossed out by England, and, as Bert Blaze, that keen and knowledgeable cattleman from the Interior, had averred, before all those aborigines had perished they had employed their pointing bones at the Answerths and those with them, and through them down through the years to their children and their children's children.

Clearing the land taken by murder had not brought good to the Answerths. Creating pastures, breeding stock, fighting fire and flood, had done them no good. They had lived by brutality and suffered from hate. Power had withered them. Greed had rotted them. The mighty white man, armed with his guns and riding swift horses, never laughed, never knew happiness. And now his abode was called Venom House.

He whose maternal forebears were of that vanished race, and in whom the best and the worst of the white race constantly warred, lingered in the evening glow and wished his wife were with him. She, also of his duality of races, would, even as he, experience the thrill of satisfaction that before those long-dead aborigines had

94

fallen to the gun, had been outraged and flogged and hanged, they had buried their sting in those who had encompassed their agony.

"Would you *mind* coming in to dinner before it's spoiled, Inspector Bonaparte?"

He turned about to see Mrs. Nash beckoning to him from the garden fence, and he hurried to the gate and joined her.

"You do right to scold me, Mrs. Nash," he told her and rewarded her with a beaming smile. "Am I so very late?"

"It's gone half-past six."

"I was day-dreaming."

"About what?"

"A problem couched in the question: 'Is unhappiness due to glandular irregularity or to the blacks pointing the bone at an ancestor?' "

Mrs. Nash laughed, and he liked that, because when she laughed her pale face glowed.

"You don't think I can help you, I hope," she said. "Cooking problems, now. . . ."

There was a daughter, but she was not at dinner this evening.

"Did you go to the funeral?" Bony asked, after the soup.

"I went down the street to see it start. They say it was the biggest funeral ever at Edison. Poor woman."

"Her life was not a happy one?"

"I think she felt unwanted."

"And her stepdaughters are not happy?"

"I can't say as to that, Inspector. Miss Mary seems to enjoy rioting and shouting at people."

"D'you think she is a little . . . er . . . touched?"

"No. Do you?"

95

"Yes. Must be. She actually told me her age. I have never known a reputedly sane woman to do that."

Mrs. Nash studied her guest, and not till he looked directly at her did she understand his mood.

"How old did she say she is?" she asked.

"Now, now! That would never do. A policeman must never gossip. What is your opinion of Janet Answerth?"

"We're not gossiping, by the way?"

"Oh no! No, certainly not. Tell me about Miss Janet."

"Miss Janet is everything that Miss Mary is not," said Mrs. Nash, and there was in her eyes that which told him here was a champion. "No one is in trouble for long before Miss Janet comes to help out. When my husband was killed in a car accident, Miss Janet paid for everything until the insurance came in. When young Carlow died, Miss Janet did everything for Mrs. Carlow. And that after what she did for her and the boys when they had to leave the farm. There are others, too, who owe her a very great deal. She is kindness itself, and we all have come to rely on her advice."

"H'm! Good. Mrs. Answerth was born in this district, I'm told. Why was she unhappy?"

"It's a long story, Inspector. My husband used to tell of her, he being born here. Mrs. Answerth was the youngest of a family of nine. 'Tis said she was a very pretty girl when Jacob Answerth married her. He was such a brute that twice she ran away from him."

"Then what happened?" Bony prompted as Mrs. Nash appeared disinclined to continue with the subject.

"Her mother was dead when she ran away the first time. When Jacob came for her, her father told him to begone. Old Jacob knocked him down and stormed into the house. He found his wife hiding in a cupboard, and

96

he dragged her back to Venom House. When she ran away the second time, her father was dead, and her eldest brother owned the property. He refused to take her in, and old Jacob refused to take her back, and went there to say so.

"He was speaking his mind when Miss Mary arrived. She told her father he was a disgrace, and she told Mrs. Answerth's brother that he was a . . . was a . . . you know. Then she made Mrs. Answerth get up behind her on the horse, and she took her back to Venom House. Miss Mary was only a chit of a girl at that time, but already she was bossing her father. And she's bossed everyone ever since. Excepting Miss Janet."

Chapter Eleven

DIVISION AND MULTIPLICATION

THE light in the men's quarters waned and vanished. The light in the small room off the kitchen continued to gleam. The light within an upstairs room of Venom House was like a fire-fly steady on a leaf. The world was invisible, for the stars suffered a high-level haze foretelling wind.

Reclining on his bunk, Bert Blaze read a weekly newspaper, and, between paragraphs, he was beginning to think of blowing out his lamp when through the open doorway flitted a dark form that silently approached the

97

stretcher and passed unnoticed until it squatted on the floor.

"You move around," calmly remarked the cook.

"Speak softly," ordered Bony. "The light in the men's quarters has just gone out, but Foster may not yet be asleep. Anyone with him?"

"No. He ain't fit for company, anyway. Got brought home by Miss Mary like something picked up by the dog-catchers. Seems she yanked him outa the pub for the cattle-dipping tomorrow."

"It happened like that." Bony made himself comfortable and rolled a cigarette. Blaze waited, and presently Bony said: "I've been thinking that you might like to give me a hand."

"Might. Depends, of course, on what."

"At locating the murderer of Mrs. Answerth."

"Then you can rope me in."

"I'm glad I wasn't mistaken in you, Blaze. Let us talk of Mrs. Answerth. Somewhere in the background of the past lurked the motive to kill her, and as we don't know the motive, it is to the past we must travel. I have gathered that no one knows these Answerths more intimately than you."

Bony offered opportunity for comment on this point, and as Blaze remained silent, he went on:

"We don't know just where Mrs. Answerth was strangled. If on the house side of the causeway, then we must concentrate on the living Answerths. If she met her death this side, then we have a much wider range of people with whom to deal. How did Mrs. Answerth come to confide in you about her home life?"

"Well, to explain all that, you've got to understand I first came here as head stockman, and that old Jacob was alive and, in addition to his freehold, he leased another fifty thousand acres and employed round about a dozen men."

The yellow light of the lamp set on a packing-case at the head of the bed was kind to the lined face and to the dark eyes which could gleam so brightly. The ex-head stockman crammed tobacco into a pipe with a broken stem.

"In them days things was good and easy," he said. "Money went a longer way, there was more men about, and they was good at their work. When the first Mrs. Jacob snuffed out, and Jacob got society ideas, he sort of left me to be a bit more than just head stockman. The causeway wasn't under water them days, and I usta go over and spend an evening now and then with Jacob.

"In them days I was pretty capable, and too independent to call the King me uncle. I knew me job, and old Jacob knew I did, too. When he shouted at me, I shouted back, and he sorta liked it.

"He'd been married to the second wife about six monse and I was over there at dinner. He was a bit sour, and he took it out of his new wife. Because she wouldn't answer back, he got up sudden and made to hit her, and I told him I'd knock his teeth down his throat. Instead of sacking me, he doubled me wages, saying I was the only man who'd ever showed the guts to beard an Answerth.

"He never stopped askin' me over, either. But he was always careful what he said to his wife when I was there, and she seemed to like me going for that reason. That began a sorta friendship, and I mean friendship and not any funny business. She'd look at me pretty miserable-like, and I'd give her a nod of encouragement, and that's as far as it went for years.

"Troubles piled up against her like the driftwood

against the coolibahs when the Diamintina's in flood, and troubles were like a pack of dingoes around old Jacob until he shot himself instead of the dingoes.

"Then I took sick and was off for months in hospital, and after that wasn't any good with horses. So I took on this cooking, and one night in this here room I wakes up to find Mrs. Answerth standing just where you're sittin'.

" 'Bert,' she says. 'Come outside, I wanta talk to you. I must talk to someone.'

"We went out and sat on a log a bit away, and she tells me all she's had to put up with from·the girls, and mostly that both of 'em are gradually getting Morris away from her."

"About how old would Morris be then?" Bony asked.

"Oh, musta be getting along for eighteen," Blaze replied. "Seems that Miss Janet decides that young Morris wants a firmer hand and less his own way, and Miss Mary disagrees with her. Then the way them two went on upset Mrs. Answerth. They wouldn't speak to each other for weeks, and neither would speak to her, even when she spoke to them. She goes on tellin' me all this till it is getting dawn, and sometimes she's crying and I'm patting her shoulder, not knowing what to say.

"She came over again another night, and after that she'd come about once a week just for a pitch about old times when she was a bride and there was visitors and people about the place. As I told you, there wasn't ever any funny business. We got to be good cobbers, and I used to get a lot off me chest, too.

"You see, my parents were speared by the wild blacks and I was brought up on a cattle station and the boss wasn't married. Exceptin' the lubras there wasn't a woman on the place. I was fifteen, or thereabouts, before

I ever saw a white woman. I never had anyone to tell me things which worried them, until that night Mrs. Answerth came over to talk about her troubles. It was the first time I got the notion I was worth a zac to anyone. And that's all of that, Inspector."

"You would be more than interested to know who killed her," Bony said, stating a fact.

"Never had no education exceptin' what I got off a Scottish lord who had sense enough to keep two hundred miles away from the nearest pub so he could go on living. I can read the papers enough to know they don't hang murderers in this State. I usta think that was best. If I finds out before you do who murdered Mrs. Answerth there won't be no trial. And that's jake."

"D'you suspect any particular person?"

Blaze shook his head.

"Ain't come to thinkin' that far. But I will."

"Any idea about Carlow coming to be drowned in the Folly?"

"Ideas! Plenty. He was on the make. I've heard a whisper or two. You know, picking up a stolen beast what's been killed and skinned all ready for his shop."

"And Carlow evaded paying the lifter what he owed him?"

"Might be something like that. Them as think themselves smart generally gets taken down. There's fellers in the forests agin which Ed Carlow was a suckin' calf."

"Men like Robin Foster?"

"No. Robin Foster's just a grow'd-up gorilla. His brother Henry's different. There's more like Henry who never miss a chance to make a quid or two easy and quiet. Me and old Jacob was troubled by them kind in the old days."

"And you think that Henry Foster. . . ."

"I'm not thinkin' nothing about Henry Foster 'cos I don't know anything," came the swift counter. "I'm putting up Henry Foster as an example of the bloke who's slick when the chance comes his way."

"Was he ever employed by the Answerths?"

"Only when he does the wool-pressing at shearin'. And then he don't actually work for the Answerths: he's employed by the shearers who contract for the job."

"Has the recent wool clip here been sent to Brisbane?"

"Yes. Several weeks back."

"How many bales—do you know?"

"Ninety-two. Branded M & J over A."

"What agent was it consigned to?"

"Parsons & Timms."

"Do you know how many sheep were shorn this year?"

"Of course. I keep in touch although I'm only a dough slinger."

"Then let us work out a little sum and check up."

Bony produced notebook and pencil, and Blaze swung his feet over his visitor's head and sat on the side of the bed that he might watch the sum being worked out.

"The clip came off three thousand, four hundred and eighty-two sheep. That right?" asked Bony.

"Correct."

"Ewes, hoggets, weaners, lambs. Wethers and rams in together. How many lambs?"

"One more'n seven hundred and thirty."

"Now mix up the rest and give me the average weight of the fleeces."

"I'd say ten pounds . . . average."

"Good. This might be harder. Average weight of the lamb fleeces?"

102

"Four pounds," Blaze promptly answered, watching the working pencil.

"Now what have we? The total weight of the clip works out at twenty-eight thousand, four hundred and thirty-four pounds. Consider again your estimate . . . because it's important . . . the average weight of the fleeces—ten pounds for the adult sheep, four pounds for the lambs."

"I stands by it," asserted the cook. "As a matter of fact, I guessed them weights before the classer worked it out on the scales in the shed."

"We'll take another step, Blaze. How many pounds of wool to a bale?"

"Three hundred . . . mostly just a bit over."

"Right! I'll work all that out."

Blaze could not follow the figures leaping to the page, but he was satisfied that this mathematician knew his work. Presently Bony announced the total number of bales to be ninety-four. Still satisfied, Blaze offered no comment.

"Mistake somewhere along the line," Bony murmured. "Our total is ninety-four. You said that ninety-two bales comprised the clip. We're out by two. I'll check."

This time Blaze did not watch the pencil. The hand which held the short-stemmed pipe to his mouth moved downward slowly to rest on a pyjama-clad knee, and thereafter his body was still.

"My figures are right," Bony said. "Sure yours are?"

"Yes."

"Sure the number sent away is ninety-two?"

"Yes. I helped load 'em on the transport; Miss Mary was there, checking the bales out. There was no more nor less than ninety-two."

"No bales left over in the shed?"

"Shed's empty and unlocked. My guesses on weights is right. My figures is right, too. If your sums is right, then two bales musta been pinched. Musta been pinched in fleeces, 'cos Miss Mary checked the baled wool outer the shearing shed and into the wool shed at the end of every day."

"The bales would be serially numbered, I suppose?"

"From one upward. Miss Mary had a boy from Edison helping with the branding of the bales and moving 'em about."

"And she would keep a daily tally of the bales received into the wool shed?"

"In her head if not in a book," Blaze replied with conviction. "That he-woman misses nothin'. I'll tell you how that wool coulda been pinched. You know the game. Shearer removes fleece. Picker-up carries it to the wool table. The classer trims it, rolls it into a bundle, puts it into one of his bins. The presser takes the fleeces from the bins to bale 'em. At the end of the day, there's generally fleeces left in the bins for baling next morning.

"That's the way it goes. Now a coupler smart fellers could sneak in every night and lift a dozen, perhaps more, fleeces from them bins."

"The classer?" purred Bony.

"Feller named Tanter. Got his own place out from Manton. Don't think he would be in it. But if the fleeces in his bins was took, he musta known."

"What about the presser?"

"Henry Foster! He musta known, too. Of course, he could. . . ."

"What?"

"Tell you how the presser could have worked it. He's

the bloke who takes the fleeces from the bins to bale 'em. His cobbers sneaks in at night and lifts say, half the fleeces left in each bin, and makes up the difference in the level by pushing in hessian sacks under top ones they leave. The classer don't notice any difference in the morning, and the presser whips out the bags when the classer ain't lookin' . . . leavin' the bags handy to be used the followin' night. And now I comes to think of it there was always a few sacks on the floor near them bins. I seen 'em there when I took the mornin' and afternoon smoke tea in."

"Wool at one hundred and eighty pounds per bale is well worth stealing," remarked Bony.

"Probably fetch more than that. Anyway, that's how them fleeces could of been pinched, if they was pinched."

"I'm glad you express the doubt," Bony said, thoughtfully.

"You musta had some idea of wool havin' been pinched."

"Merely an idea." Bony scrambled to his feet, and smiled down at the wizened old man. "What brought Edward Carlow to the logging stage where he parked his van? Or did someone else drive it into the scrub to hide it? And how was it that Carlow, who was a town butcher, came to be drowned in Answerth's Folly within five days after the Answerth's clip was baled?"

"You answer them questions. I'm only a flamin' cook."

"Answer this one, then. How did Mrs. Answerth get along with Mrs. Leeper?"

"No good. That Leeper woman was brought in by Miss Janet and old Harston. Before Mrs. Leeper, there was a woman cook who'd been there before I come. She just died naturally. Up to then Mrs. Answerth was more or less boss of the house, but when Mrs. Leeper came she had to take a back seat, and she didn't like that. Seems that Mrs. Answerth was gradually pushed out, she tellin' me that she got to be only in the way and not wanted by anyone."

"Your opinion of Mrs. Leeper?"

"A grab-all and know-all," replied Blaze. "Makes me thankful I never got meself married. She's out for Number One, but then a lot of people are like that. She certainly runs the place better than Mrs. Answerth did, and as neither Miss Mary nor Miss Janet is keen on housework, I reckon she earns her wages."

"I understand she seldom leaves the house. That right?"

"Takes a spell in Brisbane once a year. Otherwise stays put. Told me she was saving her money."

"Does she know the path over the causeway?"

"No. I rows her back and across in the boat." Blaze smiled, his eyes impish. "When she came here first, I had to take four trips over with her swags. I says to her: 'You aim to stay a long time.' And she says: 'I'm staying all of ten years.' I tells her she mightn't like staying ten days, and she says p'raps not, but she's staying ten years all the same. And by the looks of it, ten years it's goin' to be."

"When was it you were last in the house?"

"About a coupla monse ago."

"Did you happen to see Morris fishing out of his window?"

"Yes. He's always fishin'."

"Did you then notice what kind of line he fished with?"

"Course. It was reddish rope sort of stuff. First time I ever see rope like that was when Mrs. Leeper came. One of her tin trunks was bound with it, 'cos the locks had busted."

Chapter Twelve

A DAY WITH MIKE FALLA

CONSTABLE MAWSON was arranging his papers preparatory to prosecuting at the Court of Petty Sessions, scheduled to open at ten, when Bony appeared. As usual neat and debonair, Bony smiled as his eyes accepted the constable's 'Sunday-go-to-meeting' uniform.

"Not another funeral, Mawson?"

"Court day. Five cases beside what the Clerk will have entered in the register. Chairman of the Bench sick, and Bittern will take his place, so that we oughtn't to be mucking about all day. You have a pleasant evening out?"

"Delightful. By the way, what is the character of young Alfred Carlow?"

"All right . . . so far."

"Care to enlarge?"

Mawson slipped a rubber band about his court papers, and took time to consider. Bony had previously noted the constable's deliberation before giving an opinion on a person.

"Young Carlow's industrious enough," he began. "Always been a help to his mother. Seems tending to flashness, though. He's dark and good-looking, like his brother. And never forgets it. Might settle down, though."

"What precisely does he do in the business?"

"Fetches the carcases from the slaughter yard and does

the serving in the shop. The mother keeps the books, and serves when he's out delivering."

"They have a man doing the slaughtering?"

"He's a small farmer. Steady and a worker. Big family to keep him at it."

"Know anything of a man named Tanter?"

Mawson's gingery brows rose a fraction.

"Sheep man out Manton way. He's pretty solid. Does the wool classing in this district. You getting interested?"

"The present tense is correct, Mawson. Could I borrow your car today?"

"Yes. She'll want juice, I think. And don't forget to ask for a receipt from the garage for petrol and oil. The department pays. Wish I was a plain-clothes man. High-flying and all that."

"An adventurous man is he who prevents his fetters from laming him," Bony said, and added dryly: "And that is not a quotation."

It was a brilliant day and its spring warmth was joyous to feel. The street was already busy when Bony drove the borrowed car down the grade to stop outside an old shed, fronted by two majestic petrol pumps. There he sounded the hooter for service, and from the shed issued Mike Falla.

"How many?" asked Mike without dropping from his upper lip the dead cigarette-end. "Why! It's the Inspector! Gud-dee."

"Day off or something?" enquired Bony. "Seeing to those brakes?"

Mike laughed, and the sunlight appeared even brighter. He was wearing dungaree overalls, but the greasy cap was absent, and the fair hair unruly.

"Come off it, Inspector. A bloke's not a real driver if

he has to use brakes. I'm having a day off as the old man wanted to take a pig to Manton and I let him do the run. Only had two passengers, so they rode in front with him and the pig went to sleep on the back seat. How many?"

"Fill the tank, please, and check the engine oil. I'll want a receipt for the money."

"That'll be okee. Mr. Mawson has it booked. You gonna have a look at the scenery today? Wouldn't mind going with you."

"You may come if you wish."

"I can! Goodo! It'll do me. I'll tell old Lousy to look after the business. Comes in handy, he does, at times."

Having filled the tank and attended to the engine and tyres, Mike vanished inside his shed, from which had come the musical clanging of a hammer on an anvil. On reappearing, he had the same fag-end hanging from his upper lip, but the dungarees had been discarded for a pair of tweed trousers and a sports coat.

"Bit more comfortable than my old grid," he decided on easing himself into the seat beside Bony. "Yair, Lousy will look after the customers. Does a bit of work for me when he feels like it. Ninety-one not out, and a good tradesman. Only one thing crook with him. He never washed since he was christened, and he says the drought was so bad that year the parson had to do with spit instead of water. Where do we aim for?"

"Depends," countered Bony.

"I'm askin'."

"On your ability to keep your mouth shut hard on what we do and where we go."

Mike combed his hair with spread fingers, crossed his long legs, and watched the passing paddocks make way for the tall timber of the forest. As though only now brought to full realisation that he was a passenger, he produced tobacco and papers, rolled a cigarette and then, when about to lick the paper-edge, was made aware of the old butt.

"A long time ago," he drawled, "me old man tells me that to make dough in this world you have to keep one hand blinded to what the other one does. Having made up me mind, sort of, to make a lot of dough, I bears that advice in mind. Over to you."

Bony laughed, and Mike turned a little to look at this man who could be a milk inspector, a bank inspector, any kind of inspector save a police inspector.

"Enjoying the ride?" Bony asked.

"Yair. I'm liking the scenery. You was sayin'?"

"I was asking if you know the man who does the slaughtering for Mrs. Carlow?"

"Was you? Musta been deaf. Know old Jim Matthews? He's chased me outer his orchard more'n once."

"Straight goer?"

"Too right. Worries like hell about getting his income-tax return correct. Eleven kids and a wife to add to his worries, too. Three pairs of twins. Doing well, ain't he?"

"He slaughters on Tuesdays and Fridays, I understand."

"Yair."

"Tell me when we reach the turn-off to the yard."

"Okee. Bit on yet."

"Edward Carlow did the slaughtering himself, didn't he?"

"Yair. Pretty slick at it, too."

The yard was built in a natural clearing beside a running stream. It was constructed with heavy timber forming high walls of posts and rails. Off it was a smaller yard having a concrete floor, and the hoist to lift the carcases. A little to one side was an open-fronted shed, and, behind that, another shed the door of which was padlocked. The smell of blood and offal was strong. The crows whirred about like black snowflakes. It was a place that Bony hated.

"The cattle are shot, not speared nor pole-axed," he said, and Mike agreed that the slaughter-man used a rifle.

Before leaving the car, Bony slowly manufactured a smoke and studied the lay-out. This place had received no mention in the Official Summary of the murder of Edward Carlow, and Mawson had told him that, so far as he knew, Inspector Stanley hadn't come here.

Mike Falla was extremely curious to learn Bony's reason for coming, but instead of asking, he said:

"Don't think I'd choose this joint to spend a honeymoon in. Even the trees round about look sorta bilious."

Bony offered no comment, and Mike followed him from the car to the open shed, and watched whilst he poked about behind stacks of hides and sheepskins. Save for bags of salt, a tucker-box, several blackened billies and a cross-cut saw, there was nothing to strike a discordant note. Presently Bony observed:

"Sheepskins are valuable these days for the wool on them, Mike. Mrs. Carlow evidently doesn't fear thieves."

"Aw, no one 'ud come here to pinch a few skins." Mike waited for the next question and when it did not come, he added: "Any'ow, no one would pinch skins off Mrs. Carlow."

"Glad to hear it. Wonder what's in the other shed."

"Dunno. Good sort of lock on her."

"Yes. I think we'll have a peep inside while we're here.

H'm! The padlock seems not to have been unlocked for some considerable time. Find me a piece of wire. Thin and pliable." The wire was found, and Bony fashioned an open hook at one end, watched by the interested Mike. "A crime worse than entering, Mike, is breaking and entering. Should you ever think of becoming a burglar, study the law. Such study will enable you to avoid harsh sentences. If you break down this door in order to steal, you will receive six months. If you use a piece of wire to pick the lock you will receive only three months. If you shoot a man dead, be sure to say that the pistol went off. Never admit you fired the pistol. Just that it went off at a most inopportune time. Then you'll get five years instead of ten."

"You reminds me of me old man," Mike said, absorbed by the manipulation of the wire in the bowels of the padlock. The lock clicked open, and they entered the shed.

There were more hides and skins and a pack of wool sacks. On wall pegs were several saddles and bridles, throwing-ropes, and a Winchester rifle suspended by its sling. Dust proved that none of these articles had been disturbed for many months. To one side there was a stack of chaff bags, filled and tied at the mouth with twine.

Bony felt the top layer, and then untied a sack and thrust in a hand. Wool. Opening another sack lower down in the stack, that also contained wool. A sample of each sack he placed in specimen envelopes.

The curious Mike said nothing. They passed outside and Bony snapped shut the padlock to the iron bar guarding the door. Neither spoke until they were half a mile away, back again on the road to Manton. Then Bony asked where the slaughter-man lived and was told four miles out of Edison on another road. After that, Mike said:

"That wool in the sacks didn't come off sheepskins."

"Is that so?"

"Yair. Come off living sheep's backs. I seen the shear cuts on the bits you pulled out."

"Join the police, Mike. You'd go high."

"Yair. Might be more money in burglaring, though. You seem to make it that easy."

"You lose a lot of time, though . . . in gaol. Where does Mr. Tanter, the wool classer, live?"

"Out a bit from Manton. Better ring from town and find out if he's on deck."

Mike decided on another cigarette, and as he was making it they came to the junction of the three tracks at the old logging stage. A mile farther on along the road to Manton, Bony said:

"Can I hear someone shouting?"

"Yair. And a whip crackin', too. Someone out after cattle."

"Whose country is this?"

"The Answerths.' They rent it from the Government Bit of a land pocket about fifteen square miles." Mike leaned out from the car the better to locate the source of the shouting. "Bit along the track. It'll be Mary Answerth."

The cigarette was made and lit when, far ahead, a steer leaped from the road bank to the track. Bony slowed the car, and now the shouting was more distinct and the whip cracking like a machine-gun in the hands of a novice. A large bull appeared, tawny and disinclined to a siesta. Seeing the car, it began to paw the earth high over its broad back.

"Nine hundred pounds dressed," estimated Mike. "He's

113

going to spring a leak in the radiator if he gets going. Old Mawson won't like that."

Before the beast could charge, several other steers and cows leaped from the bank to the track between it and the car, which Bony had stopped. And then down the track after them rode a horseman, a man having a perfect seat, none other than the Neanderthal. He shouted and flayed a cow and herded her with other beasts to the lower side of the road. More beasts gained the track behind the still pawing bull, and these trotted to stand behind the bull as though adding their defiance to his and sooling him on to flatten the car.

It might have charged did not the Neanderthal have trouble with a dozen animals whose curiosity in the car over-rode their fear of the long, snaking stockwhip. It was then that Mary Answerth appeared in the road beyond the cattle backing the bull.

By comparison, the Neanderthal's yelling was gentle whispering. The adjectives made Mike chuckle, and Bony aghast. The woman charged the cattle behind the bull, her whip a machine-gun in the hands of an expert. The cracker at the end of the leather thong exploded in the ear of a cow and sent her upwards on four straight legs. It exploded in the ear of the others in such swift rotation that none could have heard a sound for the next week. The bull spun round on a shilling, hindquarters going up and head and shoulders going down. His little black eyes took in the charging horse and the huge woman on its back, but before he could think, an atom bomb exploded on his nose precisely between the foam-flecked nostrils.

The other cattle had vanished off the road, the Neanderthal after them to keep them on the move. The bull moaned and ran his nose along the dust of the track, and got caught with a bomb on either rump. It was enough . . . for him. He streaked for the scrub. But it was not enough for Mary Answerth. As though she hated all masculine things, and wanted to parade her hatred before the two men in the car, she followed the unfortunate bull showering him with bombs and yelling insults. Magically, the track was clear, and the uproar dwindled among the tall trees towards Answerth's Folly. There remained only memory of a huge woman, astride a small horse, who could shame every bull-fighter in Spain and every bargee on the canals of Old England.

"Bit of a doer, ain't she?" remarked the laconic Mike Falla.

Bony slipped into top gear, and chuckled to hide from his companion the thrill of admiration for Mary Answerth's horsemanship and dexterity with a fourteen-foot stock-whip. Gross, superbly efficient, as contemptuous of an enraged bull as of her head stockman whom she had tossed into her wagon like a sheaf of hay, the woman was ruthlessness personified.

"I must agree, Mike," Bony said, and gave himself to meditation until they arrived at Manton.

Tanter's house was brightly painted and the centre of wide and verdant pastures on which sheep were white dots on green. Tanter himself was short, alert, quiet.

"I won't occupy much of your time, Mr. Tanter," Bony said when they were seated in the classer's office. "I understand that you classed the Answerths' wool this year."

"I have classed their wool for the last nine years, Inspector."

"The shed routine is, I assume, the same as that on outback stations?"

"Yes, the same."

"Did you at any time note, or even feel, that anything was wrong with the fleeces and wool left overnight in your bins?"

The classer's face registered his answer before he spoke it.

"Well, that's strange you should ask me that," he said, quickly. "It was only a feeling that something wasn't quite right. Not a conviction, else I'd have spoken about it. In fact, I blamed myself, coming to doubt my memory, thinking I must be slipping somewhere."

"You said nothing of this, as you say, doubt of yourself to anyone?"

"No. Had I become certain that anything was amiss, I'd have spoken of it to Miss Mary Answerth." Tanter hesitated. "You see, Inspector, Miss Answerth isn't the kind of woman one can talk to easily. She is . . ."

"I think I understand. You, of course, placed the wool in the several bins?"

"Yes, of course."

"The only man to remove the wool from the bins was the presser?"

"That is so."

"And the presses were in the same shut-off part of the shearing shed as were your wool tables and bins?"

"Yes."

"No one worked there other than the presser and yourself?"

"No one."

"If during the night someone entered your room and took out half the fleeces in your bins, and placed sacks under the top fleeces left in each bin, you would not notice the loss?"

116

"No. The bins there aren't large, and three rolled fleeces would make a perfect top layer over sacks. But . . ."

"Well?"

"The sacks placed in the bins to take the space occupied by the stolen fleeces would have to be removed somehow to stop the presser finding them immediately he began work in the morning."

"Well?"

"The presser?"

"To employ that method of stealing wool, Mr. Tanter, the presser would have to be an accomplice of the thief . . . an accomplice at least. However, I put forward that method only as a possibility. As yet, I am not sure that wool was stolen from the Answerths' shed, so we must be careful how we proceed. Tell me, do the flocks in this wide district vary much in overall classification?"

"Not to a great degree."

"Could you determine from a sample of wool what station it came from?"

"If from a station where I classified the wool, I think so."

Bony produced his specimen envelopes. There were three, although Mike Falla had seen only two. Tanter was given the first, and from it extracted the wool and examined it.

"That's Answerth wool," he stated. "I can give you the strain, if you like."

"Give your verdict on this sample, please."

The classer opened the second envelope and said this, too, came from the Answerth flock. The third envelope opened, he gazed at the wool it contained. Then putting it back in the envelope he said:

"This has been cut by a sharp knife from the skin of a

117

dead wether. The animal isn't an Answerth sheep. It was bred on a place called Lake Nearing, which is owned by people named Smythe."

"Thank you, Mr. Tanter," Bony smilingly said. "I cut the wool from a sheepskin with my penknife. The skin was in the shed at the slaughter yard owned by Mrs. Carlow, of Edison. Obviously from an animal purchased in the course of business. You will not, I hope, be offended by my little test of your powers of judgment."

"Of course not, Inspector."

"If, in the course of a few days, I send a telegram asking you to examine wool in a place I won't at this time mention, would you oblige?"

"I would be very glad to do so," replied the classer. "I infer that you have traced wool thought to be stolen, and, like all my neighbours, I'd be only too glad to help in nailing the thief."

"Much thieving of wool and sheep been going on?"

"Of sheep, yes. Constant nibbling rather than serious raids."

"We may be able to put a stop to it." Bony rose and Tanter accompanied him to the car. Recognising the lolling passenger, he wished Mike good day with a warmth betraying long acquaintance.

On the return journey to Edison, Bony said:

"What's your opinion of young Alfred Carlow, Mike?"

"He ain't properly branded yet, Inspector. Bit silly now he thinks he's grow'd up. T'ain't him, though. That bagged wool's been in the shed some time."

"Indeed!"

"Yair. I been thinking."

Bony stopped the car, cut the engine, and proceeded to roll a cigarette.

"Take it easy, Mike. Don't think too hard. That's my job. Beside, too much thinking aloud is often dangerous."

Mike laughed, long, softly. He stretched his arms and brought his hands behind his head.

"Did you happen to notice which way them wool bags was tied?" he asked with naïve nonchalance.

"Of course I did," replied Bony. "The man who tied the mouth of the sacks used what seamen call a reefer knot. Edward Carlow was a life saver, wasn't he? He could sail boats."

"That's jake. Young Carlow couldn't have tied them sacks. You couldn't get him on the water or in it for all the dough in the Commonwealth Bank. Cripes! And I thought I was going to put one over you. What a flaming hope!"

"As you say, Mike," Bony murmured before starting the engine. The car moved on, and he added: "What a flaming hope."

Chapter Thirteen

A PLEASANT EVENING

WITH the going down of the sun it turned unusually cold, and Bony was appreciative of the fire lit in his sitting-room. He had dined well, and had dawdled at table with coffee whilst relating some of his triumphs to Mrs. Nash and her daughter, who appeared to be, and were, enthralled.

He was at work on his notes when Mawson called and was told sit and smoke until the writing was complete. That done, Bony left the table to share the fire with his visitor, and now the constable experienced no difficulty in putting from his mind the fact that his host was a V.I.P.

"Had a good day?" he asked.

"A happy day," replied Bony. "Spent it with young Mike Falla. That lad is going to make something of his life despite the lack of education set against initiative. D'you know his father?"

"One of the local characters. Any progress today?"

"Progress. I always progress once I take up an investigation. It's not absence of progress, but the speed of progress which sometimes upsets the mighty. If ever you decide to relinquish your job of collecting statistics, serving summonses and prosecuting drunks, remember to refuse to be hurried. Wait upon time. Exercise your mind with but six questions per diem, and rebel against additional problems such as irate superiors, and you are bound to succeed."

Mawson laughed. It began with a chuckle and ended in a guffaw.

"You're not serious when you say you thumb your nose at the big shots, are you?"

"I am," asserted Bony, blue eyes twinkling. "After your third successful murder case you can stick out your chest. After your thirteenth success you can stick out your neck."

"Wonder to me you get away with it and not be sacked," commented the now sober constable.

"One has to adopt an attitude of mind. When an office detective declares he could have solved a murder in a tenth of the time it occupied me, I am amused. Once you can laugh at the ignorant and ignore the frowns of the mighty, you are indeed a king in your own right.

"I have specialised in murder, Mawson, for several reasons, and one reason is that of all the crimes on the calendar murder is least necessary and therefore least pardonable. The starving man may be excused for stealing bread, and the bank teller for robbing his organisation to purchase drugs for his wife dying of cancer. The hungry must eat, and money can be refunded, but restitution of a life stolen cannot be made.

"The psychological impulses of the murderer are vastly at variance with that of the hungry man, or of the bank teller. Murder is the climax of a drama, not the drama itself, and the investigator more often than not must work back to the prologue. His progress, Mawson, is determined as much by his patience as by his mental calibre. In fact, patience is of the greatest importance, for without it the clever man often stumbles in the dust and is blinded. Interested?"

"Too right," replied Mawson.

"Ninety-five per cent of murderers have been sadists all their lives, though outwardly they might act like little gentlemen. The five per cent murder by succumbing to overwhelming fear or a kindred emotion, and do not concern us. Our ninety-five per cent are, as I have stated, sadistic beasts, many of them able to wear a halo with distinction. All are extremely vain, and it is through the vice of vanity that the investigator is given his chance. Once the crime is committed, then the murderer's vanity is in full swing, and with patience and perspicacity the investigator need only wait for the murderer to tell him, in so many actions, how he did it and why."

"Sounds easy," commented the constable. "Mind me butting in?"

"I have come to welcome your opinions, Mawson."

"Whilst waiting for a murderer to trip himself up mightn't he commit another murder?"

"It is the business of the investigator to establish who committed a murder, not to bother himself with a probable one. Naturally, if he has reason to think a person is going to be murdered, he will take all steps to prevent it, not only to save the life of the prospective victim but to use that life as a bait for the man he seeks for murder already done. Is your question related to the murders which have been committed here?"

"Yes."

"Then it would seem that you connect the two as being accomplished by the same person. You may have evidence of this. I have none."

"Both bodies were found in Answerth's Folly," argued Mawson.

"But the circumstances surrounding the one do not touch the other. Let us consider the first murder, for certain developments have encouraged me to consider probable motives actuating this crime."

As Bony related the steps by which he had discovered the theft, and then the whereabouts, of portion of the Answerths' wool clip, Mawson stopped drawing at his pipe and omitted to relight it.

"Thus we may be sure that the wool at the slaughter yard came from the bins in the shearing shed owned by the Answerths," Bony went on. "We may be sure that the theft extended over a period, that the wool was taken by the fleece not by the bale. With me, view the scene of that crime.

"After the first days of shearing, there were several bales of wool in the shed. Those bales were branded and numbered, and every day others were added to the store. To break open the wool shed would have been easy, but to steal wool in the bale most difficult unless transport could be had from the shed. The thief or thieves couldn't carry a three-hundred pound bale of wool to a transport sufficiently far away as not to attract attention.

"So, the thief or thieves, with the connivance of the wool presser, stole half a dozen to a dozen fleeces every working night from the open bins in the unlocked shearing shed. The thieves could carry rolled fleeces bound into a bundle for a considerable distance, even to the logging stage. Men who have worked hard all day, either in the shed or out of doors, sleep soundly. And that goes for the working dogs, who because of the advent of many strangers were less alert than normally.

"The shearing, remember, began on the last day of June and ended on July 27th. The wool stolen from the bins was conveyed, ultimately, to Edward Carlow's slaughter yard. He was either one of the thieves or he was the receiver of the stolen wool. Which do you favour?"

"He'd be the receiver," promptly replied Mawson.

"Until we have proof, we cannot assert either one or the other against him, because the wool could have been placed inside his shed after he was killed. Improbable but possible.

"For the moment, let us accept assumption. Let us assume that the presser, either alone or with another, stole the wool and conveyed it to Edward Carlow waiting with his van at a point where its movements could not possibly be detected by anyone at the men's quarters. On accepting the wool, he conveyed it to his shed and bagged it. The theft was completed not later than July 27th, for on that date the last fleece was placed by the classer in his bins. And five nights after the night of July 27th, Edward Carlow was attacked and made to fight for his life. A large man and still powerful, he was overcome and held under water until drowned.

"It indicates that more than one man attacked and killed him, and assuming that two men attacked him, and both were powerful men, they could have conveyed him to the Folly and drowned him. Two strong men could have carried him bound to poles like a stretcher for a considerable distance.

"Motive! Was Carlow a bilker? Did Carlow refuse to pay what the thieves thought a fair thing? Was the motive nothing whatever to do with the theft of the wool? Was it revenge? Or one of half a dozen other motives we could think of? Remember that the stolen wool was inside a shed which could be broken into by thieves who thought themselves wronged. To you, Mawson, I leave the motive for Carlow's murder. And try to beat you to it.

"Meanwhile, we wait for vanity to work in the murderer of Edward Carlow, like yeast in a bread batter. If we are sufficiently intelligent we shall detect him because, Mawson, a murderer cannot stop still. The act of murder is a door opened to let into his mind a veritable flood of imagining. Imagination drives him on to action which normally he would never even think to do. He has become to himself a person of supreme importance. By the simple act of pressing a trigger, or wielding a bludgeon, he has made himself famous. People are talking about him, reading about him. The coppers are looking for him. and when people fail to recognise him, he exclaims to his *alter ego*: 'Ah, if they only knew!'

124

"Then fear attacks, and leaden doubt replaces the volatile essence of imagination. How much do the police know? What are the police doing? Where in his build-up for escape did he make a mistake? Ah yes, he made such-and-such a mistake. What a fool he had been. He must rectify that mistake whilst there is yet time. Instead of sitting down and reading comics, or a good mystery yarn, he must . . . *must* . . . cover that mistake.

"Sometimes, as you inferred, the mistake is not killing someone else. We could say, but have no licence for doing so, that the murderer of Edward Carlow made the mistake of not killing Mrs. Answerth. It took him four or five weeks to realise his slip, then to rectify it. We could say, and fervently hope that it will not be so, that the murderer of Mrs. Answerth even now is realising he has made a bad mistake, and in the very near future will rectify it by killing another person thought to be vitally dangerous to him.

"The mistake, of course, could be any other vital omission. Thus, as I have pointed out, Mawson, the murderer cannot keep still. All his life he may have been conspicuously successful in hiding his light under a bushel, but once he becomes a murderer that, shall we say, virtue is utterly destroyed."

Mawson remained thoughtful when Bony ceased speaking. What did strike him as singular was that Bony laid no stress on the acumen of the detective, and stressed the stupidity of the murderer. He began to ponder on the theft of the wool, and the discovery of it in the murdered man's shed, when Bony interrupted the flow of thought.

"Do not permit yourself to be unduly taxed by the puzzle," he advised. "Put more wood on the fire, and then employ your mind usefully on the more recent murder. So far I cannot find any connection between the two slayings excepting perhaps in the fact that had both bodies been submerged until putrefaction raised them the marks of violence might not have been detected by the post mortem . . . in the mind of the killer.

"It would seem, according to Dr. Lofty, that the body of Mrs. Answerth was dragged either over the causeway or along the shore shallows and pushed into deep water. First, survey the people living at Venom House. Who could have killed Mrs. Answerth? Any one of them, of course. Even Morris could have killed his mother."

"But he can't get out," expostulated Mawson.

"Once his door was left unlocked, Mawson. It could have been left unlocked again that night. The padlock to the bolt is of the type like that securing the door of Carlow's shed, and I opened that with a piece of wire in three or four seconds. And, anyway, the key to the padlock on Morris's door is kept suspended by a nail in the wall close by.

"Let your mind wander freely, and take a peep at Mrs. Leeper. Having been a hospital sister and a matron, she would know the action of putrefaction on a drowned body. She could anticipate murdering the two sisters, when Morris, being next of kin, would inherit the estate, and she, being experienced in the care of the mentally unstable, could anticipate being appointed his guardian by the sisters' trustees."

"You might have something there," Mawson said, and Bony was now satisfied that the constable had been led far away from stolen wool in a murdered man's shed. Mawson pushed back his chair and rose, saying: "I'd better be off to bed."

"It's been a pleasant evening," Bony told him. "We

may not have spent it profitably, but idle speech often has the effect of stirring the moribund mind. I can hear Mrs. Nash coming with the coffee. Better sit down again."

Mawson promptly accepted the suggestion before Mrs. Nash entered with a supper tray.

"Phew! Two policemen together and I can't see across the room," she complained. "Why, it's as bad as the sitting-room in Baker Street with old Watson and Sherlock Holmes both smoking at the same time."

"There is, however, not the same degree of intellectual chit-chat," Bony pointed out, sorrowfully, so that Mrs. Nash had to laugh. "The great Holmes always raced to his solution; we dally at the roadside. He would have required barely two seconds, Mrs. Nash, to sum you up as a most delightful woman. It has taken me five days to reach that same truth."

Mrs. Nash flushed with pleasure. Constable Mawson sipped his coffee. He left at eleven, and he was asleep long before Bony stirred from his notes and his meditation . . . to go to bed at one o'clock.

Bony was on the brink of slumber when the telephone in the hall shrilled its summons. That Mrs. Nash might not be unnecessarily disturbed, he slipped into a gown and went to the instrument.

It was Mawson.

"No doubt about your idea that murderers can't stay still," Mawson said, briskly. "Another murder. At Venom House. Miss Mary this time."

Chapter Fourteen

AGAIN THE NOOSE

BERT BLAZE was waiting with the boat.

"Miss Janet telephoned for me to take you over," he announced. "Miss Mary's still in a bad way."

Mawson said sharply:

"Miss Janet told me that Miss Mary had been strangled."

"That's so," calmly agreed Blaze, holding the boat steady as they boarded it. "Not properly, though."

Pushing the craft from land, the little cook agilely climbed inboard and took to the oars, when the water-reflected lights in the house slid round to become motionless beyond the bow.

"How long ago was it that Miss Janet roused you?" asked Dr. Lofty.

"Bit less than an hour," replied Blaze.

"And she said . . .?"

"That Miss Mary had been strangled, and that she'd phoned to Mawson, who told her he'd be leaving at once. Then she tells me to have the boat ready for you. I asked her how Miss Mary got herself strangled, and she said she didn't know and that Miss Mary wasn't able to say. Didn't sound like she was dead."

"We will hope that Miss Mary is alive," Bony contributed.

"Take a lot of strangling, she would," Blaze said with conviction. "Got a neck like a sawed-off tree."

Nothing more was said during the crossing, and silently

the three men left the boat, walked over the levee and across the grass to the main entrance. There was light in the room to the left, and the stained-glass window above the door was a tall oblong of gold. Mawson knocked on the heavy door.

The door was opened to reveal Janet Answerth wearing a silken gown over her night attire, and in her right hand a weapon Bony had not previously seen outside a police museum . . . a horse pistol. The lamp suspended from the ceiling directly above the foot of the magnificent staircase cast her face in shadow, but movement in addition to her voice betrayed her agitation.

"Oh! Please come in. I'm so glad you are here. Poor Mary!"

Mawson first entered, almost sweeping Janet Answerth aside. To the left of the staircase, Mrs. Leeper was kneeling beside Mary, who was lying on a mattress. To her Dr. Lofty went at once, and Bony, seeing that the horse pistol was wavering from one to the other, firmly relieved Janet of further responsibility. Blaze hurried in last, and closed the door. Janet would have spoken, but Bony motioned her to be silent and brought a chair.

"Neck," whispered Mary. "An' back."

"Almost strangled with this cord," Mrs. Leeper said. "He dragged Miss Mary to the ground and her back is hurt, too."

"Well, well, we'll soon have you comfortable, Miss Mary," soothed the doctor. Janet began to speak and Bony told her to wait. A minute was marked off by the victim's groans and the doctor's encouraging murmurs. Presently he stood up.

"Is that the lounge?" he asked Mrs. Leeper, indicating the lighted room off the hall. "We'll have a bed put in there for the patient, instead of carrying her up to her room."

Mrs. Leeper called on Blaze, and Mawson went with them up the stairs. Bony stepped forward, raised his brows interrogatively to Dr. Lofty and received his nod of assent. Kneeling beside the victim, he was shocked by her appearance. The great bosom heaved beneath the blanket covering her. Her breathing was stertorous, but the mouth was still square and grim, and the dark eyes very much alive.

"Please don't speak unnecessarily, Miss Answerth," he commanded. "Where were you attacked?"

"Outside," the woman managed to reply. "Something thrown at me window. When I poked me head out a man asked me to go down. Didn't have a light. Went out, and when I was off the step, he got me."

"You didn't see him when it happened?"

"No. Corded me from behind."

"Did you recognise his voice when he spoke to you from the ground?"

"No."

"Did he say why he wanted you to go out to him?" persisted Bony.

"To talk about the cattle that was lifted. He got me good. . . . The swine." Dr. Lofty's sedative was now taking effect, and Bony nodded understandingly.

"You went down off the porch step and then he drew the cord about your neck?"

"Yes. Hauled on me. The step caught me back."

"Even then you didn't see him . . . even the dark outline of his head?"

"No. I can wa . . . I can wait, Inspector. I'll get me hands on him some day. I'll . . . Leave me be."

The lids drooped, fluttered, closed, as though the mind of this woman could not be subdued even by the doctor's drug. Her breathing was changed in tempo, and as Bony watched the rugged face he was forced to acknowledge that to such personalities must be given the credit that the first settlers survived to found a nation.

Mrs. Leeper came to the doctor to say the bed had been placed in the lounge, and the men lifted the patient on the mattress and carried her from the hall. That accomplished, Bony beckoned Mawson and Blaze to follow him from the room. The door was closed.

Bony gave Mary's story.

"He could still be in the house, or somewhere on the 'island'," Mawson suggested, and Bony said he thought it unlikely as a full hour had passed since the attempt on Mary's life.

"He will have gone the way he came," he decided. "In a boat, or by swimming, and we'll find his tracks at the water's edge when it's light enough to see. However, you might cruise about the ground floor and see that all doors are locked. Bring the keys. If there is a back stairway, set a trap with flour or something from the kitchen. You might accompany Constable Mawson, Blaze, as you probably know the house."

"Ground floor, anyway," agreed the cook. "There is a back stairs, with a heavy door at the bottom. Might be able to lock that."

Blaze led the way to the passage along which Bony and Mawson had been conducted a few days previously, and Bony, glancing at the hall lamp, so arranged two chairs that the light would favour him. He sat and pensively rolled a cigarette, and the house was silent and cold so that he shivered.

Now the glory of the regal window was dimmed by the funereal tint of night, and the shade of the low-hung oil-lamp banished the upper half of hall and staircase, and the panelled walls appeared to be one with the shadows. On the top floor was that young man who was training himself to be strong, and who fished from his window with a magnet attached to power flex. Above were rooms filled with old period furniture whereon the dust lay heavy. Above were the rooms occupied by two women and, till recently, another. The strangler who had failed could play successfully a game of hide-and-seek.

It was so unlikely that the man had entered the house that Bony did not seriously consider the possibility. He had the feeling that he was sitting on a brightly-lit stage, and beyond the light a large audience was waiting, silent and watchful. The audience knew what was to come, but he, the actor, was ignorant of the plot. He felt relief when Janet Answerth came from the lounge, and rose to invite her to be seated in the chair he had placed. He supplied her with a cigarette, and then sat opposite with the light behind him.

"Tell me just what happened . . . from the beginning, Miss Answerth."

Bars of colour slanted across her gown where the light was caught by the silk. It tinted her hair with living lustre. It shone greenly in her eyes. Her face was pale, and she seemed as fragile as a doll.

"Take your time," he urged. "It's been a nasty experience for you."

"Horrible, Inspector," she said. "Thank you for being so . . . so considerate. I . . . it terrified me."

"It must have done. You had gone to bed, I suppose?"

"Yes, I was in bed. I was dreaming, and it was a

nasty dream, too. I dreamed I was out on the causeway, and something I couldn't see was chasing me. I slipped, and then knew it had me, and I screamed and woke up.

"I was thankful for my little bedside lamp, and was chiding myself for being so frightened by a mere dream, when I heard a peculiar noise, a noise I'd never heard before and so couldn't say what it was. I went to the door and listened. Then I opened it a little way. I could hear nothing until Mrs. Leeper called me from downstairs.

"I went into the dark passage and along to the gallery above the hall, and I looked down and saw Mrs. Leeper on her knees beside Mary. There was a lamp on the hall floor beside Mrs. Leeper and it was smoking terribly. Then I thought I must be still dreaming and was walking in my sleep. I have done that, you know. I went down to the hall, and Mrs. Leeper told me to lock the front door, and telephone for the police.

"I asked her what had happened, and she said that Mary had been strangled. So I telephoned to Edison and the operator told me to wait, and I had to wait such a long time before Constable Mawson spoke to me. I . . . I . . ."

"A little brandy, perhaps," suggested Bony.

"There's some on the sideboard in the dining-room." She made to get up, but he stopped her, saying he would bring it, and she nodded to the room opposite the lounge. Aided by his flashlight, he found a decanter and glass.

"Thank you, Inspector. Where was I? Oh, yes. After I told Constable Mawson what had happened, Mrs. Leeper asked if there was a gun in the house, and I remembered there was an old pistol in the escritoire in the lounge. So I managed to go in there in the dark and light a lamp. I was dreadfully frightened, but I had to do it.

"Mary was groaning, and I thought Mrs. Leeper was fighting with a snake. Then I saw it was a piece of Morris's fishing line and I meant to ask her what it was for when she told me to stand guard with the pistol and shoot if a man appeared. She went out to her room and came back with her mattress and a blanket, and we managed to pull Mary on to it. Once Mary screamed out that her back hurt frightfully, and Mrs. Leeper said she must bear it and wait for the doctor to come. We asked Mary if she would like some brandy, but she said she couldn't swallow. That is, we thought she said that. She couldn't speak clearly, you see."

"When you came downstairs, the front door was open, you said. Was it wide open?"

"Yes, Inspector. The draught or something was making Mrs. Leeper's lamp smoke. She blew it out when I lit the hall lamp."

"You heard no strange sounds in the house, after you came down?"

"No, not a thing."

"Where is your sister's room?"

"Over the lounge," replied Janet. "Mine's over the dining-room. And Morris's room is over what used to be the library. It's been locked up for years, and there's nothing in it, no books or anything."

Mawson returned with Blaze, to report having found nothing unusual. They had locked the door to the back stairs. Blaze said, eyeing the decanter:

"The fire's alight in the kitchen stove. What about making some coffee?"

"Oh, yes, please, Blaze," Janet said, just forestalling Bony. "And cut sandwiches, too. You must all be starving."

"What happened to the flex you mistook for a snake?" asked Bony, and Janet said it was rolled into a ball and left under the telephone. The instrument was in heavy shadow at the rear of the hall, and Mawson brought the flex. "Why was it put there?"

"Oh! Mrs. Leeper whispered to me to put it out of Mary's sight. Poor Mary was so terribly upset, we thought it might make her worse if she saw it."

Bony shook the flex free and took up the looped end to examine the manner in which it had been fashioned with sewing thread. Passing the other end through the loop, he then had a noose, and such was the condition of the two twisted cords that he was surprised by its flexibility. It was probably far from new when Mrs. Leeper used it to fasten her trunks.

Bony passed the flex to Mawson, and the constable tested the freedom of the noose before placing it with the pistol on a side table. Not speaking, Janet Answerth continued to sit stiffly on her chair, her gaze concentrated first on one man and then the other, her slim fingers opening and tightening on her handkerchief. There reached Bony a distinctive perfume, and this was recorded on his mind only when Mrs. Leeper was asked to take Janet's chair, when Janet was released to supervise Blaze in the kitchen. The perfume from Mrs. Leeper was of carbolic.

"I was wakened by a noise I thought at first came from somewhere on the Folly," the cook-housekeeper began her statement. "When I heard it again, it seemed to come from inside the house. I was wondering what it was when I heard what I thought was a door bang. So I said to myself: 'Ah! they're at it again.' I lay still . . ."

"Who, did you think, was at what again?" interrupted Bony.

"They have arguments, Inspector," replied Mrs. Leeper. "Miss Janet riles Miss Mary, and Miss Mary loses her temper and throws things and bangs doors and thumps along passages. Sometimes Miss Janet calls her insulting names, and then Miss Mary swears, and her language is shocking."

"Has this behaviour occurred in the middle of the night?"

"No. They're quiet enough at night, but at night you never know when you'll come on one or the other prowling about in the dark. As I told you, Inspector, you or I would carry a lamp when moving about a large house like this, but they don't, and more than once I've got a fright when they'd step from a room or appear in a dark passage."

"Disconcerting, Mrs. Leeper. What happened when you heard the sound of a door bang?"

"The next sound I heard was like someone calling, and I lit the hurricane lamp I always keep handy, and went out to the passage leading to the hall. It was then I heard someone groaning and calling for me. When I reached the hall, the first thing I noticed was the front door wide open, and then I saw Miss Mary at the foot of the stairs on her hands and knees.

"I asked her what had happened, and she said she had been attacked and strangled. She didn't say it as easy as that, though. I got her to lie down, and she moaned of pain in her back.

"Then I noticed she had something caught in her left hand, and I had the silly idea it was a snake. I moved the lamp to see what it was, and saw it was a length of flex."

"Had you seen that type of cord here before tonight?"

Mrs. Leeper nodded. She looked like a very fat koala

bear as she sat easily and well protected by a grey woollen
dressing-gown.

"I think the flex I found clutched in Miss Mary's hand
was some I secured my trunk with when I came here
first."

"You do not know that Mrs. Answerth was strangled
with similar cord?"

"N . . . no." The long-drawn negative could be due
to rising horror. Bony persisted.

This time the negative was sharply uttered.

"What did you do with the cord after removing it from
about the trunk?"

"I don't remember. Probably dumped it into a cupboard. I had no call to remember it."

"You shouted for Miss Janet to come down from her
room?"

"Yes."

"How long after you called did she appear?"

"At once. I think she was actually on her way down
when I called. She probably heard Miss Mary trying to
call for assistance. Anyway, when she did come down I
asked her to shut and lock the front door, and then to ring
for the police."

"Before, or when asking Miss Janet to ring the police,
did you tell her that Miss Mary had been strangled?"

Mrs. Leeper hesitated before saying she could not
remember having done so.

"Exactly when did you realise that Miss Mary had been
partially strangled?"

"After I could make out what she was saying, I think.
And then the mark round her neck was deepening . . . in
colour."

"Well, what next?"

"When Miss Janet had called the police, I asked her to stay with Miss Mary while I went to fetch a mattress. It would be some time before the police could get here, and I couldn't leave her lying on the floor. And, Inspector, I couldn't know just how hurt she was, and had to move her as little as possible till the doctor came. We managed to get her on to the mattress and make her a little more comfortable, and then I went to the kitchen and started the stove.

"After that, I came back to Miss Mary, and Miss Janet said she thought she was unconscious. But she wasn't. She opened her eyes, and I asked her if she'd like a drop of brandy. She wouldn't take anything. I went back to the kitchen and filled hot-water bottles, which I placed at her feet. There was nothing else I could do till Doctor came."

"Your room is near the kitchen, I think you said. Is the back door locked at night?"

Mrs. Leeper smiled grimly.

"How they can be nervous of burglars, I don't know, Inspector. With all the water round the place, and the only boat chained to a stump on the other side, no one could come across the causeway. No one knows the path over it excepting these women and the men's cook. But every night before going to bed, those two see to it that all the windows are fastened and the doors locked. I . . . No, that isn't possible."

"What isn't possible, Mrs. Leeper?"

"I've seen Morris with flex like that I had on my trunk. He uses it to lower a magnet from his window to catch metal things. Just for the moment, I had a bad idea about him."

Janet came back pushing a supper wagon, and Bony

warned Mrs. Leeper he might have further questions later on. He walked to the front door and out upon the porch to stand on the step. The hall lamp cast a broad ribbon across the porch and down the step, to end at a distance on the sward. The step followed the line of the house front, and was immediately below the large stained-glass window.

Sitting on the step, he rolled a cigarette and lit it before placing himself in the position of Mary Answerth when pulled to the ground. She said she had been strangled from behind, and that indicated that the man must have stood to one side of the door as she came from the house. Having slipped the noose over her head, he found he was unable to complete the deed, and so hauled on the cord and thus brought the heavy woman down upon her back.

It did seem that his only way of escape without being seen and possibly recognised was into the house, because to have broken into the open he would have had practically to leap over his victim.

According to medical theory, the body of Mrs. Answerth had been hauled through shallow water by the cord about her neck.

The Three Sisters were well down to the westward and told Bony it wanted at least three hours to daybreak. He had been right to refrain from instituting a search of the ground about the house, for the tramp of men in the dark might have ruined vital tracks. And if the attacker had taken Blaze's boat, well, he would have to reach the shore somewhere, and from that place could be tracked no matter what he did to evade pursuit.

Dr. Lofty came out to tell him that the coffee tasted good, and was invited to sit on the cold step.

"I'll not keep you longer than a minute," Bony said. "Can you tell me how that woman saved herself?"

"Luck and brute strength saved her, I think," replied Lofty. "Plus animal instinct to counter attack. When the cord fell about her head, she must have felt it touch her hair and was in time to thrust a hand upward between it and her neck. The cord cut the back of her right hand, such was the pressure exerted, and where the right hand would be held against the neck there is no mark of the cord.

"The neck ligaments are badly wrenched, and her back could have been broken on this step. She'll be up and about again in a week. You or I would have been in hospital for a couple of months . . . if we had managed to get clear of the noose."

"You will visit her again tomorrow?"

"In the afternoon, if there are no complications. Fortunately, this Leeper woman has had hospital training."

"She'll be out to your dope for the rest of the night?"

"And well into the day. Must keep her quiet. What about that coffee?"

"I need three cups."

They passed inside and Bony relocked the door. Janet Answerth was seated. Mrs. Leeper stood by the wagon and poured. Blaze offered the sandwiches.

With a coffee cup in one hand and a sandwich in the other, Bony stood close to the golden banisters to admire the sheen of the exquisitely carved wood. He heard Blaze offer the sandwiches to Dr. Lofty, then froze because he heard movement at the top of the stairs. There was a soft padding of feet.

The doctor was complimenting Janet Answerth on the

coffee. The soft padding was now on the stairs. The hall light cast the edge of its shadow midway up, and from the shadow into the light came a slippered foot. The companion foot followed, and then a pyjama-clad leg. Bony stood back. He didn't see, but felt Mawson beside him.

Down the stairs slowly came Morris Answerth. His eyes winked in the light. On his face was a smile. He waved to them all, and then particularly to Bony, and at the bottom of the stairs he said:

"I'm out again."

Chapter Fifteen

THE LAMP AND THE ROPE

THERE was nothing sinister in the voice, no wild emotion on the bearded face, no cunning triumph blazing in the dark eyes. He had but stated a fact, the importance of which was burned from his mind by the suspended lamp swung low above the foot of the stairs. The people to whom he had waved were forgotten. He stood with his hand pressed against his side, head back, gazing at the lamp.

"What a beauty!" he exclaimed.

Janet Answerth slipped past Bony and took his arm in her two hands. Her voice was gentle, her words urgent. Submerged in voice and words was steel.

"Morris! You oughtn't to have come down in pyjamas and dressing-gown. Can't you see we have guests? This will never do. Come along at once. Back to your rooms, please."

She pushed him almost off balance before he was aware of her. He saw Mrs. Leeper stepping forward, and he frowned. Janet shook her head, and Mrs. Leeper stopped.

"Come, Morris, at once, please."

Her arm imprisoned his against her side. She whispered something they could not hear, and he said:

"You will, Janet? Oh, thank you."

Together they went up the stairs, and it seemed that the shadows came down to take them into their darkness. Nothing was said. Dr. Lofty frowned into his coffee cup. Mawson stood rigidly, regarding Bony, waiting. Blaze struck a match and lit his pipe, and Mrs. Leeper sat down. Presently Janet came down the stairs.

"I don't understand it, Inspector," she said. "I am certain I snapped the padlock to his door-bolt and put the key on the nail."

"When was that?" he questioned, and, regarding him with wide eyes, she replied:

"Shortly after ten o'clock this evening. I'd been up with his supper tray and made sure he was comfy in bed for the night. I remember quite clearly bringing out his tray and the lamp and placing both on the passage floor so that I could bolt his door. Then I hung the key on the nail, and took up the tray and the lamp and came downstairs."

"Where is the key now?"

"On its nail."

"Where was it when you took Morris up?"

"In the padlock. Someone. . . . I don't know. I'm positive I locked his door."

"Then we must be doubly sure there is no stranger in

142

the house. Please go to your sister and remain by her bedside. Mrs. Leeper, be good enough to remain seated until we return. If you, Doctor, would mount guard at the front door. . . . Withdraw the key and keep it in your pocket. Shout if a stranger appears. Mawson, come with me. Blaze, bring that hurricane lamp and follow me."

Arrived at the head of the staircase, Bony asked Blaze if the two wing passages joined at the rear of the house, and Blaze said that the left passage ended at a bedroom door. The right passage ended at the top of the back stairs, at the bottom of which was the door which he had locked and passed the key to Mawson.

With the exception of the rooms occupied by Morris Answerth, they searched the top floor, and returning to the ground floor searched there, even to the two cellars. They found nothing of interest save the several rooms which had not been occupied for . . . in Mawson's opinion . . . a hundred years. Bony then called on Mrs. Leeper to conduct him to the room occupied by Mary Answerth.

Again passing up the stairs, Bony was taken to the left wing and to the first room on the left. There was no light other than that cast by his torch. He went in first, and the torch beam swept the room for the second time that night, stopping to reveal the ordinary oil-lamp on the bedside table.

"Please light that lamp, Mrs. Leeper. Matches?"

The lamp banished the silhouettes, created shadows to hide behind the furniture. The heavy four-poster with its canopy of heavy material was congruent with a massive wardrobe and an equally massive tallboy. The dressing-table could have come from the boudoir of an empress.

Upon it, a modern brass petrol-lamp was an affront.

The bed had been slept in. The clothes were thrown back as though the sleeper had left it without haste. On a chair was feminine underwear, a pair of men's tweed trousers, and by the chair was a pair of men's golf shoes.

The window was open. It was of the leaded, diamond-pattern casement type. A ratchet catch kept the window open, and into the room entered cold air to tease languidly the heavy curtains.

Leaning out over the sill, Bony directed his torch beam downward, and within the circle the dewy grass glistened as though covered with diamonds. The light circle moved left to stop at the wide step bordering the porch. Outward from the step moved the light, to follow the tracks on the diamond-littered ground made by the police party from boat to front door. Then back it came to the ground beneath the window where the glistening dew was unmarked.

No one had stood immediately below the window, to arouse Mary Answerth and then to persuade her to go down, but Bony had to accept the possibility that the man could have been standing below the step of the porch, when his tracks would have been blotted out by those of the police party.

"Do you believe it?" Mrs. Leeper asked as he was re-fastening the window.

"Believe what?"

"The yarn about a man throwing stones or something against the window and asking her to go down?"

"I have as yet no reason to disbelieve Miss Mary," he objected. "Have you?"

"I disbelieve her on principle," declared Mrs. Leeper. "Believe nothing these people tell you . . . nothing.

She said she went down to see a man about stolen cattle. Didn't she say that?"

"She did."

"Why come here to talk about stolen cattle in the middle of the night? What's the matter with the day-time? They won't have visitors here, but they're not that hostile that they'd shoot a rare one on sight."

"H'm! How often does the rare visitor call?"

"About once every third blue moon. Mr. Harston mostly, and now and then Bert Blaze or the old man who comes across to do the chores."

"Are Blaze and the old man regarded as visitors?"

"Why not? They come that seldom. But I didn't mean that they come into the house by the front door. The lawyers came twice this year, and they came in by the front door. And five or six weeks ago that butcher came to see Miss Janet."

"You refer to Edward Carlow?"

"The same," replied Mrs. Leeper. "Came to get Miss Janet to fill in his income tax forms, so she said. The parson came about twelve months ago . . . the Methodist parson. They took him in and gave him afternoon tea, the pair of them, and after he had gone back in the boat they ordered Blaze to return, and they dressed him down for bringing the parson over without their orders. Told him he was never to bring anyone to the house unless told to."

"And you don't believe Miss Mary was attacked outside the house?"

"No, I don't. She must have let him in. She let him in because she knew him, and she told the tale because she's made up her mind to deal with him herself. I think it was Morris. Miss Janet forgot to bolt his door, remember.

The last thing Miss Mary would admit is that Morris tried to strangle her."

"There may be something in what you say," Bony conceded, and noted the gleam of satisfaction in her eyes.

They returned to the hall, and Bony instructed Blaze to sit by the front door. He drew Dr. Lofty aside.

"I want you to accompany me on a visit to Morris as I'd like to have your professional opinion. We'll take Mawson in case additional physical weight is needed. Agreed?"

"Yes, of course . . . you're welcome to my opinion . . . with reservations."

Mawson was asked to bring the petrol-lamp from Mary's bedroom, and when arrived at the padlocked door Bony knocked. At once, Morris Answerth said, his voice coming from under the door:

"Do you want to come in?"

"Yes. Have you a light in there?"

"Janet always takes the light back when she goes off to bed. But I can see." They heard soft laughter. "I play games in the dark when Janet has gone to bed. She's not out there with you, I know that. There are three of you. Yes, you may come in."

The padlock was removed from the bolt. They entered, Bony holding aloft the lamp. Morris was seen with his back to the table and, as Bony advanced, he blinked at the fierce light, his face white, his hair and beard black by contrast. As Bony passed him to set the lamp on the table beside the toy railway, Morris turned to watch the light and the brass reflecting it. He was so interested in the lamp that Bony and the doctor, and Mawson who remained just inside the door he had closed, were seemingly forgotten.

146

"Good light, eh?" Lofty said, cheerfully.

"I . . ." Morris stood back, rubbing his hands as though controlled by ecstatic wonder. "Is it yours? Will you give it to me?"

"Have to ask Miss Mary first," Bony told him. "Anyway, would you like Doctor Lofty to tell you how it works?"

"Oh, I would." Morris maintained concentration on the lamp. Bony felt himself completely ignored, and was delighted. He nodded encouragingly to Lofty, and the doctor began a lecture with the incidence of petroleum. Quietly, Bony went to work aided by his torch.

The room off this large one was the young man's bedroom. It was clean and neat. The three-quarter bed had been occupied, and Bony tried to estimate the period since Morris had left it. By touch, he decided that the bed had not been occupied for several hours.

There was but one window to this room, and no other door save that leading to a small bathroom and lavatory. The walls were calcimined blue, and there were pictures cut from books, framed but minus glass. The one window opened to the end of the house, and this received careful attention.

Like those in the larger room, it was of the casement type, with small diamond panes. It opened as far as the outside steel lattice permitted, a bare eight inches, and Bony proceeded to test the lattice. It was firmly fixed to the outside of the wall, and by touch he found one of the studs having a squared head to take the spanner to screw it in.

He was able to move the stud with finger and thumb. He took it out. As easily, he removed other studs so that he was able to push the lattice away from the window and further open the window wide enough for a man to pass out. As easily, he replaced the studs and closed the window. He spent five minutes searching the bedroom and the bathroom for a rope, and found nothing which would enable Morris Answerth to reach the ground and return.

Shoes in the wardrobe were dry. The linoleum-covered floor under the window was dry. The clothes in the wardrobe were clean and unscarred. There were five Eton jackets of several sizes, and several pairs of hard-wearing grey trousers. The chest of drawers contained nothing of interest, save that the bottom drawer was crammed with toys. There was nothing under the bath, and the floorboards were as firm as cement.

Standing again beside Morris when Dr. Lofty's lecture was withering for the want of inspirational rain, Bony rolled a cigarette and dropped his matches. He knelt to retrieve them, and lightly touched Morris's slippers, to find them dry. Then at last he was rewarded.

Beneath the table ribbons of cloth had been tacked to form a web, and this web supported firmly against the table-top a rope of plaited blanket, a pair of trousers and a pair of canvas shoes. There were other oddments which Bony at once found of no interest. The old canvas tennis shoes were distinctly damp. For a moment he was held by memory of Morris Answerth supporting the table on head and hands when rising from a kneeling position, and he blamed himself for not having noted the hiding-place when the table must have been higher than the level of his eyes. He heard Morris say with startlingly simple conviction:

"I want the lamp."

"By the way, Morris," Bony said, rising like Phœnix.

"Show Dr. Lofty how you throw a lasso. I've been telling him how wonderful you are with it."

"Then will you give me the lamp? It's a beautiful lamp, and I want to keep it. I've never been allowed to keep a lamp, and I'm tired of playing in the dark all the time."

"We'll have to ask Miss Janet about it," Bony told him.

"When I tell Janet that you gave me the lamp, she will let me keep it. I'm sure she will."

"But the lamp belongs to Miss Mary, Morris. She mightn't like it if we left it with you. Whatever would she say if we told her what we had done with her lamp?"

"Mary won't ever know." Morris Answerth stiffened. The scowl of frustration gave place to a smile. The smile vanished. He moved so quickly that neither man could offer a counter. With his left hand, he swept up the hissing lamp and held it high. He was Ajax . . . if Ajax had red hair and a red beard and blue eyes which shone with rage. "If you come to take the lamp, I'll strike you with it."

Slowly and sadly shaking his head, Bony held out his hands.

"We'll do something about it later on, Morris. You must always trust your friends. Please let me have the lamp."

The anger faded. The lips trembled. The eyes filled with tears. Bony accepted the lamp and placed it back on the table.

Chapter Sixteen

MORRIS MUSTN'T TELL

"WE haven't said you cannot have the lamp," Bony pointed out. "Be a good fellow now, and talk about other things like you did when I came to see you last time. The lamp belongs to Miss Mary, not to us. We cannot give you what doesn't belong to us, can we?"

"No, you cannot do that. I am very sorry for behaving so badly. Will you overlook it this time?"

"Of course. Now do show Dr. Lofty how you can throw a lasso. We'll speak to Miss Mary about the lamp for you."

Morris pinched his lower lip, alternately regarding his visitors. His expression registered doubt.

"You could leave it with me, though, as Mary will be ill for a long time. Didn't you hear she has been strangled?"

"Yes. How did you come to hear about that?"

"A little dicky-bird told me. He tells me lots of things." Gone was the frankness of the boy of ten, the naïveté of the simple youth. The blue eyes were masked by craftiness, and their silence was what Morris looked for, for silence meant to him breathless curiosity.

"Wouldn't you like to know who tried to kill Mary?"

"Perhaps we do know," Bony said.

"Oh! Who?"

"You tell."

Morris chuckled and shook his head. He looked again at the lamp, and Bony hoped his attention would not be recaptured by the bright light. He rubbed his hands together, turned back to his visitors and again laughed.

"Then perhaps you would like to know who killed Mother?"

"What I am sure about, Morris, is that Doctor Lofty would like to watch you throwing your lasso."

"Would he?"

"I certainly would," said the doctor. "Who did kill your mother?"

"I won't tell."

Morris's laughter this time was prolonged.

"Oh, never mind who killed your mother," Bony exclaimed, impatiently. "It's the lasso we want to see. Come on, Morris! We want to see you in action, and we can't stay all night."

"I don't know what I've done with the lasso."

"That is a pity. Especially after I told Dr. Lofty about it. Well, I suppose we had better be going, Morris. It's long after your bed-time."

"Yes, it must be, Bony. I'm sorry about the lasso. I am very angry with myself for forgetting to remember what I did with it. I found the magnet. I'd left it on the mantel over there. I made another line with string, but the string isn't heavy enough to use for a lasso."

"What you really want is some light rope, Morris," Bony told him. "Would you like me to bring some when I come again?"

"Thank you, Bony," said Morris, abruptly grave. "That would do very well."

"The magnet, you say, you found on the mantelshelf?"

"Yes. I must have left it there." Morris went over to the fireplace and with a finger indicated the exact position. Bony accompanied him.

151

"D'you ever have a fire?"

"Oh no! I hate fires. Once a fire burned. It came from a match in a box Janet brought. I told her she had left it, and she told me to fire one of the matches and it burned me. I don't like fire."

"But lamps are fire, and you like lamps, don't you?"

"Yes. But lamps don't burn if you know all about them. Janet says I know nothing about them, and that's why she won't let me have one."

Bony again examined the mark on the wood made by the incessant blows of the lasso about the cloisonné vase. Then, sinking to his knees, he looked at the empty grate and up the chimney. He fancied he saw a hanging spider's web, and he brought out his torch and turned the beam upward. At about the level of the mantel, two iron bars crossed the inside of the chimney, previously used to suspend hooks to support iron kettles over the fire. The spider's web was a strand of red flex, for on the bars rested a rolled length of it. He pulled it down, shook it out over the floor. There was neither soot nor dust upon it. It was very much reduced in length.

"Well, that's what you did with your fishing-line and lasso," he told Morris, but Morris wasn't interested. The torch completely captivated him, and when Bony returned the torch to his pocket, he cried out:

"Oh, please don't put it away. What is it, Bony? Let me see."

"Don't you remember putting your lasso up the chimney?" persisted Bony, merely wasting breath because Morris insisted on looking at the torch. It was brought out and flashed on and off and on again, whilst Bony softly said: "Would you like me to give this lamp to you?"

"Give it to me! Why, it's lovely. It's better than the other one. Oh, I would. Thank you, Bony."

"If I give this little lamp to you, you should give me something in return."

"Of course. I'll give you the lasso."

"I'll give you the torch if you tell me who killed your mother."

The torch vanished into Bony's side pocket, and Morris Answerth stepped back, and from the pocket his gaze rose slowly to meet Bony's eyes.

"I'll give you the lasso for the lamp," he insisted.

"But I don't want the lasso."

"Then I'll give you something else. What would you like?"

"You to tell me who killed your mother."

Morris's white teeth chewed the under-lip. The struggle was obvious, and Bony became confident of victory.

"I mustn't. . . . I mustn't tell who killed Mother."

"That's just too bad, Morris." Bony turned away to the doctor standing near the table. With his back to the man-boy, he was thankful to see Constable Mawson standing stiffly at the door. "Well, Doctor, we had better be going. Morris seems reluctant to show you how he throws a lasso."

A large and capable hand was rested lightly on his shoulder and, turning again, he looked into the appealing face and eyes.

"I mustn't tell," Morris cried. "I promised not to. I mustn't tell you . . . I mustn't. I'd be whipped again if I did, and I can't bear to be whipped."

"Who would whip you, Morris?"

"Janet."

153

"But you are ever so much stronger than Janet," Bony argued. "She couldn't whip you."

"Oh, she would if Mary held me."

"Well, who told you about Mary being strangled tonight?"

"No . . . I won't say. I won't say, Bony."

"Did you strangle your mother and try to strangle Mary? Tell me," thundered Bony.

Morris wept, standing like a dying tree swaying in a windstorm. Shaking his head he continued to murmur:

"I mustn't. I mustn't."

Bony motioned to Lofty to take the petrol-lamp from the table and, when the doctor had joined Mawson by the door, he said gently:

"Never mind, Morris. Let us still be friends. I'll come and see you again. This time I'll take your lasso and you may have my lamp." The flaring joy on the bearded face was pathetic. "See, you hold it so. That's right. Now press upon the little button. Now lift your finger from the button, and the light goes out. Good night."

He backed to the doorway, watching Morris Answerth flashing the torch on and off, holding it from him that the beam be directed to his delighted eyes. The room darkened as Lofty carried the petrol-lamp into the passage, and from the doorway Bony paused a moment to see Ajax bathed in lightning flashes. He closed the door, shot the bolt and padlocked it. Having returned the key to the wall nail, he said:

"I would regard it as a favour did both of you say nothing of this visit to Morris Answerth."

They could hear Morris singing as they passed along the passage to the gallery crossing the hall, and the echo lived in their ears as they went down the golden staircase.

Lofty said he would visit his patient, and Bony sensed that the little doctor wanted time to bring his reactions to Morris into focus before giving an opinion. Blaze rose from the chair beside the door, his old eyes undimmed by the vigil, and Mrs. Leeper was sent after the doctor.

"Doing any good?" Blaze asked, regarding Mawson with suspicion and wondering if he did actually see the constable 'pouring' flex into the doctor's bag where already was the cord which had almost choked out Mary Answerth's life.

"May do better after daybreak," replied Bony. "Take a peep outside and see how far off it is. Don't go from the porch."

Bony sat in the chair vacated by Mrs. Leeper, and Blaze returned to say that in less than thirty minutes it would be light enough to gather mushrooms. When Bony relaxed and closed his eyes, the cook returned to his chair at the front door. He heard the lounge door open and close, and didn't bother to see who came out. His mind was racked by questions the answers to which could be only problematical, based as they were on an incomplete survey of this scene of attempted murder.

There were, of course, facts which had emerged from the latest visit to Morris Answerth. One fact was that he had been in the habit of leaving his room by the window, roaming about outside the house, and returning the same way. Another fact was that Morris Answerth was not the simple, polite little boy as first impressions would give.

There was the fact that Morris admitted knowing who killed his mother and who attempted to kill his half-sister. Mary Answerth had said she had told Morris of his mother's death, and no doubt Janet had told him of the attack on Mary when she returned him to his room.

Morris could have been out of the house and witnessed both the murder and the attempted murder, and thus known the killer. However, to Mary he had evinced no emotion when informed of his mother's death, and he had betrayed no emotion save one of childish triumph when asking if he, Bony, would like to know who killed his mother. It certainly indicated that he was bereft of the power of affection.

It seemed obvious, too, that Morris had to tell someone that he knew who killed and tried to kill, and this accorded with abnormal psychology, a superficial survey of which Bony had but a few hours previously given to Mawson. One thing fairly certain was that no one knew Morris could have and had left his room via the window that very night Miss Mary was attacked. He could have killed his mother, and dragged the corpse over the causeway, and in opposition to the statements that only the Misses Answerth and Blaze knew the hidden pathway, there was the inescapable fact that from his window Morris had repeatedly watched them cross over and return, and therefore could have the pathway charted on his mind. He could have met and pounded Carlow into insensibility, and then dragged him to the Folly and drowned him. He could be the man who induced Mary to leave the house.

There was the flex. The small loop at one end of the flex used in the attempt to strangle Mary Answerth was of the same size, although bound with sewing thread, as that fashioned with twine to make the noose of Morris's fishing-line-lasso. The neatness with which both loops had been made indicated they had been bound by the same person.

Janet could know who killed Mrs. Answerth, and do all

in her power to prevent the killer becoming known. Mary could know that Morris had attacked her. Both, for the same or different reasons, could be determined to protect their stepbrother at all cost. They hated each other, but there had emerged no evidence that either hated Morris. The whipping he had received, following his escape, was probably administered as corrective punishment.

Bony was now feeling the cold of the hall and rose to stretch and stifle a yawn.

"Bit fresh this morning," remarked Blaze, and for the first time Bony noted that he was wearing only shirt and trousers.

"Could be a frost outside."

"Cold enough."

"Why didn't you say so much earlier? Without a coat you must be as cold as mutton."

Blaze grinned and struggled to set his lower denture into place.

"You townies are too soft," he managed to say. "Not like us old bushwhackers. You going out?"

"Ought to be growing light. Prove your hardiness by coming with me."

Bony opened the door and the dawn light was like new steel. They passed out to the porch, and Bony closed the heavy door. The air stung. The grass glistened with dew almost frozen, and the dead trees on the Folly beyond the levee were white splinters against the distant back-drop of varied greens. The birds were united in their anthem to the new day.

"Now I can breathe," Bony said, and old Blaze chuckled and declared he preferred a blacks' wurlie to a house, and in the greatest storm would choose a five-wire fence to the shelter of Venom House.

"I want you to accompany me," Bony told him. "I want you to see what I shall see, and give me your opinion. And remember what I told you Miss Mary said had happened to her and where. First, from this porch to the levee are the tracks made by you, by Doctor Lofty and Mawson and by me."

"Don't appear to be no tracks right under Miss Mary's winder," Blaze said, rubbing tobacco into shreds for his pipe.

"Do you think anyone could throw something against her window when standing on the porch step?"

"Take a glancing shot to do it."

"But it could be done by a person aware of the tale-telling dewy grass. Our four pairs of tracks are plain enough, and they do not entirely obliterate those left by Miss Mary when she stepped down from the step. Right?"

"Correct."

"A man could stand just left of the door and not be noticed when she came out. If expert with a lasso, he wouldn't need to come forward to make his throw. In the dark, he could slip by the woman when she was on her back on the porch and struggling to release herself. Think so?"

"Correct again," answered Blaze. "And I see tracks coming and going along the house front . . . or going and coming. There was dew on the grass when them tracks was made, and a lot of dew fell on the tracks after they was made."

They left the porch and, keeping wide of the two sets of tracks, followed them to the corner of the house, round the corner to halt beneath the second window.

"Now, what do you think?" asked Bony.

Blaze faced to the house and the window on the ground floor. Then he looked upward to the window above it, a window guarded by steel lattice. Pointing to the lower window, he said:

"He came out of that room. Usta be the library. Nothing in it now, so I was told. He came out of the library, sneaked round the corner and walked to the porch, and came back the same way."

Bony stooped and indicated several short lines about the clearly defined shoe prints.

"D'you think those lines could have been made by a rope?"

"It would be a pretty hefty-sized rope," Blaze contended, his eyes screwed to bright brown points. What he saw in Bony's quizzing smile brought a frown.

"A rope made of torn-up blankets," Bony suggested, and the cook exclaimed:

"Cripes! Not him?"

"Those short lines were made by the tail end of a blanket rope let down from Morris Answerth's bedroom window."

The cook sucked in his breath. He followed Bony back along the tracks to the porch step, and was then asked to follow the tracks to the levee to see if his boat was still there. On his return, he watched Bony stooping and angling his body that he could observe the tracks near the porch step, and to himself said:

"They's born with it . . . them abos. Trick 'em! Not on your life." Coming behind Bony, he said that the boat was where he had tethered it.

"Take another look at these tracks, Blaze. What do they tell you?"

Blaze, who had once been renowned for his bushcraft,

now took his time. Having lost one bout with this half-abo, he wasn't going to lose another . . . as easily. Bony stood back to give him room as from various positions the old man crouched and angled to sight the tracks.

"He come from round the corner," Blaze eventually began his summing up. "He came along to here, and he stepped up on to the porch. Then he stepped off the porch and went back the way he'd come. Funny! He stepped off the porch backward, and he walked backward to there before turning round and walkin' away in proper style."

"Point out just where he turned."

"Here's where he turned . . . a good twelve feet from the porch step."

"Yes?"

"And when he turned, he set off almost running."

"That's so," agreed Bony. "He hurried away as far as the corner. From the corner to his rope, he walked at normal gait. Most interesting, isn't it?"

"Yes. He'd have been the last I'd picked."

"I wonder, Blaze, if you could answer just one question."

"I'll give her a go."

"Why, Blaze, did Morris Answerth step off the porch backward."

"Why . . . Hell! How d'you expect me to know?"

"I do not expect it," countered Bony.

Chapter Seventeen

BONY IS DISPLEASED

Mawson opened the front door and Dr. Lofty appeared, to ask if he might now return to his home and his labours.

"Of course, Doctor. Blaze will row you over at once. Mawson! You may return, too."

At the levee, Bony drew the doctor aside.

"You will be paying Miss Answerth another visit . . . when?"

"Some time this afternoon. She's comfortable, and I've given Mrs. Leeper instructions."

"Did you leave any drugs, a sedative, with Mrs. Leeper?"

"Only sleeping tablets. I've treated the abrasions, and will bring back a supply of ointment. They had a good embrocation in the house which will do for her back."

"How many tablets?"

Lofty's brows shot upward. A little stiffly, he replied that there were one dozen in the bottle he had left with Mrs. Leeper.

"What do you think of Morris?"

"Arrested intellect. Mind you, I'm no psychiatrist. Physically he's an extraordinarily fine specimen, and that is extraordinary in a man confined all his life to two rooms."

"D'you think it essential that he be continuously kept to his room, never permitted to take the air? Do you think his mental condition warrants that?"

"Not having a history of the case I am not competent to give an opinion. From a somewhat superficial examination, I'm inclined to agree with your doubt."

"Your opinion of Mrs. Leeper? She is really a trained nurse?"

"Oh yes. I tested her. She's worked in hospitals. I'm quite satisfied to leave the patient with her."

"And Miss Answerth will be abed for a week, I think you mentioned."

"Should be in bed for a week at least. I doubt that she'll consent to stay there that long. However, Mrs. Leeper will do her best to persuade her."

"Thanks. I'll wait over here till you come this afternoon." Bony turned to Mawson. "I'll be staying, Mawson. Telephone if necessary. Squash any rumour in Edison that Miss Mary is even suffering a headache. Where is Mrs. Leeper now, d'you know?"

"In the kitchen preparing breakfast."

"And Miss Janet?"

"She's with Miss Mary. I heard 'em arrange that she was to stop with Miss Mary until Mrs. Leeper called her to breakfast and could take her place."

"Well, that's about all. Blaze! I'll telephone you if I should want to be ferried over before Dr. Lofty returns this afternoon. Meanwhile, don't repeat the story of the little aborigine boy who tracked his sister to the lagoon where she was taken by an alligator."

The cook nodded and grinned, nearly lost his empty pipe whilst holding the boat steady for his passengers, and pushed off. Bony watched the boat for a full minute before turning back to the house.

As though he were the owner, he strolled into the hall and looked into the room opposite the lounge that now was a ward. He had previously entered this room with Mawson and Blaze, but on that occasion had remained by the door while they searched by the light of his torch. Despite distance from the kitchen it was used as a dining-room, being furnished with an exceptionally long and solid cedarwood table. At the table stood twelve cedar-wood chairs. There was a vast cedarwood dresser which because of its antiquity was not incongruous. Above the fireplace hung a portrait in oils of a man who had lived in a bygone era and who could have been anything from a pirate to the official flogger. As Mary Answerth looked something like him, Bony guessed he was one of her forebears.

Almost languidly, he passed up the staircase to pause on the gallery once again to admire the window. Anguish and blood, toil and sweat and brutality, had gone into the erection of this sombre house, and a ruthless man had conceived and brought into being the glory of this stair-case, and the window to emphasise its beauty, making of it a wondrous jewel in a cold, stone casket. Perhaps he it was whose portrait hung above the mantel in the dining-room.

Proceeding into the wing opposite that where Morris had his rooms, he entered the bedroom normally occupied by Mary Answerth, again examined the window, and leaned out to observe the position of the porch below. The next room, Mrs. Leeper had said, had been Mrs. Answerth's bedroom. It was clean and dustless, but the four-poster bed was stripped, and the chest contained neither linen nor blankets. Standing before the window, he watched the boat now drawing close to the opposite shore, and he unfastened the catch and leaned out to estimate how far he was from the window of Mary Answerth's bedroom.

He looked into four more rooms before arriving at the end of the passage beyond the right-angle. All these rooms had been undisturbed for decades. At the end of the passage was a curtained recess, and nothing there excepting two pails, several scrubbing brushes, and brooms flanking a water tap. The pails were dusty. The brooms looked as though never used, and two wall brooms reminded him of his wife, Marie, who appeared to like nothing better than to whisk imaginary cobwebs from the ceiling of his study when he was working there.

He descended to the ground floor by the back stairs, noting that Mawson had returned the key to the door at the end. Hearing Mrs. Leeper in her kitchen, he passed its door and sauntered to the refreshingly modern room in which he had first met Janet Answerth.

This room was so markedly dissimilar to the rest of the house that to enter it was like emerging from a dungeon into a sunlit garden. The risen sun flung wide bars of gold across the rugs in effort to reach the baby grand of natural walnut. The divan was aloof but the chairs said let me caress you.

From a small table he took up a copy of *My First Two Thousand Years*, and wondered how Janet Answerth reacted to the adventures of The Wandering Jew. Taste in literature is invariably an excellent guide to character. A wide, glass-fronted bookcase drew him. Next to a set of Bishop Thurlow-Elswick's *Notes on the Book of Revelations* were two beautifully bound volumes of *The Decameron*. Jane Austen's work was well to the fore, with Somerset Maugham representing the moderns. A volume which made Bony's heart ache with envy was Milton's *Paradise Lost*. With the exception of the tale of the lass who went to sea without a chaperon, works by Australian authors were conspicuous by their absence. Not a fraction of an inch was given to mystery fiction.

Doubtless, the music sheets and albums would have assisted him in his reading of character, had he understood music. The few pictures were originals, their subjects so varied as to give no clue to the psychologist. And women of all ranks are buyers of sleek magazines devoted to cosmetics and clothes.

There was a further door, and, receiving no acknowledgement to his knock, he entered a room whose outer wall was entirely of glass. The parquet floor was lightly waxed. The furniture was voluptuous . . . what there was of it. There were several easels bearing paintings in varied stages of development, and upon the wall facing the window was an art gallery. All these pictures were unsigned, and amateurish even to Bony, whose taste was old-fashioned. Save that the artist favoured the out-of-doors, they told him nothing. He found no weapons, no phial of poison, no flex, no treatise on the art of garrotting. He glanced into the drawers of a roll-top desk, and found no reports of inquests on drowned bodies.

Again in the sitting-room, he was sure that these rooms were solely occupied by Janet, for he found no evidence of her sister Mary. Even the spittoon Mary had brought in during that first visit was gone. Surely no two sisters could be more widely apart than these.

On his sauntering into the kitchen, Mrs. Leeper turned from the immense wood-burning stove to regard him with undisguised astonishment. Her house frock was almost wholly concealed by the starched apron, and once again Bony was sharply reminded of the advertisement for the pot and pan polish.

"I thought you had gone, Inspector," she said.

"The aroma of bacon and lamb cutlets detained me, Mrs. Leeper. Am I in the way?"

"No. You will be staying for breakfast?"

"That is the ambition at the moment."

"Then I'll prepare more cutlets. One of the advantages of working here is that you can eat the meat they kill on the place."

"My wife and I are thinking of turning vegetarians," Bony lied, seating himself in a chair at the centre table. "On my meagre salary, we can no longer afford to pay a shilling for one small, stringy chop from an animal who lived to the age of twenty. Did you suggest a cup of coffee?"

"I didn't. But I'll pour you one."

"You haven't been able to recall what happened to that flex you used to tie up your trunk?"

Mrs. Leeper sighed as though her patience was taxed by yet another mental invalid. Without speaking, she filled a coffee cup and placed it before him. She brought a dish of cutlets from the refrigerator, added several to the grill and returned the dish. She sighed again, then made her pronouncement.

"When I accepted a position in a lunatic asylum, I learned the art of self-defence. Pressure on certain nerves in the neck will cause temporary paralysis. If the pressure is maintained on another nerve for five seconds the patient will not survive. I've often felt like committing murder, Inspector. If ever I do it won't be with power flex."

"I've heard of that jujitsu hold," Bony said, blandly. "You must try it on me sometime. Meanwhile, I feel I ought to point out that there are necks and necks. There are swan necks and bull necks, and, Mrs. Leeper, there are hippopotamus necks. I suggest that one might meet

166

with difficulty when trying to apply pressure to the nerve you mentioned, in the alleged neck of Miss Mary Answerth."

"I wouldn't find it difficult," boasted the cook.

"I was not so impolite as to infer that you tried to murder Miss Answerth," proceeded Bony, and added thoughtfully: "Although you could have used that long-handled wall broom upstairs to tap against Miss Mary's window from the window of the room next to hers, and then followed her downstairs and out to the porch. By the way, you are quite sure that when finding Miss Mary on the hall floor the front door was wide open?"

"It was wide open, and breaking a hippopotamus neck is easier than breaking a swan neck." Mrs. Leeper completed the loading of a tray. "Take the passage to the left if you want the bathroom. Breakfast's ready . . . in the dining-room."

Thanking her, Bony passed from the kitchen, hearing behind him the rustle of the woman's starched apron and feeling himself rebuked by one to whom cleanliness was greater than life and death. Refreshed by cold water and the application of a pocket comb, he entered the dining-room to be greeted by Janet Answerth, who rose from the table.

"What a surprise, Inspector! Do come and eat. You must be famished."

She was wearing a yellow linen dress with Chinese collar of white, and in the dimness of the room her hair was the colour of old copper. Petite and vital, it occurred to Bony how peculiar it was she had not married.

"How is Miss Mary?" he asked, when helping himself to a cereal.

"Still sleeping, Inspector. At least I suppose her

167

drugged condition could be called sleeping. Doctor Lofty said she would wake about eleven, and told us to be very firm if she insisted on getting up. She has to stay in bed for a week."

"My study of her causes me to think she will rebel."

"Mrs. Leeper will win," Janet said with the vocal tones she had used with Morris. "Mrs. Leeper is a very capable woman."

"That is my opinion also. It is her ambition to own a mental hospital, she tells me. She is experienced."

"I am not aware of her ambition, but of her experience. She is a good cook and a reliable housekeeper, which is all that interests me. I am much more interested in you."

"In me?" Bony pretended to be startled more than he actually was.

"Yes," Janet said slowly. "You know, you don't look a bit like a detective. Are you an Australian?"

"I am Australia," Bony claimed, a pause between each word.

"But you have such a wonderful accent."

"Due, perhaps, to the fact that I was reared at a Mission Station with children of the aboriginal race who speak English like the Dubliners of Ireland. Not having been to Dublin I cannot vouch for it."

"And you are actually on the same level as Inspector Stanley?"

In this light, the large eyes were grey, and Bony was sure of it as he looked deeply into them. There was a limit to the depth, however, and he recognised a clever woman so absurdly foolish as to believe in her power over *all* men. Well, why disillusion her? In his grandee manner, he murmured:

"Madam, I have the same rank as Inspector Stanley, but I am far above his level, intellectually."

"I am sure you are, Inspector Bonaparte. I found Inspector Stanley rather dull. Do you think you will ever discover who murdered poor Mother?"

"Naturally, Miss Answerth."

"You have reasons for being confident?"

"Yes."

"Oh! Do tell me."

"One reason is because I have never yet failed to finalise a murder investigation."

Her lips were still and slightly apart, and her eyes wide with admiration until scepticism crept into them.

"But some murderers are very clever, don't you think?" she said. "Not all murderers are found out."

"They would be were there a dozen Napoleon Bonapartes instead of but one. I am myself unable, Miss Answerth, to investigate every crime of homicide."

"Of course. You think, then, that this case won't defeat you?"

"I am sure of it. The murderer made one mistake, and will make others. They all do, Miss Answerth, but often when a crime is investigated by men like Inspector Stanley, the murderer outwits them. By the way, during my wanderings about the house before breakfast . . . to make sure that the man who attacked Miss Mary isn't in the house . . . I found myself in your sitting-room, and entered the studio. Are all those your paintings?"

"Yes. I spend quite a lot of time there. I found I had to do something to keep myself alive. Do you like them?"

"Very much. Especially those of the Folly. I thought your treatment of light on the water-killed trees particularly good. You play, too?"

"I love the piano. Outside Morris, my music and my painting are my chief interests. Father was wise in his dealings with us, Inspector. He sent me to school in Brisbane. Poor Mary was too boorish to bother with. Often she is horribly crude. I'll never forgive her for bringing that beastly spittoon into my sitting-room. Her place is at the men's quarters. Do tell me what mistake the murderer has made."

Bony looked doubtful. He was not pleased that this Janet Answerth should have the effrontery to think he could be ensnared by her feminine charm and beauty, to think that he, with all his experience of life and people, would fall at her feet and pour from his palpitating heart all his secrets. So he smiled into her eyes, and played her game, just a little better.

"You wouldn't mention it to anyone, would you?"

"You may trust me, Inspector."

"I feel that I can, Miss Answerth. Well, you see, the man who killed your mother also attempted to kill your sister. His mistake was in twice using a lasso, betraying the fact that he was an expert. When I find the man who is such an expert, I shall arrest him at once."

Chapter Eighteen

WRITING ON THE WALL

THE day was growing up . . . an unruly child. On Bony's emerging from the house after breakfasting with Janet

Answerth, he found that the sun was Chinese yellow instead of Australian gold. The wind was coming from the nor-west, and already little waves were throbbing against the island called Venom House.

Standing on the levee, he could see the mark in the bank made by the prow of Blaze's boat. There were several similar marks obviously older than twelve hours. He could not observe marks made by a swimmer wading to and climbing over the levee. To be sure that no one had swum or come by boat to the island the previous night, he followed the levee clockwise.

The levee, of earth and stone, was sufficiently broad at the top to provide a pathway six to eight feet above the water. Half a dozen sheep were feeding inside the levee, and they followed him with the expectancy of hand-fed animals until a fence stopped them.

Beyond the fence was the vegetable garden, the fowl pens, the woodstack and, protected by tarpaulins, the sawing-bench and the oil engine to power the circular saw. Here Bony was at the rear of the house, and he paused to watch the busy hens, among which were two mothers fussing with many chicks, at the same time noting the position of the kitchen and back doors. There was much more land on this, the north, side, and the rising wind was vigorously flapping the clothes on two lines. Near the kitchen door was built an open-fronted shed containing the split wood. The man who came over specially to saw and chop wood, and do other chores, might be worthy of examination. At the moment, the situation of the covered sawing-bench and oil engine in the lee of the stack of unsawn wood was of greater import.

Eventually the levee conducted him to the east side of

171

the house and so opposite that corner where Morris Answerth had his rooms. There was nothing out of position with the steel lattice guarding the bedroom window. The casement was open a few inches, but he could not see Morris, probably because he was sleeping after his exciting night. The thought brought awareness of his own need of sleep.

On coming again to the causeway, he was sure that no stranger or unauthorised person had landed from a boat or had emerged from the water to attract Mary Answerth's attention and so lure her out of the house, and thus there could be no argument to contest the fact that her assailant lived at Venom House.

Bony turned to gaze once more at the front of the mansion, for mansion it was. He fancied someone was watching him from the lounge. The front door was open as he had left it, but long since the dew on the grass had vanished, and with it the tracks which he had read as easily as the printed page. There was slight movement at the first of Morris Answerth's two living-room windows and he saw the hand from which a dun-coloured line was creeping down the grey stone face. Morris was fishing, not sleeping. It would be Janet who watched from the lounge, as Mrs. Leeper would be in her kitchen.

Just why was Morris Answerth confined to those two rooms? Unable to swim, the 'island' itself was for him a prison. Was that eternal confinement dictated by periods of violence when restraint was difficult even to such a pair as Mary and Mrs. Leeper? Save for the one exhibition of violence when Morris had threatened to throw the lamp, Bony had seen nothing indicating that he required such constraint.

On the occasion when he had escaped from the house, he

had taken the boat, aimlessly rowed on the Folly and landed to play with young lambs. Blaze had supported that story, in addition to Mrs. Leeper. The thought that Morris, by watching his sister and others wading over the causeway, also knew the pathway hidden by the muddy water, had previously been explored by Bony. Had he managed to escape on occasions other than when he had rowed on the Folly? It inferred, of course, that his door had been accidentally left unlocked, and this in turn inferred a habit of forgetting to lock his door. That no one knew of his escape via the window could be accepted.

The hiding-place of the blanket rope, the old trousers and the sand shoes was sufficient proof of planning and cunning to outwit his sisters. He was much more than an obedient, polite boy of ten or twelve years, and Bony wondered how much, if anything, had his mother contributed to that part of his seemingly arrested mind.

Bony walked to the magnet being lowered from the upper window. The string was ordinary parcel twine and the magnet was large and powerful. On touching the ground, the fisherman manœuvred it as much as the window opening would permit, and it collected a toy railway line, two nuts and a metal knob which had probably come from the top of a chair. Although the fisherman could not have felt the 'bites', the magnet was drawn up and disappeared through the window.

Bony noticed many metal objects lying so wide that the fisherman would never catch them, and, the magnet again being lowered, gently he moved it to catch so many objects that it fairly bristled.

This catch eventually disappeared, and a hand was thrust far out and waved to him. Again the bait was lowered, and again raised bristling with the catch. Then a shower of objects fell from the window, and the game was continued.

It was played for half an hour, and might have continued longer had not Janet Answerth appeared on the porch and come to investigate. Solemnly, Bony loaded the magnet, and, solemnly, he watched it being drawn up by the fisherman.

"Whatever are you doing, Inspector? Why! Playing at fishing with poor Morris."

"Your brother is happy because never before has he caught so many fish in so short a time, with such little effort," Bony said. "Wait and see. Dear me . . . I'm being quite political . . . Churchill and Asquith."

The magnet came down, rested on the ground, lifted to sweep in narrow arcs, gather a Meccano part, a bolt. Bony picked up other objects and dropped them against the magnet, and presently the loaded 'hook' was moving slowly up the wall.

"Morris will want to play all day, Inspector. And I've to tell you that Blaze has just rung up to say he advises coming over to fetch you, as very soon the Folly will be too rough for the boat."

"Oh! In that case I'd better accept his advice. It means, too, that Dr. Lofty will not be able to visit his patient this afternoon. Has Miss Mary wakened?"

"No, not yet. Mrs. Leeper says that she can do everything the doctor tells her by telephone. She's quite a good nurse."

The sun said it was ten-thirty, and Janet knew by the manner in which Bony estimated the house shadow that he was satisfied to know the time by this method rather than to look at his wrist-watch.

"The doctor told us that Mary ought to waken about eleven," she said, calmly. "You are, of course, very welcome to stay as long as you wish. But if the Folly grows too rough for the boat, you may have to stay until tomorrow. We should be rather glad to have you."

She had perfect control of her eyes and her face, but slipped a trifle with her voice as many a hostess does when secretly wishing the guest to the devil. Bony decided to leave as soon as Blaze could come for him, and he was taken to Janet's sitting-room for morning tea whilst waiting.

Later, on looking back, Bony could find no note of discord. There was neither probing nor shying away from the purpose of his presence. They discussed her pictures, when she admitted that her study of art had been terminated by her father's death, whilst her knowledge of world events proved that mentally she was not limited by her life at Venom House. When interested, as well as when emotional, the lisp was absent.

Buffeted by three women, Bony felt a trifle less spiritually buoyant than usual, for he realised how far apart in mental stature he was from the Emperor Napoleon Bonaparte, who had claimed: "All the women in the world would not make me lose an hour." Bony was perturbed when admitting to himself how little he knew of feminine psychology. An intelligent woman like his wife would have talked nineteen to the dozen, noted voice inflection, eyes and mouth expression and, having added all together, would have multiplied the answer by intuition, divided by imagination, and thus accurately summed up these three women. An hour! They had cost him six hours in a row.

Three women under the one roof! One able to kill by

pressing on a nerve in the neck. Another able to crack a whip hard on the nose of an infuriated bull. And the third conscious of her power over men and silly enough to believe herself infallible with all men. And with these three women under the one roof, a subnormal man of twenty-seven who claims with impish triumph to know who strangled his mother. As the outback bushman, like Blaze, would say: "Things is crook."

Standing on the porch, Janet waved to him. His acknowledgment was also accepted by Morris Answerth, and old Blaze shouted to make himself heard:

"Gettin' a good send-off. In a manner of speakin' you're going to get a good welcome. I got summat to show you."

"That sounds good."

"Reckon you'll think so. Robin Foster and the lad are away shifting sheep, so you can take your time. Did she give you a cuppa tea?"

"She did. Any fish in this lake?"

"Plenty. You like fishin'?"

"Yes. My favourite sport."

With the wind astern the crossing was fast, and, having locked the painter to the stump, Blaze led the way to the men's quarters. At the kitchen door, he said:

"What I got to show you's in the wool shed. I was doing a bit of moochin' around when I seen it."

"Can we enter without being observed from the house?"

" 'Fraid not. Why worry?"

"True . . . why worry. Tell me, is the pathway over the causeway very difficult to follow?"

Blaze stopped when between the kitchen and wool shed that he might not miss the effect of his words.

"You aiming to make it one night?"

"I might be. What do you think of the idea of Morris watching Miss Mary and you crossing and returning by wading, and charting the hidden pathway in his mind so clearly as to be able to make it himself?"

"Let me stew a bit."

The little cook went on and together they entered the wide door of the wool shed. It was completely empty, and there Blaze again confronted Bony.

"There's a sort of knack of getting over that causeway," he said. "Going from this side you take a sight at the left corner of the house, and coming back you keeps your eye on the right corner of the shearing shed. There's four big holes and one small one you got to get by. No, I don't think Morris could make it, no matter how he nutted it out from his winder. I'm sure he couldn't in the dark of night. Takes me and Miss Mary all our time not to get slewed and fall into deep water after dark."

"Thanks. Pass it. What have you to show me here?"

"That."

Blaze pointed to the wall, on which figuring had been done with blue raddle. Rows of figures had been lined out, and others substituted above them. There was a number tallying with the number of sheep recently shorn. There were many small sums of addition, and of division. And there were the figures 94.

"So Miss Mary worked out the theft of the wool the same way that we did," Bony murmured.

"Thought you might like to see it," Blaze said with enormous satisfaction. "Now why in hell didn't she squawk about that stolen wool?"

"Tell me."

"I could tell you easier how many seven-ounce glasses of beer ought to be in a niner. You say, Inspector."

"One day I will. Meanwhile inform me on another point. Tell me who goes over to saw and split the wood."

"Old bloke by the name of Winter. Does that and other jobs about every three months. Been doing it for years. Had a lot of bad luck in his time."

"Indeed!"

"Yes. When he was a young feller he went to sea and fell down a hatch. Just happened to bite his tongue off as he was going down. Never talked since. Anyway, he kept going to sea until he got that deaf he couldn't hear the orders, so he took to growing pineapples, and one night the house burned down and he couldn't get his wife and daughter out.

"Twenty year ago that was. He sold the farm and come to Edison 'cos he'd be near the sea, and took a job as yard-man at the pub. Been there ever since, and takes a break by coming here and making a raft outer logs and polin' it over. Decent old coot."

Bony warmly thanked the cook for his co-operation, and began the four-mile walk to Edison. He had proceeded half a mile when his mind focused on old man Winter who was deaf and dumb. Had the idea of employing him at Venom House emerged from Boccaccio's *Decameron*?

178

Chapter Nineteen

A GUARDIAN FOR MORRIS

Bony left Answerth's Folly shortly after eleven fifteen, and at eleven forty-five he made himself a couch of leaves on the bank of a running stream, and slept until three. Being fortunate to thumb a lift, he was in Edison by half-past three, and took time off to shave and bath and make himself presentable to Mr. Samuel Harston at five minutes after four.

"Yes, Inspector, what can we do for you?" asked the large, bald man with the sharp, dark-brown eyes and the office-white hands. "Sit down. Smoke?"

Mr. Harston's private office was, like himself, large, pleasant and comfortable. The outer office manned by two clerks was additional evidence of the prosperity he enjoyed. Bony settled himself with the air of a man prepared to relax for several hours. Having rolled a cigarette, he looked up at the stock and station agent before striking a match, and placidly opened what he knew, and the other now suspected, was to be battle.

"How many cattle have the Answerths lost this year?"

"I don't know that. . . . Have you a reason for asking?"

"I never seek for information. . . ." Bony lit the cigarette and added ". . . without a reason."

"Yes, of course, Inspector. I was thinking that Miss Mary Answerth would be in a better position to supply that information."

"Miss Mary Answerth is indisposed."

"I'm sorry to hear it. I didn't know."

"I had it hushed up by Constable Mawson," asserted the omnipotent censor. "Last night Miss Mary Answerth was strangled."

The effect exhibited by the agent was not overdone. Bony's statement raised him from his chair to lean with his hands upon his paper-littered desk and stare for long moments at his visitor. The visitor stared at him, and he was the first to wilt.

"Strangled!" breathed Mr. Harston. "I don't understand."

"She will recover," calmly announced Bony. "Dr Lofty, who accompanied Mawson and me to the house last night, left her in the charge of Mrs. Leeper, who, as you probably know has had extensive nursing experience."

Mr. Harston sat down, and from a drawer took a cigar and lit it with a match which trembled. He waited for supplementary data, and Bony supplied it.

"Having been lassoed with power flex, and then hauled backward to the ground, Miss Answerth found speech most difficult. That was before Dr. Lofty gave her a sedative, from which, when I left late this morning, she had not awakened. Someone called her from the house in the middle of the night, and attempted to kill her. Only her unusual physical strength and mental agility saved her. I hope you will not make the matter public. Miss Janet concurs with me that publicity would be harmful to the family."

"Of course, Inspector, of course. . . . Dammit, these crimes cannot be permitted to continue."

"My only interest in these crimes," Bony said, coldly, "is to establish who is committing them. Miss Mary being out of circulation, forgive the idiom, I have to turn to you for information she doubtless would give me. How many cattle have the Answerths lost this year?"

"I understand that the number to date is twenty-nine, but how many were actually stolen, and how many merely strayed and will subsequently be recovered, remains for time to prove. Not a few farmers and pastoralists have suffered losses this year. Last year, too."

"Have any losses been reported since the death of Edward Carlow?"

The agent gazed hard at the questioner and shook his head.

"What of sheep losses, Mr. Harston?" was the next probe.

"The figure is much higher."

"How many sheep have the Answerths lost this year?"

"Only the other day Miss Mary told me she thought she had lost well over a hundred since March 16th, when the entire flock was yarded."

"Do you know if she suspects any particular person of stealing her stock?"

"I think she does," replied the agent. "However, she was never explicit on this point. Suspicion, of course, isn't proof."

"There would be fewer criminals at large if suspicion were enough, Mr. Harston. Tell me . . . this Edward Carlow was a very prosperous butcher, was he not?"

Bony could see the growing caution in the other's brown eyes.

"Yes, he was, Inspector. He opened this business just where and when it was badly needed here in Edison."

"Would you say he was extremely prosperous?"

"I think I can say that."

"Pardon my pertinacity. Was he more prosperous than even the circumstances of his business warranted?"

"These are prosperous times, Inspector. Everyone is prosperous."

"Excepting me, Mr. Harston. Let us discuss wool. You marketed the Answerths' clip?"

"I did."

"What was the number of the bales?"

The brown eyes flickered.

"Ninety-two. They are to be offered at auction in the second series."

"Did either Miss Mary or Miss Janet tell you they had lost wool?"

Mr. Harston was now decidedly uncomfortable. Doubtless, stepping down from the Bench to be cross-examined like a witness wasn't to his liking, and it was really odd how the examiner could hide himself behind eyes of bright blue.

"Miss Mary told me she suspected some of the wool had been stolen during the shearing," he felt compelled to answer.

"When was it she told you this?"

"It would be some time after the shearing. We went into the figures, or rather we checked the figures Miss Mary had worked on."

"Taking the number of sheep and lambs, working on average weight of fleeces, and deducing a loss of approximately two bales?"

"That is so." Mr. Harston was admittedly astonished, and Bony said:

"I also am intelligent. Was the loss reported to the police?"

"I think not."

"Why not? Two bales represent a lot of money. To a tax-riddled salary like mine, anyway."

"Well, it was like this, Inspector. The position was a little obscure. The early losses of cattle were reported to the police, and when, later, some of the cattle were found to have strayed, subsequent losses were not reported. Miss Mary . . . you have met her and assessed her character . . . isn't easily influenced. I advised reporting the matter of the wool to Constable Mawson, but she refused to listen, saying she would track down the thief or thieves and exact her own justice. But, of course, she didn't."

"How can you be certain that Miss Mary did not?"

"Well, I . . . I cannot be certain, Inspector. But, having known the Misses Answerth for so many years, I am quite sure that Miss Mary didn't really mean what she said. Mind you, I am sure that if she suspected a particular man, she wouldn't go to Mawson, but if she held proof she would report the matter to him for action."

"On what date did Miss Mary tell you she would exact her own justice?"

Mr. Harston took his time over this one, frowning the while at his silver inkstand. Patiently Bony waited, rolling himself another cigarette. Harston didn't know it, did not realise that this dark man's patience was inexhaustible. Otherwise he might have saved himself the trouble of trying to escape from the trap he felt had ensnared him.

"I really cannot recall the exact date," he replied.

"Try, Mr. Harston. It is important."

"Now look here, Inspector. As I told you, I've known these Answerths for many years. The original Answerth was a thorough blackguard, and his son and grandsons were almost on a par with him. But these two women, Mary and Janet, are at heart kindly folk. Miss Janet is renowned for her generosity and good works, and although Miss Mary is often unorthodox in her approach to a problem, calling a spade a spade when it is actually a garden trowel, she would not . . ."

"The date, please, Mr. Harston."

Mr. Harston sighed.

"It was the day after the shearing was finished."

"When Miss Mary discussed the wool loss from her figures?"

"Yes."

"And five days later the body of Edward Carlow was found in the Folly. Did you not consider it probable that Miss Mary had exacted her own justice? Pardon me, that's not a fair question. Do you think that Miss Mary is physically capable of handling a man of the weight and strength of Edward Carlow?"

"To that, Inspector, I must answer yes. One afternoon at the hotel across the street Miss Mary tackled a bar full of men. Five needed Dr. Lofty's ministrations. But murder . . . no! I'll never consider the possibility. It's . . . it's damnable."

"I agree," murmured Bony. "However, I have to weigh and assess every possibility. What do you say when I tell you that Edward Carlow had in his slaughter-yard shed the wool stolen from the Answerths' shed?"

"That I still refuse even to consider that Miss Mary killed the man. When a little tipsy, she loves a brawl. But murder . . . no! Murder in cold blood . . . preposterous!"

"Miss Mary says she was awakened by someone throwing earth against her bedroom window. A man standing below asked her to go down to him as he wanted to talk about the theft of her cattle. Only by exploring every avenue can I settle the questions who and why. My long experience shows me that a threat spoken in anger dies at birth."

Mr. Harston was instantly mollified, unaware that Bony had not yet finished with him, and feeling that he himself had been at fault. Bony moved to fresh pastures.

"Tell me why the causeway hasn't been maintained," he pressed. "The property, though comparatively small, appears to be in good and efficient order. With the ruling prices of meat and wool, there must be plenty of money."

Mr. Harston relit the stub of his cigar, made a mess of it and killed it on the ash-tray. Having lit a fresh one, he said:

"I don't think I can answer your question, Inspector. Meaning that I'm doubtful that I know the answer. As you mentioned, there's no lack of money. The fortunes of those two women must be considerable, and I have no idea just how much they're worth today." Harston chewed the cigar, caught himself in the act and refrained before it was ruined. "I have not been unaware of changes these last ten or a dozen years, changes towards me due much less to anything held or imagined against me than to something which has been building up in them."

When the agent paused, Bony encouraged:

"Perhaps you would care to elaborate."

"I'll try. When old Jacob Answerth was alive, my work as his business agent was smooth. His views were consistent, and more often than not he acted on my advice. After he died, the daughters were content to carry on under my general supervision, that is, with marketing and finance, the actual management of stock being outside my province. However, as time went on they became ever more independent of my advice, and more reticent in financial matters. Time appeared to effect changes in them, too, and I cannot explain these changes excepting that Mary seems to have become even more intolerant and Janet more secretive, or shall I say . . . oh, I don't know. My wife says they should have married. I am inclined to think they were born under most unfavourable stars."

"Janet, I understand, is something of a philanthropist," Bony suggested.

"That is so," conceded Mr. Harston. "Janet is least like any of the Answerths. She is brainy, cultured, likeable. We have three churches in Edison, and she never fails to hear their appeals for financial assistance and personal effort. When old Carlow died, and the farm was bankrupt, Miss Mary insisted on letting it to other people, and Miss Janet rescued the Carlow family and set them up, Edward in the butcher's shop.

"Miss Mary is equally generous in her way. She's hostile to the churches, but generous to the local hospital and the aged. Janet seems to like people knowing about her good works. Mary appears to be indifferent to what people think of her, good, bad or half-way."

"When Miss Janet took under her wing Mrs. Carlow and her two sons, what was Miss Mary's attitude?"

"In this very office she called Janet a hypocritical little bitch. They were here to settle the lease of the farm to new tenants. She also said, very much to my surprise, that Miss Janet's only interest in the Carlows was Edward. Miss Janet was furious."

"H'm!" Bony's face was masked. "Who does the booking . . . household accounts, and such things?"

"Miss Janet. She's a clever little thing, you know.

After she came home from school she studied accountancy, and when her father died she compiled the Stock and Income Taxation Returns. Which is why I do not know just what their financial position is."

"They would not spend money on the causeway, I think you said."

"I did. When it was again apparent that the causeway would have to be raised, they said that the Local Council should bear the cost, or that the Government should open the river mouth. The last time work was done it cost a thousand pounds. This time the estimate was treble that amount. I pointed out that it might be wise to build a house to the right of the men's quarters, a modern house with up-to-date amenities, but they wouldn't hear of it. Mary said that what the first Answerth had built she would never desert, and Janet produced the hare-brained idea that if the water rose high enough it would itself burst out to sea.

"Eventually, they employed an elderly man by the name of Winter to build a boat. Although deaf and dumb, the old chap is a good boat-builder, and a reliable handyman. When needed, he rafts wood over to the house and saws it into required lengths."

"He has been going to Venom House, how many years?"

"Oh, a full dozen, might be more."

"Visitors, I understand, are not welcome."

Mr. Harston shrugged.

"They have never entertained like their father used to. Miss Mary thinks only of work and the stock." The big man smiled. "I could not imagine Miss Mary in a lounge, or at a meeting of our literary society. Miss Janet occasionally comes to town to spend an evening with one or another, or to attend a charity meeting or church function. But no one is ever invited to Venom House."

"Mrs. Leeper appears willing to stay there. What do they pay her?"

"Twice as much as they need to employ a cook-housekeeper." The agent looked grim. "I imagine that she believes she earns it."

"Tells me she is saving to acquire her own mental hospital," Bony said, casually, and the agent agreed a trifle too readily. "Seems a capable woman."

"Very. Just the type to manage the family."

"You found her for them?"

"Yes. Her credentials were excellent. It was I, in fact, who suggested to them that they ought to employ a nurse to help with Mrs. Answerth and Morris. They both said Morris was well cared for, but they did realise that Mrs. Answorth was growing old."

"Is it correct that Jacob left all his money to his daughters and nothing to his wife and son?"

"That is so. I knew nothing of his intentions until the will was read. I wanted the daughters to settle an annuity on the wife, but Mrs. Answerth wouldn't hear of it. Said she didn't want any of Jacob's money. She had a little of her own."

"The Misses Answerth have had their wills drawn up, I suppose?"

"Yes. They sought my advice about that."

"Who did they appoint their executor?"

"That I don't know."

"Who inherits the bulk of the money?"

"I don't know that either, for sure. I think it is to be held in trust for Morris. I advised it."

"That implies a guardian," Bony murmured. "Who has been appointed?"

Mr. Harston coughed, and rose as though to indicate that the interview was ended. His eyes were uneasy. His face was flushed. When Bony declined the hint, and remained in his chair, the agent said, angrily:

"You know, Inspector, I think I ought not to continue this particular subject. After all, I am breaking a confidence. The solicitors, perhaps, may have another view. Mark and Mark, of Manton, are the solicitors."

Blandly, Bony regarded the agent, and negligently waved him back to his chair. Mr. Harston sat. He glared.

"Solicitors are always difficult," Bony said. "Their training and practice withers in them the precious gift of imagination. May I accept the point that you have at heart the welfare of this Answerth family?"

"Of course! Of course! I've known them since they were babies."

"I am happy to have your assurance, Mr. Harston. You see, I have two objectives. One is to establish who murdered Mrs. Answerth, and in addition, who attempted to murder Miss Mary Answerth. The other is to prevent another Answerth from being murdered. Therefore, I may claim also to have the welfare of this family at heart. I may expect your willing co-operation in my efforts to prevent another murder?"

Bereft of words, Mr. Harston nodded as though counting.

"A detective's job is to suspect everyone until they are proved to be innocent," Bony went on. "His job is to gather evidence amounting to proof with assertion that a particular individual is guilty. Among many who it is

189

now my job to suspect of strangling Mrs. Answerth is . . . you."

Again the agent was on his feet.

"Me!" he came close to shouting. "Why me?"

"Have I not explained? I suspect everyone here in Edison, everyone at Venom House, everyone in this district, and I shall continue doing so until Mrs. Answerth's slayer is named. You could have killed her, Mr. Harston. That you cannot deny. So, too, could Constable Mawson, Robin or Henry Foster, one of the station hands, an Answerth, even the guardian appointed by their will. Who is the guardian?"

Mr. Harston waved his hands helplessly. He saw nothing of the dark face: only the enormous blue eyes. The voice was like a gimlet another twist of which would enter his brain.

"The name of the guardian, Mr. Harston?"

"Mrs. Leeper," whispered Mr. Harston.

Chapter Twenty

MRS. CARLOW'S FRIEND

THE sun was a rusty cannon-ball embedded in the western celestial wall. The wind tormented the trade signs above the pavements of Edison, and blew dust into eyes and debris against feet and legs. The air was warm when it ought to have been crisply cool, and it brought to the nostrils of Napoleon Bonaparte the aroma of baked sand-dunes, of burning eucalypt leaves, of the essence of the bush which has no beginning and no end. The wind annoyed business-men and shoppers: what it brought from the endless plains and the low ironstone hills and rivers that seldom flowed, and then uphill, delighted Bony. It stirred his blood and quickened his imagination.

The butcher's shop was clean and about to be closed. The meat had been removed from the marble-floored window and the heavy hooks on bright steel runners. A young man was scraping the huge block, and an elderly woman was counting money in the small, glass-fronted office.

"Just in time," said the youth without looking up from his work. "What d'you want?"

"You."

The youth straightened and turned to Bony. He was tall, athletic, good-looking. His eyes were dark, his hair was dark, and both gleamed with robust health. Insolently he stared, and Bony nodded towards the shop door.

"Might as well close it," he said. "I shall be here some time."

"And who the hell are you?"

"Oh, I'm sorry. I forgot to mention that I am Detective-Inspector Napoleon Bonaparte."

Mrs. Carlow came from the office, removed spectacles from tired grey eyes, and waited at the end of the counter. She said, simply:

"Yes, Inspector?"

"I take it that you are Mrs. Carlow, and you are Alfred Carlow," Bony said, easily. "I'm investigating the the circumstances surrounding the death of your son,

Mrs. Carlow, and thought you would prefer not coming to the police station where I have my temporary office. I'll not keep you long."

Mrs. Carlow sighed. She was neatly dressed and could have been a school-teacher, such was the compression of her mouth, the steady appraisal, the vertical lines between her brows.

"I hope you find out who murdered Edward," she said, and waited.

"I shall, eventually. Perhaps you would like to complete your office work while I talk to your son for a few minutes."

"Thank you. I will."

"Now, Mr. Carlow, I want to ask you several questions, hoping that your answers will greatly assist me," Bony said when the woman had re-entered the office. "I understand that on leaving school you began in the butchering trade, and since your brother's death you have undertaken much of the work he did. That right?"

"That's how it is, Inspector," agreed the youth a trifle more cordially.

"Like it?"

"Better than the farm."

"You'd come in contact with more people, and that kind of thing." Bony smiled. "Be near the pictures and the dances, eh!"

"Yes, there's more life in Edison."

"Of course. Well now, let's go on. I understand that when your brother was alive he did the buying of carcases, and did the slaughtering when sheep and cattle were bought on the hoof."

"That's right, Inspector. We slaughter our own meat as well as buy it from the wholesalers."

"I suppose occasionally you went with your brother when he slaughtered?"

"I went with him once or twice, not more. He said he could look after that end, and mine was to serve in the shop when he was away."

"You began working here some time after your brother started the business, I think?"

"Year or two."

"And then after he was killed, a man was employed to do the slaughtering and you ran the van to fetch the meat to the shop?"

"That's right."

"At the yard there's a padlocked shed. Where's the key kept?"

Although ready, Bony failed to see any alteration of expression in the dark eyes which had been and remained frankly curious. Without hesitation, Carlow replied that the key was in the office.

"When were you last inside that shed?"

Carlow's hesitation was natural.

"I don't know," he replied. "Could be a year ago."

"You haven't been inside the shed since your brother died?"

"No."

"Why not? You have been to the yard often to fetch the meat."

"Didn't have no reason to go in. Old Jim Matthews is in charge down there. He tells us on the phone what beasts are in the yard, and we tell him what to kill. Always been a good bloke, and he keeps on the right side of the Health Inspector. Been a butcher by trade before he went farming."

Concern and curiosity were now plain in the dark eyes,

and Bony told him he would like to talk to his mother. He proceeded with his work of cleaning-up for the day, and Bony was invited to take the spare chair in the office.

"I hope, Mrs. Carlow, you won't mind if I am very frank. I may have your fullest co-operation?"

"Yes, Inspector."

"You know, Mrs. Carlow, there is much in a detective's life to sadden him. He is continually confronted by tragedy in the hearts of innocent people. The sympathies of the thoughtless and stupid towards the condemned criminal always become vocal at the conclusion of his trial. There is little sympathy extended to those dependent upon the victim of murder save in the hearts of men who track down the slayer. Now tell me about your son. Was he a good son?"

Slowly the woman nodded before saying:

"Always. We worked hard on the farm, but my husband drank what we worked for, and after he died Edward took charge of us and worked twenty hours a day to put this business on its feet. He denied Alfred and me nothing."

"Was there trouble with the Income Tax Commissioner after your son died?"

Again, slowly the woman nodded before saying:

"Edward must have taken money from the till every evening before he gave the takings to me to enter in the books. Not a great deal. We think it was something like five pounds a day. He earned it, anyhow."

"You have kept the books from the time the business was opened?"

"Yes. There was no fault found with the books."

"Who prepared the income tax returns?"

"Edward. He was helped by Miss Answerth, Miss

194

Janet Answerth. Miss Janet has always been the soul of goodness to us ever since my husband died and Miss Mary insisted on turning us out. She rented these premises for us and advanced the money for the fittings. She even lent the money for Edward to buy his first delivery truck. It was an old one, but it was a start. Edward paid back all the money. Then he bought a house for us and furnished it. All the trouble with the Income Tax people has been about the money he paid for it."

"How soon after your son was murdered, did the Income Tax people pounce on you?"

"They began on us three weeks ago. They found that the takings after Edward was killed were much higher than before. Someone in Edison must have written to them. It wouldn't have been the police, would it?"

"I can tell you that it was not."

"I don't understand it, Inspector," Mrs. Carlow said, desperation in her voice. "My husband turned out no good, but he was always honest as the day. And then something that the Income Tax men said to me about the house and the new furniture and the new van coming out of the business on top of the money repaid to Miss Janet, and all in so short a time, has made me think bad things of poor Edward."

"I'm afraid he did engage in business not strictly orthodox," Bony said, gently. "There's no doubt that he spent much more than this business could rightly provide. I regret having to back that statement, Mrs. Carlow. Stacked in the locked shed at the slaughter yard is wool known to have been stolen from the Answerth station during the shearing. Your other son tells me he did not enter the shed since Edward was murdered, and I've proof that no one else did."

195

"But . . ."

Mrs. Carlow wept, and quietly Bony said:

"The theft of that wool doesn't greatly concern my enquiry. I want to know who killed your son. Your son might have been tempted to make money too fast, but he was entitled to his life. His life and who took it is our objective . . . yours and mine. Someone associated with your son killed him. It wasn't accidental. Someone in his life hated him enough to murder him, and you probably know this person along with others who were in his life."

"No one to my knowledge could have hated him like that, Inspector."

"People who hate strongly enough to murder seldom show it, Mrs. Carlow. It is for such as I to burrow and dig and burrow again to unearth him. From something which you think unimportant I may find him, and so please answer my questions frankly, and keep from your mind that I am interested in the damned Income Tax people, or that I am concerned with the theft of wool . . . unless the theft leads me to the murderer. Now, tell me. Did your son ever complain of being injured by someone?"

"No. We all felt injured when Miss Mary turned us out, but there was justice on her side. My husband hadn't paid the rent for four years, and we were left without a chance to pay it."

"Did your son have friends, or associates, who did not fully meet with your approval?"

"No. Only those who led him to gamble a little, and drink sometimes." Mrs. Carlow hesitated. "I'm sorry, Inspector, but Edward did get to be living too fast. And he had ambitions, too."

"What were they?"

"Just ordinary ambitions of a young man wanting to ge on."

"Such as . . ."

"Well, he wanted to go on the Shire Council. He put up at the last election and Miss Janet helped him, but he was beaten for all that. He could talk well enough. I taught him to speak properly long before we left the farm.

"He was always talking of making a lot of money, and selling this business and going back to the land . . . buying a real sheep station and being a pastoralist. He often said how he hated doing the slaughtering because he'd never get anywhere while people knew about it, and when I told him that if he gave up the gambling and the drink he could employ a man to do the slaughtering, he said he couldn't trust anyone else to do it."

"Is it true that, earlier on the night he was killed, he told you he was going to Manton to see a girl?"

"Yes."

"Who is this girl?"

"I don't know any girl in Manton who interested him."

"Was he keen on any local girl?"

"He could have been. They were all mad about him. He was a handsome boy, Inspector."

"I have seen his picture. Alfred is much like him. D'you think there was anything between him and Miss Janet Answerth?"

"He never told me straight out. I think he had hopes in that direction. I don't know what to say."

"Just say what is in your mind, Mrs. Carlow."

Mrs. Carlow fingered a pencil. She looked at it being twirled by her fingers, but she was not seeing it. Bony, who knew when to wait, waited. Suddenly, she was looking at him, and seeing him.

"I think it was more on her side than his. When Edward was speaking at the local hall at election time, Miss Janet was sitting beside me I happened to glance at her and I saw the way she was looking at him. I ought to have been proud, but I wasn't. She's too old for Edward, I thought. And then I remembered who she was and I hoped just a little."

"Was that, do you think, as far as it went?"

"Yes. Mind you, Edward might have asked her later on, but he was very ambitious. He used to tell me, when I teased him about having no real girl friend, that first things had to come first, and the first things were money and position. I don't know . . . Oh, I don't know why he stole the wool, and why he kept the money from the till. We were so very happy together, and hardship and want were far behind us. I . . ."

Bony stood and patted the woman's shoulder as she wept.

"I'll come to see you again, Mrs. Carlow," he told her, and added, softly: "as a friend."

Chapter Twenty-One

THE FOX OFTEN WINS

HALF-past six, and the windy dusk deepening upon Edison was almost eerie. The long cloud bank to the north was dull red, and all the world below the township was darkly mysterious.

Mawson decided to wait no longer, when Bony came

in, his steps crossing the outer office betraying haste.

"Won't keep you, Mawson, more than two minutes," he said, sitting at the desk to roll a cigarette. The wind had tossed his hair and the dust had stained his cheeks, but Mawson noted how brightly the blue eyes gleamed. "What did the slaughterer have to say?"

"Says, of course, that he knows the shed very well. Doesn't remember ever seeing it unlocked. Never asked the Carlows about it and didn't need the key, because he had no cause to enter. The hides and skins from the animals he kills he stacks in the open shed."

"Your impressions, please."

"Speaking the truth."

"It fits, Mawson. What about that niece of yours?"

The weathered face expanded, and one knobby hand carelessly combed the fine gingery hair. Mawson recited:

"Would she listen in to any calls for Venom House? No, certainly not, Uncle! Did she ever listen in to conversations? How dare you, Uncle! Well, would she, as a very special favour, listen in to calls for Venom House from now on and report same to her doting uncle? He wasn't her doting uncle any more after trying to persuade her to betray her trust as a telephonist. Yes, she was interested in the maintenance of law and order. Yes, she liked Inspector Bonaparte, who was her mother's paying guest, but . . . Oh, all right, as a very special favour she would note the time and the name of anyone calling Venom House. Further than that, no, a thousand times no . . . with two stamps of the foot. And that's how it went."

"You saw her, at what time?"

"Round about twelve o'clock."

"I shall meet her at dinner. Did you examine the exhibits?"

"Yes. D'you want to see 'em again?"

"No. Give me your conclusions."

"Two lassoes. One is thirteen feet long, the second is eleven feet. They've been made the same way . . . a small loop or eyelet at one end. The eyelet binding of the longer lasso is light twine. The binding of the other eyelet is strong sewing thread."

"The long one being recently in the possession of Morris Answerth," Bony pointed out. "And found in the chimney."

"Yes. The eleven-footer half-strangled Miss Mary, and the thirteen-footer strangled Mrs. Answerth. Don't know that I'd use such stuff to choke anyone with. The pistol wasn't loaded, and hasn't been fired, I'd say, since it blew off old Jacob's head. Must have took a full hour to load and prime it before pulling on the trigger with both hands."

"The noise must have been terrific," Bony said, standing. "Well, we had better go along, or we'll be unforgivably late for dinner. Doing anything tonight?"

"I was thinking of listening to a favourite radio session."

"I do hope it is not entertainment by morons for morons, Mawson. I shall spend my evening in pursuits more elevating."

"Such as . . ."

"Communing with the stars. Meditating upon the weakness of man and the wiles of woman. There is, I believe, no place more conducive to meditation than the old logging stage. I'd be grateful if you would run me out after dinner."

"I'll be through in half an hour," Mawson said as he locked the exhibits in the safe. "Wouldn't like a nice companion to meditate with?"

"The solemnity of the occasion dictates solitude. Some

other time, perhaps. When will this wind go down?"

"Might keep up for a couple of days."

"Think it will rain?"

"Might before morning . . . if the wind swings to the west."

They parted, Bony to walk smartly up the street to his lodgings, where at the gate he was met by Mrs. Nash's daughter. She had her mother's eyes and Mawson's pleasing smile.

"Good evening, Inspector Bonaparte."

"Ah! I seem to be for it. All my friends call me Bony."

"Did you happen to ask my uncle to get me to eavesdrop on telephone calls?"

"I did suggest it," Bony gravely admitted.

"Then why didn't you ask me?"

She was facing the line of now white cloud, and he saw with amusement that her candid eyes were seeking to impale him. Ah . . . these women! So direct when it suited them: so evasive when intuition warned. Like a small boy placating an irate teacher, he replied:

"Well, you see, Miss Nash, it was most important to my work here, so important that I felt the matter ought to be placed before you with all possible personal influence. Knowing how much your uncle thinks of you, and you of him, I, well . . ."

She began to laugh, and taking him by the arm, said:

"Come along in to dinner. You're terribly late. I'm sorry I couldn't do what you wanted . . . not without the postmaster's consent. So I did the next best thing. Here are the calls to Venom House."

"This is generous of you. You won't be on duty tonight?"

"No. I'm on again at eight in the morning."

"Perhaps tomorrow you would continue . . . ?"

"Maybe I will, Bony."

"Ah, that's better. Now all is well."

Within his sitting-room he studied the memo, reading:

'4.51 p.m.   Mr. Harston to Venom House.

6.19 p.m.   Mrs. Carlow to Venom House.'

Venom House! Everyone naturally referred to the house on the lake as Venom House. He wondered if the Answerths had objected and, finding objection of no avail, accepted it.

As he walked to the police station, the day was dead and the night very much alive. The stars looked unhappy. Shop signs complained as though rebelling against working after hours. Save for windows alight above shops and offices, the only street lamps were the red one over Dr. Lofty's door and the blue one in the wooden arch over the police-station gate. Mawson's car was parked at the kerb.

"Right!" Mawson said from behind the wheel, and Bony, on sitting beside him, switched off the dash light. Silently the constable released the brake and allowed the car to roll down the street and out of town. Before switching on the engine, he made an observation.

"Light rubber-soled shoes. Black scarf instead of white collar. Old suit and cloth cap. Torch in the inside pocket of the coat. Where d'you carry your gun?"

"A gun is gangsterish, so crude, Mawson. Near the logging camp I noted a heap of old German fencing wire. Stop there, and I'll obtain a length of about four feet, and make a hook at one end to use as a handle."

Mawson chuckled. "You'd sooner stick a man than shoot him."

"Slashing a man across the throat with a length of

heavy wire doesn't make a noise, Mawson. Neither does he."

"What are you planning?" asked the constable, more than curious.

"Officially, I may be away for several days. Between ourselves, I'm going bush, and during my peregrinations I may exercise a suspected talent for burglary. I would like you to keep close to your telephone for three days at least. If you have to leave town, try to keep in close contact with your niece at the exchange."

"All right. Go on, I'm liking this."

"Your niece was co-operative. I told her I thought you would be so pleased you would give her a pair of those Italian shoes."

"The hell you did! What d'you think I am?"

"A doting uncle."

"You don't cotton to the fact that her wages are almost as much as mine, and that mine is about as much as quarter pay to a wharf labourer."

"Money," scoffed Bony. "What is money?"

"Featherweight stuff the boss hands out and the Government takes off you."

"Precisely, Mawson, and so milk your bank for as much as possible. It isn't worth the germs sticking to it, anyway. Shoes patterned with gold, now, would . . ."

"What she gave you is a better subject."

"Having spoken of cabbages and kings with Mr. Harston, I left him at 4.50 this afternoon. At 4.51 he rang Venom House. The subject of my conversation with Mrs. Carlow was kings and cabbages. I left the shop at 6.17, and at 6.19 she rang Venom House. As Mr. Harston did not know till I told him that Miss Mary had been strangled, his call was doubtless to ascertain her condition.

203

Mrs. Carlow, however, did not know and I didn't mention the attack on Miss Mary."

Mawson said nothing for a quarter of a mile.

"Well, what are you making of that?"

"Oh, I wasn't thinking of it, really. Those shoes . . . beautiful."

Mawson laughed without restraint.

"You reckon the info's worth the price?" he managed to say.

"I do."

"Oh no, you don't, Bony. You pay for the shoes yourself. We're right near the logging stage. Whereabouts is the wire you want?"

"Left side. Pull up here and switch off your lights. Keep them off for a full minute after I leave you, and then go home to the radio. If at the end of seven days you don't hear from me, start dragging the Folly."

"H'm! Cheerful, I must say."

"Don't worry. I'll not be that careless. If my headquarters contact you about me, tell them I've gone fishing, and may be away for a week or two. If they become too fresh, tell them not to be childish . . . with my compliments. Between us, Mawson, I am expecting another attempted murder, and I rather want to be present. The slightest interference would delay the attempt, possibly for several weeks, and I cannot be mooning around for so extended a period. Thus intererence from headquarters, or from you, would be offset by my displeasure."

"Ye gods!"

"Meanwhile, if Robin Foster or his brother come to town, keep your eyes on them. Note what the Carlows do, especially the lad. Note, too, if either Janet Answerth or Mrs. Leeper appears in town . . . who they visit, time and what not."

"I get it," assented Mawson. "And if any other d. comes down from headquarters, I'm to go dumb?"

"Dumb or stupid. Some of the cleverest men in history pretended to be stupid. Now I'll be on my way. Rest easy on my behalf. Remember that Burke said: 'What shadows we are, and what shadows we pursue.' I leave you to become a shadow."

Silently Bony opened the door, and without a sound closed it. Mawson waited two minutes, and for him they were long minutes.

It was then a quarter to eight, and at nine o'clock Henry Foster was lying on the bunk within his tent, and reading by the light of a hurricane lamp set on a packing-case. Beside the lamp were pipe and tobacco and matches, and a tin pannikin containing coffee dregs. Outside, sheltered by a half-round sheet of iron, was his dog. The dog was chained to a stake, and the dog winged as though hard on the trail of a flea. That the dog did not bark remained long in Foster's memory, for it was the antithesis of the well-fed, slumbrous lap-dog. Foster knew nothing of Bony, until the tent flap was raised and Bony entered.

"Good evening!" was the polite greeting.

"Gud-dee!" answered Foster, sitting up.

"Come to the fire. I want to yabber."

"Cripes! Who's camp's this?"

"Yours . . . for tonight at least."

Bony withdrew, and Foster found his boots and proceeded to pull them on. Normally he would not have laced them. On emerging from the tent, he found his visitor squatting on his heels beside the fire he had replenished, and as similar visits by strangers were not entirely outside his experience, he dragged a case forward and sat opposite Bony.

"I," said Bony, "am Detective-Inspector Bonaparte. You are known by the name of Henry Foster, and you pressed the wool at the Answerths' shed."

The branch which had been taken from the fire to light the pipe became motionless in the hand of the man as strong as Robin Foster, but over six feet in height and less ugly. He watched Bony light a cigarette before lighting his pipe with the flaming brand. After that he waited, waited with the passive tensity of the bushman.

"As you probably guess, Foster, my job is to ascertain who killed Edward Carlow."

No response, no movement other than the rhythmic puffing of the pipe. The wind tore through the surrounding trees, tormented the bright fire wanting to burn in peace. Beyond the near trees, nothing.

"In a long report left with Constable Mawson," Bony went on, "I detailed how you hoodwinked the wool classer and stole a large number of fleeces from his bins. The report also deals with a visit I made, accompanied by a competent witness, to the shed at the slaughter yard once owned by Edward Carlow and, too, the result of my visit to the wool classer, who identified the wool as that from the Answerth clip. Further, six years ago you were working on Jonton Brothers' station, and only just escaped conviction for theft of cattle, two other men being sentenced to three years.

"As I mentioned, I am investigating the murder of Edward Carlow. I am not officially interested in the theft of the Answerth wool, and this will have some bearing on what I shall presently say to you. What did Carlow pay you for the wool?"

"What d'you think I am?" Foster asked with dangerous calm. He watched Bony idling with a length of stout fencing wire, and because such a weapon is the choice of anyone thinking to meet a snake, he wondered, with a part of his mind, why this man carried such a weapon at a time too early for snakes to be about.

"The situation, Foster, is too serious for facetious questions," Bony said sharply, and outlined the details of the theft, ending with: "And after the camp was asleep, you and your brother carried the day's 'lift' away in bags and handed it over to Carlow, who was waiting with his van. What did Carlow pay you for the wool?"

"Robin been talkin', eh? We was to get half what Carlow got for it."

"Edward Carlow was murdered too soon after receiving the final consignment of wool for you to think he had double-crossed you. Therefore, as I am interested only in the murder of Edward Carlow, I am willing to trade for information with my evidence against you in the theft of the wool"

Foster pondered before saying:

"Must be a catch in it somewhere."

"There is no catch. I am merely being pressed for time."

"Who can trust a copper?"

"I am not concerned with whether you trust me or not. I am trading you the chance of remaining out of gaol. Remember, when you are found guilty, the judge will have in his mind your close shave at the Jonton station. Shall we look into his mind and estimate the term as five years?"

"All right. What d'you want to know? You hold the whip."

"I want to know fully and exactly what Miss Mary Answerth said to you about the loss of her wool."

"And get carted away to hospital! No fear. Five years of the best would come easier. Crikey! You don't know that woman."

"She need not perturb you, Foster. She was strangled last night."

The eyes staring at Bony were reflecting redly the firelight. The hand holding the pipe fell to rest on the case. Thence the man's stillness in anyone not a bushman would have been remarkable.

"You don't go to market about the wool if I talk?" he persisted.

"I have said so."

"That report . . ."

"Mawson will either return the sealed report to me or hand it to his superior officer if I fail to claim it."

"All right, I'll talk. The day after I got me shearing cheque, I was up to Edison paying me bills and having a few drinks with Robin and the boys. Robin wanted me to stay with him at the pub, but I wasn't having any as I aim to buy a bit of land and build a house. I came out of the pub about half-past five and rode out of town, and when I'm half-way to the logging stage, Miss Mary catches up with me in her wagon.

"She says: 'Where's my wool, you bastard?'. She's itching for me to have a go at her for calling me a bastard, and I wouldn't have taken it from her, either, only I sorta knew I was in the wrong. Anyway, if I'd made a smack at her, I'd been half-killed. So I told her what had happened to her wool."

Foster relit his pipe.

"Then she blames me for pinchin' her sheep, and that's

too thick 'cos I never lifted no Answerth sheep, and I'll swear to that. Mind you, I know who did, and I won't tell her 'cos I'm not falling foul of certain blokes. She wants to know what happened to them. And to some cattle what's missing.

"What got me is how she knew about the wool. Aw, well, she knew, and I couldn't do nothing with her. She says to me: 'Look, Henry Foster, you tell me who bought them stolen sheep and who got them cattle, and I don't say nothing more about the wool.' Any'ow, it ends up with me telling her who I'm pretty sure got the sheep and the cattle in carcases from the lifters who'd slaughtered 'em in the scrub, and that feller was the local butcher, Ed Carlow."

"She says: 'Foster, if you says a word to anyone what you've told me, I'll hunt you out of the last rat-hole on earth and shove you inter the jug meself. I exact me own justice, in me own time and in me own way, and that's why I won't say no more to you about thieving me wool. You do it again, though, and I'll . . .' "

Foster broke off to chuckle, compelled to render tribute to Mary Answerth's language. But he sobered quickly enough.

" 'Ed Carlow!' she says, and then describes Ed Carlow. That woman is a wizard, Inspector, a wizard. There was never no woman like her. Poor old Ed oughter have been tipped off, but I . . . I don't mind a fight any time, but not with Mary Answerth. She does things in a fight what isn't fair to a man. She comes up to me and gets a holt of the slack of me shirt, and she says: 'You interfere in my business, Henry Foster, and I'll see to it that all you'll ever do in future is to crawl round on your hands and knees.' And with that she gives me a push what sends me flat on me back. And I'm no pup."

Foster fell silent. If he hoped that Bony would speak, he must have been disappointed. He was now revealing the signs of tension, and Bony still waited.

"And then Ed Carlow is found drowned in the Folly, in shallow water, and him the best swimmer in the district. She says she'd exact her own justice, and I believe she did right up till now when you tells me she got strangled."

"Why do you not believe it now? She could have made Carlow tell her from whom he had bought her sheep and cattle," Bony said, and Foster sat stiffly and stared at the fire.

"Yes," he agreed. "She could have done that before she dragged him into the Folly. And then she could have gone after them blokes what lifted the sheep and they took to her. Where was she done in?"

"Just outside Venom House," conceded Bony. "It seems that someone threw clods at her bedroom window, and that she went down to talk to whoever it was. The man was heard to say that he wanted to talk to her about some cattle that had been stolen."

"Well, that about tears it." When Foster stood he towered above Bony, and the fire between him. "Looks to me that Mary Answerth done in Ed Carlow all right and that some of Ed's friends took it out on her. I won't be taking no chances . . . with Ed's friends. I'll be doing a get, and you won't stop me, see."

"I shall not hinder you, Foster, or break my word about the wool. Make your destination South Australia."

"South Australia!" echoed Foster. "I'll stop some place a bit further on than that."

Bony stood up, tucking the rapier-like piece of wire under an arm.

"Be advised," he urged. "Start before dawn."

He stepped backward to the limit of the firelight. The dog winged and wagged its tail. Foster witnessed the night devour his visitor. Again the dog winged, and he glared at the animal, saying:

"Now why in hell didn't you bark?"

Chapter Twenty-Two

THE PERSISTENT WATCHER

To move through a dark night without betraying progress requires obedience to two commandments. You must not collide with an object, and so create sound. And you must not impinge yourself upon a lighter shadow and thus be seen. Though the night sky be heavily veiled by clouds, it is a Judas.

To have approached and mastered Foster's dog without that animal once barking its alarm was an accomplishment less than that of reaching the kitchen at the Answerths' men's quarters without arousing even one of the several dogs chained to various kennels for the night. This depended on wind-dodging, moving without producing sound vibrations heard by animals, and moving without being seen by animals able to see farther in the dark than in broad daylight.

Blaze was mixing a bread batter in a large tin dish when he was conscious of someone looking at him. His bush education had begun when a toddler, his teachers being the aborigines, and the crafty crows, and cattle when that indefinable something termed herd instinct is in the ascendant at night.

While completing the mixture of yeast and flour, he determined that the watcher wasn't outside the window, or the door, but within the dark pantry. He covered the dish with a cloth, carried it to a chair beside the stove, and wrapped it about with a hessian bag that the temperature might be maintained till morning. Only then did he turn directly to the pantry and see Bony just beyond the doorway, and beckoning.

Aware that entry had been effected through the pantry window, and that not without good reason, Blaze lit his pipe and casually closed the kitchen door, as casually lowered the blind masking the window, and finally crossed to the pantry.

"You on the flamin' warpath?" he asked.

"Have to work now and then," confessed Bony. "Lend a hand?"

"Two hands and both feet."

"I want enough tucker to keep going for three days. I'd like it in a sugar-bag with a rope to sling it over a shoulder."

"Bread, meat and brownie, eh? Tea and sugar and a billy?"

"No. The lake water will have to do. The lake's rough, I suppose."

"Yes. You aiming for the house?"

"That is where I am going."

The cook's old pipe gurgled. Casually he asked if Bony could swim, and on being answered affirmatively, went on: "If the Prime Minister was here and says to me, you take me over to Venom House tonight and I'll word the King to make you a lord, I'd tell him no deal. There ain't a hope of wading over the causeway, and the boat's more'n likely to sink."

"I must make the effort," stressed Bony. "You bring the tucker in the bag, and I'll row the boat over. I'll set it adrift and it can be thought it broke its moorings."

Blaze departed to the kitchen. He had the sugar-bag well stocked on his return, and Bony noticed he had kicked off his slippers.

"Thanks," he said. "I'll be seeing you again in a day or so."

"Getting on all right with the job?" Blaze asked, slipping on an old dungaree coat.

"It's coming to the boil."

"Good! The sooner it does, the sooner the old lady will sleep easy. You go outer the window first. I'll foller on."

On leaving the building, Bony proceeded parallel with the Folly for a hundred yards before turning down the slope to the water, Blaze recognising the objective of keeping windward of the dogs. The boat had been freed from its tree stump and drawn high up on the beach, and when sliding it down to the water, Blaze took command.

"Knowing the set of the tide, I'll take the bow oar. We gotta keep her off the causeway."

"But you're not coming?"

"Too right I am. Can't have this boat wrecked. Everyone'd know she couldn't have been washed off and wrecked. Work her round so's we can shove her in bow first. You be ready to get to that stern oar. Once she swings broadside to the waves she'll spin over and under like an alligator with a bullet in his belly."

Bony was drenched before he shipped his oar. Unseen giants pounded the craft, and it seemed that the boat had to take ten terrific waves to the yard.

"East!" snarled the cook. And "Give it to her!" came his order. Ghosts came and disappeared on either side. There was no sky, no earth, no sea, only the ghastly ghosts. And labour. Fortunately for Bony, he could manage an oar, knew when to feather it, when to dig deep, when to slip clear. All this he was doing for about a week when abruptly the ghosts vanished for good, the boat rode easily, and over his shoulder he caught sight of a tiny light seeming a hundred miles away.

With a hard jerk, the boat was stopped by the levee.

"Give us your rollock, and pass your oar," ordered the captain. "I'll have the wind astern going home. Anything you want done?"

"No. And thanks very much."

"Push her off."

At once the boat disappeared, and Bony strode over the levee and made for the light. The light became no larger, no brighter. It became the centre of an oblong frame, the window of the lounge at Venom House.

It was a tiny bedside lamp placed on a small table at the foot of a low bed. Dimly the shape of Mary Answerth was outlined by the bedclothes. At the head of the bed was a chair, but no attendant nurse. The door was half-open. There was no light in the hall beyond.

Having tested the window catch, he passed along the house front to the porch. The door was locked. Beyond the porch, the dining-room windows were fastened. Round the first corner, the library window was locked, and on looking up and thus placing the house top against the barely discernible sky, it was only by the expenditure of time and patience that he was assured Morris Answerth's lattice-guarded bedroom window wasn't wide open.

To miss obstructions at the rear of the house, he walked to the levee and followed that. There were lights in three of the rear rooms. In the first Mrs. Leeper sat writing at a table. The second was the kitchen and unoccupied. In the third room Janet Answerth played her piano, a shaded standard oil-lamp bringing to sharp relief the music sheet, the fluttering hands, the hair of gold. Her face he could not see.

Seated on the damp levee, he could observe all three rooms. The spray from the Folly fell upon his back, but failed to wet him more than he was already. The wind continued from the north and warmly. The night was filled with noise. The time . . . it was of no importance.

Janet ceased playing and closed the piano lid. Swinging round on the stool, she left it to pass to a small table, took a cigarette and lit it. She glanced once to the door, dropped the spent match to the ash-tray, and slowly came forward to stand at the window.

She could see nothing but the sheen of the lamplight on the glass. Slowly smoking, she remained there till it was necessary to return to the ash-tray with the butt. Having stubbed it without haste, she walked to the door, and vanished.

Mrs. Leeper, in her room, put down her pen and listened. Janet appeared in the kitchen, where she gathered a cup and saucer, a plate of biscuits, and two apples, which she peeled and quartered. Finally, spooning something from a tin into the cup, she added boiling water, and left the kitchen with her tray.

Mrs. Leeper rose from her table and, on her toes,

215

moved to the door, remaining there with the door ajar, listening. Then she opened the door and went out in the manner of a marionette.

Guessing Janet's destination, Bony hurried along the levee to gain position opposite that corner of the house enabling him to observe both living-room and bedroom occupied by Morris. He was in time to see a lamp being carried across the living-room and into the bedroom.

Janet stayed about an hour, and when the light was again crossing the living-room, Bony moved nearer the front entrance and watched the stained-glass window colour with light and gradually dim out as Janet left the hall.

The light in the lounge suddenly became stronger and Bony almost ran to the window. Carrying a hurricane lamp, Janet was standing at the foot of the bed. She was holding the lamp too low for the light to fall upon her sister's face. Mary was still asleep. From Mary, Janet turned to the table. Her elfin face was expressionless, and her pose became still. She could have been registering her sister's breathing. She did not notice the movement of the door. It was being slowly opened, and movement stopped when the opening was four or five inches.

Beside the little lamp on the table was a carafe of water, a roll of cotton wool, bandages, salve and smaller bottles containing tablets. For what appeared a long time, she remained still, merely looking downward upon these articles. She appeared unconscious of the lamp she held. The door closed a fraction.

Slowly her left hand went forward to take up one of the bottles of tablets, and she appeared to be counting them. From her, Bony's attention was distracted by movement on the bed. Mary was raising herself to see what Janet

216

was doing, and, from her expression, not without effort and pain.

Mary's face was almost as white as the bandage about her neck. Drawn on the square face, the mouth was a straight dark line, and the eyes were twin black discs. Janet could have been counting the tablets in the bottle, she could have been reading the directions on the label. Having satisfied herself, her hand slowly fell to replace the bottle, and, more quickly, Mary eased her head to the pillow.

On Janet beginning a turning movement to the door, the door closed. She crossed the room, passed out to the hall. The little lamp on the table betrayed no movement on the bed.

Returning swiftly to the rear of the house, Bony saw Mrs. Leeper again seated at the table and now reading a book. Carrying her lamp. Janet appeared in the kitchen, where she extinguished the lamp and made herself a hot drink. Eventually she left the kitchen and appeared in her sitting-room . . . when Mrs. Leeper was again listening at her door. Janet took up a book, extinguished the standard lamp. The room in darkness, she was no longer visible. The tense Mrs. Leeper remained at her door for another fifteen seconds, when she vanished into the passage.

It was clear that neither woman believed Mary's story of the man who invited her to talk outside the house. Neither Janet nor Mrs. Leeper evinced the slightest sign of being conscious of the unmasked windows, confident of the security given by the 'island', especially during such a night of wind and rough water.

It began to rain, but Bony ignored it. The wind died away to permit freedom to the many sounds of the Folly.

Not far from him, and inside the levee, gentle quacks told of wild ducks taking shelter.

He was decided that Janet must have gone upstairs to her bedroom without carrying a light and that Mrs. Leeper was so assuring herself, when aware of being cold and that the wind was coming from the south-west.

Mrs. Leeper appeared in the kitchen, where she heated milk, cut thin bread and butter, filled a hot-water bag. The remorseless Bony watched her rouse Mary Answerth, persuade the patient to drink and swallow the bread and butter, slip the water-bag under the blankets, give her tablets from one of the small bottles. They spoke, but he could not hear what was said. Mary was made comfortable for the night, and Mrs. Leeper attended to the little lamp and went out . . . leaving the long bell rope attached to the head of the bed.

Bony saw Mrs. Leeper wash the utensils in the kitchen, drink a cup of tea, put out the light and retire to a room beyond that where she had been sitting . . . and listening. When her light went out, he passed round the house to sit with his back against the wall under the lounge window.

He managed a cigarette without making light to be seen two yards away. Thereafter he stood keeping watch over the patient, the rain beating upon him, the wind mercifully gentle and causing a minimum of cold through his saturated clothes.

When the roosters crowed, he crawled under the tarpaulin covering the saw-bench, removed his clothes and burrowed deep into the sawdust.

Chapter Twenty-Three

SOWING SEEDS

BONY woke twice during the day, heard the wild south wind rampaging about the saw-bench and the wood-stack, and slept again. When he woke the third time, the wind was tired out, and the silence was returning like a jackal following departure of the lion.

The next hour he spent doing nothing save trying to recall the exact phraseology used by Disraeli on the subject of meditation. It went something like: "The art of meditation may be exercised at all hours; enabling one to retire amidst a crowd, be calm amidst distraction, be wise amidst folly." He was still not satisfied that he had it aright when he lifted the hem of the tarpaulin. It was quite dark, the rain had stopped, the stars remained dead, the water birds were happy, and all was well.

Dressing with care not to cut his throat by contact with the under part of the circular saw, he crawled out, and with the soundlessness of a raindrop sliding down a window gained the levee and the Folly, to scrub his teeth and wash. Back again under the tarpaulin, he combed his hair, felt his unshaven chin, and ate heartily. On setting out to earn his salary, none could say he was unpresentable.

The cook was in her kitchen, the mistress sat sewing in her sitting-room, the patient lay abed reading a farm journal, and, doubtless, the man of the house was playing his games in the dark. The front door was locked and all the ground-floor windows fastened. Only the open kitchen door offered a road in . . . but not to Bony.

He slipped the catch of the dining-room window and took that road. Memory, assisted by the tip of his wire 'sword', took him to the door without upsetting the furniture.

Because lock and handle might need oiling, the operation of opening the door occupied a full minute. Beyond was the hall, and directly opposite was the lounge door. The hall was unlit. The lounge door was wide open, and the lamp by which Mary Answerth was reading made of the doorway an oblong sheet of ancient copper. To the right, a darker oblong marked entry to the passage leading kitchenwards.

Bony flowed into the hall and up the grand staircase to the spanning gallery. There it was completely dark, for the comparative light without failed to penetrate the magnificently coloured window. The house was as completely silent as it was completely dark on this upper floor, and he drifted along the right passage until his cat's whisker stopped him at Morris Answerth's door. A finger-tip found the bolt home in the door frame, and the padlock to keep it there. The key hung from the wall nail.

Down upon the floor, he brought an ear to the inch-wide space between door and floor. The room beyond the door was also dark and silent until he detected what at first defeated him . . . Morris humming a tune. It was 'Three blind mice, See how they run. . . .' In accordance with the bee's position to the door, so did the sound wax and wane. Presently, the humming ceased, and the silence was next interrupted by a scratching noise, difficult to define.

Following the scratching, another long silence ended

by soft and rhythmic breathing. The breathing was close . . . very close to Bony. On the far side of the door, Morris was lying with an ear hard against the space at the bottom, and probably not more than four inches from Bony's ear. The situation amused Bony, but he feared to smile lest laughter betray him. With lips parted, he controlled his breathing, and was glad that the advantage was with him.

He was first there, and the light draught under the door was from Morris to him. He could smell the very faint aroma of the oil on Morris's head, and he hoped that no one below would open a window or a door and thus reverse the draught, when Morris might smell him.

Unaware if Time governed Janet's habits, with particular reference to her stepbrother, Bony had to accept the probability that at any moment she might ascend with Morris's supper tray and thus curtail the period required to move himself from the door. The door faced the passage to the gallery and the hall stairs: in the other direction the passage terminated at the top of the back stairs. That way offered strategic withdrawal.

To roll away from the door without so much as a bone creaking or a shoe scraping the floor occupied a full minute, but Bony was satisfied that what he could not himself hear would not reach Morris. Thereafter, to drift was easy.

He entered the room beyond the captive's bedroom, closed the door and dared to switch on his torch to pin-point stacked furniture and a way through it to reach the window. Pocketing the torch, he eased the catch, which had not been moved for years, and silently opened the window.

Having returned to the angle of the passage, he had to

wait a half-hour before the darkness towards the gallery was suddenly pierced by a mounting light. When Janet appeared with her tray, he retreated to the unused room.

Passing swiftly to the window, he leaned out as far as was possible, when he could just see the night-glint on the panes of the window next-door. That window was opened as far as the lattice permitted. Within that room, the bed softly creaked when taking Morris's weight. The seconds lagged before Janet's light coloured the window-panes. Then came Janet's voice, distant but clear.

"Asleep, dear?"

"No, Janet, not quite."

"Poor boy! I wasn't able to come up earlier, but I've been thinking of you. I've brought you a cup of cocoa and a few of your favourite biscuits. The fruit, remember, you must eat first thing in the morning before you get up. We must keep the body cleansed, you know, and the cheeks rosy."

"Thank you, Janet. What have you been doing this evening?"

"Oh, just working on my accounts. What with one thing and another, I'm very tired tonight."

"I am, too. I have been waiting for you," Morris said.

"So you really miss me. I cannot imagine what I'd do if I hadn't you to care for, Morris, if I didn't know you were always waiting for me. I'm so proud of you now you are growing up such a fine strong boy."

There was a pause during which Bony heard a cup being placed on its saucer. Then:

"Is Mary better?" Morris asked.

"A little better, I think. Soon she will want to come to see you. You will be good, won't you? You must always try not to lose your temper, because if you do, you might forget how strong you are, and how easily you could place one of your hands under her chin, and the other behind her shoulders, and then push up and back and snap her neck like a carrot. You will remember, won't you?"

"Yes, Janet, I'll remember."

The man's voice was almost toneless, and Bony marked it because the voice had been animated when directed to him. He wondered if this front to his sister had long been adopted to conceal from her his true personality, as he concealed from her so many other matters. She spoke again, and Bony would have given much to have observed her face.

"You must never forget, too, how I told you to behave when a stranger comes to the house. Doctor Lofty might come again tomorrow to see Mary, and he might want to come up to see you. We Answerths always mind our own business, as I've told you so often, and we never permit anyone else to know anything of it. Remember the story of the little boy who talked to the strange man and was taken to the forest and left alone to die there. You will remember, won't you?"

"Yes, Janet. I'll tell Doctor Lofty nothing at all. Do you really think Mary will soon be well enough to come up here?"

"Yes, dear."

"I'm sorry."

"Oh, Morris! Why?"

"I want a lamp," replied Morris.

"Please don't go over all that again, dear. You know quite well that Mary says you are not to have a lamp. She has said a thousand times that you might upset it and burn the house down."

There was a pregnant silence till Morris asked:

"If Mary had been killed, you would let me have a lamp, wouldn't you, Janet?"

"I would certainly think about it," cooed Janet.

"Would you give me a lamp like the one Bony gave me?"

Instantly the dove changed to a hawk.

"Bony gave you a lamp! Did you say that Bony gave you a lamp? Answer me."

"Yes. Please don't scold me, Janet. It was a beautiful lamp, but after I had played with it for a little while it wouldn't work. I took it to pieces to find out why it wouldn't go when I pressed the tiny knob, and I couldn't make it light again. Please, Janet! I don't like your face."

"Why did Bony give you the lamp?"

"Because . . ."

"Don't think, Morris. Why did he give you the lamp?"

Morris, however, had gained time to think. He replied:

"He wanted to know who killed Mother."

"Go on."

"I didn't know, Janet. I only asked him if he'd like to know. He said he would like to know who killed Mother, but I wouldn't tell him. I wouldn't tell him anything, Janet. Now, please take that look off your face, Janet. You know it frightens me. Please, Janet. Please."

The man's voice now contained more colour, more tone. Janet didn't speak, and Morris began to sob. After a little while, Janet said, soothingly:

"There, there, dear. It's all over now. I'm glad you didn't tell him about Mother. Now dry your eyes. What else did Bony ask you?"

"He asked me . . . if I could read. I said yes, I could. And Doctor Lofty asked if I could write and I said I could

224

just a little. I showed them the books, and my train and Meccano set."

"That was kind of you. What else did they ask you about?"

"Only about the lamp, Janet. You see, they brought a wonderful bright lamp with them, and they said it belonged to Mary. And when I asked if I might have it, they said no, as Mary would not like me to have her lamp. I think I was rude to them, Janet. I'm ever so sorry, truly. So I asked them to forgive me before they left, and Bony gave me his lamp."

"Bring me the lamp, dear."

Janet's voice was calm. Bony could not pass a fraction further out of the window without losing balance, and still was unable to see into the next room. He ached to observe Janet's face during the period when, he was sure, Morris was in the outer room. Then he heard Morris say:

"Here are all the pieces, Janet."

"Every one of them?"

"Yes."

"I'll take them away on the tray, and later I'll slip out and throw them into the Folly. They must never be seen by Mary, and you know what she would do if she found them. Don't you, Morris?"

"I . . ."

"You do know, but I'll tell you what she would do. When she found out why Bony gave you a lamp, you would have to tell her about asking him if he'd like to know who killed Mother, and she would go very red in the face and her eyes would have red fire in them, and she would make me whip you while she held you.

"So you mustn't tell her about it. Or say anything about Mother to anyone who may come to visit you. If

225

they find out who killed Mother, they'd take you away and lock you up in a bare room. Just a bare room, mind you, where there's nothing to play with, and where I wouldn't be allowed to see you. And they would stick red hot bodkins into you, until you screamed and screamed."

Bony could hear Morris sobbing.

"Now dry your tears, dear, and go to sleep. Lie down and I'll tuck you in. That's right, now. Just forget about the lamp. Mary will never know now. And as you are falling asleep keep on saying over and over: 'I must not tell about Mother, not to anyone.' Say it aloud to me."

Morris repeated the phrases.

"Now good night, dear. I'll always stand by you. But do remember how strong you are, and how easily you could kill Mary if you lost your temper. We would be so very happy without her, Morris, and if she died you might have a nice lamp like the one Bony gave you. But that won't be for a long time, because it wouldn't be right to kill Mary, bad as she is."

"Do you forgive me, Janet?"

"Yes, and here's my forgiving kiss. You did upset me, though, but never mind, I'll take an aspirin to cure my headache. You have said your prayers?"

"Yes. Good night, Janet."

Janet's voice came so softly that Bony barely detected the words: "Good night, dear boy. You must always love me like I love you. Sleep well."

"Sleep well, Janet, and good night."

The light waned from the diamond-shaped window-panes. Through that open window, Bony heard the door to the passage being closed, and, immediately after, the bed creaked violently as Morris sprang from it. There followed unbroken silence. Bony waited a full five minutes, expecting to see the steel lattice being pushed open, the blanket rope being let down to the ground. He waited another five minutes and then decided that Morris was lying on the floor at the foot of the outer door.

Chapter Twenty-Four

THE POT BOILS

BONY drifted down the stairs to the door at the bottom. The steps were of stone, and the door, like the front and all the room doors, had been made when craftsmen built real houses. It opened to the kitchen opposite the range.

So solid was the door and so close-fitting, the voices in the kitchen were reduced to a barely audible murmur. Bony felt for the key, a real gaoler's key he remembered seeing Mawson replace. It was not on the inside, and there wasn't a bolt, and as light failed to pass though the key-hole, he knew the key was in the outside of the lock. Since Mawson had replaced the key, someone had changed it.

He remembered, too, that the handle was of iron and not easy to turn. When he had tested it, the rusty catch squeaked like a mouse, and now when trying to peer through the key-hole he smelled oil.

Under slow and steady pressure, the door handle turned without making the mouse-squeak. And when there appeared before his eyes a perpendicular hair-line, he stopped moving the door, and listened.

". . . Miss Mary?"

"She was comfortable enough when I looked in after washing up the dinner things," replied Mrs. Leeper. "I left her with papers to read and the bell rope quite handy, and I'll be making her right for the night in a minute or two."

"How was her poor neck?" cooed Janet.

"She said it was no better for the asking, but I know it's better than it was this morning. In spite of what Dr. said, she'll be up and around by Sunday. That's if she doesn't catch the bed alight and burn herself to death."

"Oh!"

A dish clattered at the sink, and Mrs. Leeper said, conversationally:

"Don't let the idea burn holes in you, Miss Janet. They can tell by the ashes if kerosene caused the fire."

"That will be enough, Mrs. Leeper. Has Miss Mary said anything more about the attempt on her life?"

"No, but she's full of steam and says she will exact her own justice when she gets up. Just in case she has all her angles wrong, you lock your door. I'll be locking mine. And be sure not to walk in your sleep, for she might be doing that, too, and there's no knowing what might happen if two sleep-walkers met in a dark passage."

"I am so thankful you are in the house with me," Janet said, sweetly.

"I'm glad to hear it, Miss Janet."

"You will, I suppose, be thinking of leaving us when you've saved enough money to buy your own hospital?"

"Perhaps I won't be leaving. After all, experience is money, and I am certainly learning something at Venom House. Then there's Morris to look after if anything should happen to you and Miss Mary at the same time. You didn't forget to padlock his door?"

"I didn't forget, Mrs. Leeper. I'm going up now, and will read myself to sleep. Good night!"

Bony closed the door and retreated up the stairs. He sped along the passage to Morris's door, paused to touch the padlock and the key on its nail, and made for the hall. He was behind the dining-room door, when Janet passed up the stairs in the dark. He heard her bedroom door being closed and the key turned.

Why the hall lamp was never lit save when tragedy dictated, why there was rarely a lamp of any kind burning in the hall, he could not understand. The saving of kerosene was trifling: walking about in the dark so unnecessary. When Mrs. Leeper appeared, she carried a hurricane lamp.

Mrs. Leeper entered the lounge, leaving the door open, and he heard her say:

"Now, Miss Mary, it's time to go to sleep."

"Don't feel like sleeping," Mary objected. "Why the hell don't you leave a woman alone? I can put meself to bed without you mucking about."

"Now, do be original, Miss Mary. You're not telling me anything I don't know. Please let me have the papers, or you'll tear them. It has gone eleven, and all patients should be asleep. Also, I am entitled to a few hours in bed."

"To hell with you, Leeper, if that's your name. All right, take the blasted papers. I'm not swallowing any more of them tablets."

"Doctor says two at eleven p.m. Now I'll just straighten the clothes, and if you move your head a little I'll be able to freshen your pillows. That's right. How are your feet? Let me feel. Ah, warm enough."

Mrs. Leeper's voice was the voice Bony remembered

hearing on those occasions he had been in hospital. Only very small children or delirious patients were stupid enough to argue with it. Mary, probably being without hospital experience, continued to object.

"Of course me feet's warm. The bed's like a damned oven," she rasped.

"You won't do your throat any good by too much talking."

"I'll talk as much as I want."

"Lie still while I refix the bandage."

"Stinking stuff. If that jackass of a Lofty knew as much as a vet, he'd have ordered plain liniment."

"And taken all the skin off your neck."

"Not my skin it wouldn't. My skin's been brought up right by the sun and wind, not by the filthy muck you la-de-da women smear on your dials. Lipstick! Cream, and eye-wash and scented cow's milk . . . what for?"

"I don't use lipstick, and I'm not la-de-da, Miss Mary."

"Never said you was. I was meaning dear Janet."

"Well, you just mean to open your mouth and swallow these tablets."

"Ow! Blast you, Leeper. You're hurting me neck. Oh, give me the tablets."

"That's right, Miss Mary. Now I'll see to your lamp, and you will be asleep long before I can go to bed."

"That's what you think. Why don't you give Morris a fistful of tablets? What's Janet doing, the lying little bitch?"

"Reading herself to sleep . . . I hope."

"You let her read in bed, don't you? You don't say nothing to her, do you? The mealy-mouthed little . . . What you doing with that lamp?"

"Trimming the wick."

"I'll do a bit of trimming when I get up," swore Mary. "I'll show that Janet and you and young Morris who's the boss when I get outer this ruddy bed. I've had it, Leeper, see? I've more'n had it. Now get out, and don't nag me any more."

The voice said:

"Yes, yes, of course you will, Miss Mary. Now good night. Pull on the rope if you want anything. I'll hear the bell."

Emerging from the patient's room, Mrs. Leeper proceeded upstairs. Her slippered feet softly thudded along the passage beyond Janet's room, stopped at Morris's door, and returned. When her light retreated along the passage to the kitchen, the little lamp in the lounge painted a narrow oblong of colour upon the blank wall of the hall.

Bony could hear Mrs. Leeper washing utensils in the kitchen. He sat on a chair he had moved forward to the dining-room door, and from which he could watch the lounge door marked by the soft light of Mary's lamp and, too, the window of the dining-room, expectant that Morris might slide down his blanket rope and come testing all the ground-floor windows.

What had he said to Mawson? Proceed calmly, without haste, and Time will give you the murderer. Murder is the climax. After the climax, the murderer must behave abnormally. He cannot help it. If you are clever enough, he will give you the proof of his guilt on a silver salver.

The murderer of Mrs. Answerth was inside this house. The person who had killed Carlow, and had attempted to strangle Mary Answerth, was now within fifty yards of Detective-Inspector Napoleon Bonaparte. No matter when the murderer again tried to kill, Bony would be there right behind him. You don't go to your murderer: you whistle, and he comes to you. Provided you refuse to be rattled. Provided you have the gift of patience.

Bony heard a door close beyond the passage to the kitchen, and assumed that Mrs. Leeper had gone to bed. The clock on the dining-room mantel softly ticked away Time which he ignored. Not at once, but slowly, the house became itself, a personality freed now that the human beings had retired. And slowly the personality grew in power, slowly made itself felt by the alert Napoleon Bonaparte.

Men had placed stone upon stone, rafters upon walls, a roof upon the rafters. Their hands had worked with cunning while their minds were plotting evil. They planed and carved and polished that glorious staircase, and raised the great coloured window to enhance beauty. They loved beauty even when loving evil, and the evil of their thoughts sprang forth to leap into these inanimate stones and panels and beams, there to be imprisoned for ever. From the laying down of the foundations of this house, was ever a loving word spoken?

This house lived only in the dark. The light it feared. It was jealous even of the small light at the foot of Mary Answerth's bed, trying to smother it with its hatred. And succeeding!

A few seconds passed before Bony was sure that the light in the patient's room was going out for want of oil.

Had Mrs. Leeper intended the lamp to be short of oil?

Was Mrs. Leeper about to reveal abnormal activity?

Was Janet responsible?

Was the expected second attack on Mary's life about to be attempted?

The lamp was going out, slowly, inevitably. Motionless, Bony waited. Presently, there was a faint flicker upon the oblong surface of the opposite door, and the shape vanished.

Bony slid across the hall to stand beside the door of the lounge. His wire became a rapier feeling in the dark for a heart to pierce. Used like a sword to twang upon a skull, he could grapple with the murderer partially stunned and losing blood from a split scalp.

The seconds ran like endless mice across the hall. The procession was cut by the knife of sound coming from the lounge. The patient's bed faintly creaked, waited a moment to creak again. Had Morris gained entry through the window? Was he even now finalising the life of his half-sister?

Under normal circumstances the breathing of someone just within the lounge would not have been registered by ears trained to hear. The 'breather' could have been not more than a yard from Bony's back, when he slipped to one side of the open doorway. Without sound, the invisible 'breather' passed into the hall, and Bony's nostrils registered the smell of oil of wintergreen used as an ingredient in salves.

If Mary Answerth needed anything, she had but to tug the bell rope to rouse Mrs. Leeper.

The fact that the sleeping tablets, in which both Dr. Lofty and Mrs. Leeper had such faith, had had no effect on this patient was of less import at the moment than the fact that Mary Answerth had passed from the lounge into the hall without causing sound enough to be heard by Bony standing within two feet of her.

A noise did reach Bony from the passage to the kitchen, but this did not completely satisfy him that Mary

Answerth was the cause. Down that passage to the right slept Mrs. Leeper. Down that passage was the kitchen, and from the kitchen rose the stone stairs to the upper floor where Morris and Janet slept. Bony felt like the man in the haunted house listening to the clock striking the awful hour of midnight. He had whistled for the murderer and the murderer. . . .

It could have been caused by a mouse, but wasn't. The sound was like suds exploding against the ear, and yet with rhythm. It was produced by cloth moving over polished wood. It came from near the front door. Instinct warned him that someone was approaching and he moved away from the lounge door, his back against the wall.

The perfume of flowers came through the darkness to touch his nostrils, as once it had done in the radiance of the lamp suspended over the golden staircase. As certainly as though he saw her, he knew that Janet Answerth had passed by to enter the lounge. Exultation carried him, filled him with ecstatic expectancy.

No light was born within the lounge. No sound issued from the room. Bony neared the door frame, leaned sideways that his ear might protrude beyond it. The melodrama and its possibilities forced him to bunch his toes within the canvas shoes.

Had Mary set out to attack Janet, and had Janet set out to counter-attack? That would mean wits pitted in battle fought out in the dark. And what a battle! Hate fears not the dark, for itself is of the darkness.

The lust to kill can easily subjugate fear, can proceed to satiation without regard for personal safety. If these two women should realise that each was stalked by the other, the resultant encounter would be of supreme interest to the psychologist. Physical strength to the one, craftiness to the other . . . the trident and net against the sword and armour.

If people wishing to be evasive would but keep their mouths open! He heard Janet's breathing as she approached the door. He drew away. Again he smelled flowers. He waited for the perfume to vanish. It remained. Janet was standing either in the doorway, or, like himself, against the wall. The perfume in her own nostrils would prevent her smelling him. Had he counted seconds, he would have reached fifty-seven when the perfume waned, vanished. Janet had gone.

Thinking thus, Bony should have been greatly concerned with the prevention of murder, but a child could be expected more readily to leave a Punch and Judy show midway than he to strike matches and light the hall lamp, or flash on his torch. Janet had gone from his side, but where, he could not detect. He was sure she had not gone up the stairs, else she would have collided with someone descending them.

Like her sister, Janet was good at this game in the dark. The person coming down to the hall had had far less practice of moving about a silent house silently, but was trying hard to learn. The hand upon the banister was sliding along the wood . . . the act of an amateur.

A rustling sound came from the direction of the stair-foot, and then to Bony's nostrils came the first hint of carbolic. The smell grew stronger, waned, and the last he heard of Mrs. Leeper was when she misjudged the entrance to the passage leading kitchenward.

Of the three women, Janet was the most adept, having made the fewest mistakes.

For something like a quarter-hour no sound reached his ears, no smell reached his nostrils. At the end of that period he was unaware of the tension in himself, unaware that the rough U handle of the wire sword was raising a welt on the palm of the hand clenching it, and the bunched toes were locked so long that they were to give pain like the sting of ants. As with the wild man in the chase, physical feeling was suspended.

Morris! He had forgotten Morris, who without doubt could play this game in the dark so well as to make his sisters appear ridiculous. If Morris joined in this present game, if he were released to join it, and should meet with Mary, well . . .

Bony drifted to the front door. With care he removed the key, that no one would unlock it to admit Morris. He floated into the dining-room and refastened the window by which he himself had entered the house. He drifted up the stairs, prepared to meet the perfume of flowers, of oil of wintergreen, of carbolic, meet one of those impalpable substances emanating from the person of a woman. And meeting it, receive a split second to evade physical collision.

At the top of the stairs he paused with his hand upon the railing of the gallery. Whilst there, he heard as distinctly as the cat hears the mouse behind the wainscot a door being closed in that wing where Mary's bedroom was situated. He passed on in the opposite direction, came to Janet's bedroom door, and with his free hand found the door shut.

He went on. His cat's whisker entered the shallow recess at the passage angle where, like that other recess at the far end of the opposite passage, brooms were kept. The whisker passed by the recess and so came to meet Morris's door. He moved left and reached with his other hand for the key on the nail. It found the nail. The key was gone. It flashed downward to touch the bolt, the padlock. The padlock was loose, the key in it. The bolt was drawn. The door was ajar.

Chapter Twenty-Five

THE ANSWERTHS AT LARGE

BONY refastened Morris's door and pocketed the key. If Morris hadn't found his door unbolted, so much the better. Who had unbolted his door was of less import now than the probability that he was a participant in a game which Bony hoped he might finalise before it ended in tragedy.

The obvious course was to make himself known, light a lamp or two, bring the inmates together and prod them to explain their antics. However, invest the Law with personality and you find . . . the insane. Prod these people to produce explanation, and where would that lead him, and what would it achieve?"

Precisely nothing and nowhere. These people would offer a very good reason for being outside their rooms in the dead of night. They would say they were awakened by an intruder whom they sought to hold until the police arrived. And the only person illegally engaged in this game in the dark was Inspector Napoleon Bonaparte.

As the Chief Commissioner delighted to inform him, he wasn't a real policeman's bootlace, and the association of the Colonel's face, when animated by blood-pressure, with a bootlace in a constable's boot somehow produced miles of red tape wrapped about a volume of 'Powers, Duties and Prerogatives of the Police Officer'. Not included among these 'Powers, etc.' was entering private premises without authority in the form of a warrant. Even he, who thumbed his nose at 'Powers, etc.' wouldn't get away with this entrance to private premises. It was open defiance of Magna Carta, or the Constitution or Something, at which to thumb one's nose is unpardonable.

One event only would excuse him. The event hadn't happened . . . yet. If it did not occur, he must leave as he had entered, unseen.

He failed to hear Janet, or detect her approach until her perfume met his nose. She wasn't loitering this time, and she envinced no interest in Morris's door. Only when she rounded the right-angle of the passage did he hear her breathing. It was a trifle fast. She managed her bed-room door very well . . . for a white woman . . . betraying herself only by making a sound when turning the key with unsteady pressure.

The key would be on the inside. It was a pity, Bony decided, otherwise he could have locked her in.

Without doubt Morris was the expert. With intelligence, he would have been a worthy competitor with Bony to reach perfection in the art of scouting. He omitted an important point. Had he rolled himself in the mustiness of those abandoned rooms ruled by spiders . . . after washing his hair with scentless soap . . . he might have passed Bony undetected. His hair oil was a torch for Bony to see him for five seconds.

Janet had been in a hurry to reach her room. Was her haste occasioned by the stalking Morris?

Bony was still unsure of the answer when he smelled

Janet. She was standing before Morris's door, and within reach of his free hand, and tiny sounds told him she was touch-examining the bolt and padlock. She remained there for a full minute, and he felt relief when she departed towards the back stairs.

He decided to remain pressed within the shallow recess, for he was as well here as anywhere. Unlike those others, he had no immediate objective. His rôle was a waiting one. He contemplated leaving the house and pounding on the front door, demanding admittance to interview one or the other on the pretext of official necessity. That course might prevent tragedy this night, but it would not advance his investigation or prevent tragedy in the future. Confusion of purpose was due to the unusual behaviour of Mary Answerth.

Right now she should have been in bed and asleep, her light on guard, and Inspector Bonaparte keeping both eyes on her door. Instead, she was sweeping past him on the smell of wintergreen.

Some time afterwards, sound erupted to fill every corner of the mansion. It seemed to come from the back of the house, and it began with the beating of two trays against plate glass, dwindling to the rising crescendo of bass drums, and ending by each of a thousand devils tearing a sheet of canvas. Because of the unexpectedness of it all, the shriek of someone being killed would have been a lullaby. Silence squatted again.

Bony could hear the heart of silence throbbing like a distant tom-tom. The beat changed in tempo, but not in volume. It came from a human throat. Close to him, Morris Answerth was striving to control his laughter. From which point he had come and to which point he departed, Bony was uncertain.

For some time after that, none of the players came his way and he heard not a sound until a voice said:

"Got-cher!"

At last the event . . . perhaps. Stone walls distort sound. He could not tell whose voice it was or be sure that the second word was 'cher'. If the back-stairs' door was open, the speaker could be in the kitchen. The other point was the hall, and the hall was nearer.

Moving from the staircase, Bony gained the dining-room doorway, leaned against it and waited. He had been there for perhaps three minutes, when the lounge door was gently closed.

He assumed that Mary Answerth had retired from the game.

Feet softly padded along the passage upstairs. They came padding down the stairs. They padded across the hall to the front door. The handle was turned without attempt to stifle the sound. The feet re-crossed the hall, padded up the stairs. There was haste in the sound. It was like a rat realising it was trapped and frantically seeking escape. Bony heard the padlock to Morris's door-bolt being handled.

Bony followed, and at the gallery he paused to listen and could hear nothing. The point of the wire sword prodded the yielding void before his face, seeking obstruction. He advanced along the passage, passed Janet's room, was halted by the clink of metal. Yet again the perfume of hair oil met his nostrils, and he was aware it was not advancing to him but he to it. He continued to advance till the tip of his cat's whisker contacted some part of Morris's body.

"No! I'm sorry. I want to go in. I . . ."

"Stand aside, Morris, and I will open the door."

"I'm frightened. I want to go in."

Bony was gripped by his left arm, and the pressure was painful. He managed to free the padlock and open the door. "Go in now," he said, and with a stifled whimper Morris scurried back to his prison.

There remained at large Janet Answerth and Mrs. Leeper.

Traversing the passage to the back stairs, he floated down the inclined stone tunnel to the heavy door at the bottom. Soundlessly he entered the kitchen, and instantly was assailed by a perfume different from those others. A tiny particle of ice struck between his shoulders. Magically it grew in size, spreading up the back of his neck, spreading outward to cover his scalp.

The strange odour was registered by instinct rather than by the senses which recognised the perfume of flowers. During seconds, Bony was stripped of the veneer laid upon the white man by education, training, experience. During those seconds he was elemental, completely subjugated by fear of the dreaded Kurdaitcha: the Thing Who walked the earth and left no tracks because It soaked Its feet in the blood of men and to the blood glued the feathers of eagles: the Thing having something like the face of a man, the teeth of a dingo, and the nose of a mopoke: the Thing from which there is no escape for the aborigine It catches away from his camp at night.

The sweat dripped from Bony's face.

Then prevailed the pride of Detective-Inspector Napoleon Bonaparte, who prospected for the body and with his wire whisker found it on the hearth hard against the stove.

The night beyond the window failed to provide the merest glimmer to illumine the scene. Slowly Bony's knees bent to permit his erect body to sink while his eyes continued to probe and his ears to strive with the silence. His right hand touched cloth, discovered the outlines of a female body. The fingers found the face and explored the features. His arm slid under the body, and the wire sword was discarded that the left hand could hold the woman's head. That Janet Answerth's neck was broken could not be doubted.

Mrs. Leeper was the last at large . . . unless Mary Answerth had once again left her room.

With unabated stealth and cautiousness, Bony left the kitchen. At the closed lounge door he listened with an ear to the key-hole. He heard nothing. Within was no light. Entering, he listened. Slowly he crossed to the bed.

Bending over the foot of the bed, at last he caught the sound of soft but regular breathing, and as now the event had happened to release him from questions concerning his presence inside Venom House, he switched on his torch, aiming the beam at the floor.

The woman on the bed didn't stir. The reflection of the light revealed the outline of her massive form. The position of her arms caused the light beam to slant upward to the ceiling, when the reflection became stronger. Mary Answerth was lying on her back. Either she was asleep or unconscious. Each wrist was lashed to a bedpost, and the divergent range of bedclothes ended at each of the foot posts. Her feet were likewise bound.

Pocketing the torch, and aided by his wire whisker, Bony went hunting for Mrs. Leeper. Again in the hall, he could hear nothing of her. She was not in Janet's studio or sitting-room. She was not in the kitchen, nor in her own sitting-room. He came upon her in Janet's bedroom, and from the doorway directed his light to encircle her.

She was on her knees before a chest of drawers. About her was a great litter of clothes and oddments. She spun round to face the shattering light beam, and always politely formal in dramatic situations, Bony enquired:

"For what, Mrs. Leeper, are you searching?"

Astonishingly agile, she sprang to her feet. Her white face expressed incredible relief, but her voice was shrill with hysteria.

"Inspector Bonaparte! They've hidden all the matches, and I can't find what they've done with them."

Chapter Twenty-Six

MORRIS WON'T TELL

BONY touched a lighted match to the wick of the lamp on the bedside table. Replacing the glass, he stepped away.

"I can't say how glad I am you're here," Mrs. Leeper said, obviously recovering from the shock produced by his advent.

"Indeed! Why?"

"There's been fine goings-on in this house tonight. They hid all the matches, and foxed me in the dark while I hunted high and low for one to make a light with. And Mary . . ."

"We will discuss it in the hall, Mrs. Leeper. Take the lamp and lead the way."

Her gaze held to the wire cat's whisker, rose to meet his steady eyes. He looked very tall, and extremely sinister, and she almost snatched the lamp and hurried from the room. Arrived at the hall, he said:

"Light the large lamp, please."

She brought a tall stool to stand upon, and he turned the handle of the old-fashioned wall telephone and raised the Edison Exchange. She heard him ask the operator to call Constable Mawson, and he waited while she lit the suspended lamp and returned the stool to its place under the stairs. Then he motioned her to sit down, and she heard him ask Mawson to come at once and bring Dr. Lofty with him. That done, he sat opposite her.

"Now, Mrs. Leeper, let us try to fit this story together. Did you go to bed after you retired to your room?"

"I did, Inspector. I blew out my lamp and went to sleep. What woke me, I don't know. Something did, and I thought I heard a strange noise in the kitchen. I wasn't afraid of burglars. The people here have been up to tricks before now, and, what with one thing and another, I sat up feeling more than suspicious. And anxious about my patient.

"I remembered that before blowing out my lamp I had no matches on the bedside table, but I didn't trouble because I had my flashlight. I found the flashlight in the dark, but it wouldn't work, and when I opened it I discovered that the battery had gone.

"Then I was sure someone was up to tricks. In the dark I went along to the kitchen, and rummaged in the cupboard where I always kept several packets of matches. They were all gone. There was always a box or two on the mantel, but there weren't any then. As I'd left the lamp alight in Miss Mary's room, I took my lamp there. But

244

her lamp was out, and that made me uneasy. You see, she and Miss Janet hated one another, and I thought . . . I didn't know what to think.

"Anyway, I knew there was a box of matches on her mantel. I went in and felt my way to the mantel, and the matches weren't there. Then I realised I couldn't hear Miss Mary, and I felt for her and found she'd gone. I was scared then, and sat on the bed and wondered what I'd do.

"Instead of swallowing the tablets Doctor ordered, she must have spat them out when my back was turned. That meant she was up to no good, and whatever it was took her from her bed must have been driving her, because she was in pain when I attended to her last thing."

"You didn't call for Miss Mary?" Mrs. Leeper shook her head with returning confidence. "Why not?"

"You never let that kind think they've beaten you. You go after them, just to prove to them they're not as cunning as they think. Once you let them think you are frightened of them, you might as well give up. I wasn't really frightened tonight until I found Morris's door unbolted and the door ajar. Then I was. But I had to go hunting for a match. I went into Miss Janet's bedroom, and into Miss Mary's bedroom, and everywhere I thought I might find a box. They'd taken every one."

"It wasn't long before I knew that the three of them were playing with me. If I went to my room and locked myself in, they'd probably end up by murdering each other. If I kept on, one might murder me. But I've learned how to take care of myself.

"I did, too, when Mary collided with me in the hall. At first I didn't know which one it was. And I didn't pause in finding out. Anyway it was Mary, and I had her rocking in a second, and I kept the pressure on her while

I carried her back to bed and lashed her to it like a starfish."

"You carried her! A woman of her weight!"

"Oh yes, Inspector, it's easy when you know how."

"Did you cause all that crashing noise?"

"No."

"Did you collide with Miss Janet?"

"No. Otherwise I'd have spread-eagled her on her bed, too. Then I found that Morris's door had been bolted and locked, and I felt easier. I thought that it must have been Miss Janet who had taken all the matches, and probably hid them in her room, so I went there again, and then you found me. And I'm telling you, Inspector, I was very, very glad. After tonight, I'm finished with the place. They got me to be Morris's guardian if anything happened to them, told me I'd be well off for the rest of my life while I looked after him. But I'm not waiting for that."

"H'm! We'll look in on Miss Mary. You take the lamp."

Mary Answerth was very much awake. Her dark eyes glared at them, and either she fought to find words or waited for one of them to speak. At the foot of the bed, Bony removed the lamp glass. The wick was turned too low to take the flame from his match. The oil reservoir was more than half full.

"Release Miss Answerth," he said.

"What in hell are you doing here?" Mary asked, icily furious.

"To ask you a few questions, Miss Answerth."

Mrs. Leeper first freed the woman's feet. When she came to her hands, she looked at Bony, and he nodded. Freed, Mary, with genuine difficulty, sat up, and swung her legs from under the clothes. Her face was distorted with anger.

"Get out of my room, you. Go on, get out before I heave you through the window."

She stood, and Bony drew forward a lounge chair.

"Please be seated. I have questions to ask concerning the murder of your sister."

Mrs. Leeper didn't move. Mary advanced to stare malevolently at Bony. Almost carelessly he indicated the chair. Then she sat, and said:

"You're the first man who hasn't feared me. What's this about Janet being murdered? Seems too good to be true. I hope it is."

"Why did you leave your room and go upstairs in the dark?"

"Because, early in the evening, Janet had come here and done her smoodging about my neck, and she thought I didn't see her take the matches from the mantel. The way she done it told me she was up to her schemes. And I went upstairs to find out if she'd let Morris loose, and she had."

"What did you do then, Miss Answerth?"

"Went in and found he wasn't in bed. I went down the back stairs lookin' for him. I went up to Janet's room, and she wasn't in bed. I went lookin' for her. Good job I didn't lay me hands on Janet. I might have squeezed the life out of her if I had. I met up with Leeper instead, and she wouldn't fight fair, not her. Still, I can wait, Leeper."

"Did you make that startling clatter?"

The anger vanished. Mary Answerth chuckled.

"I fell into a booby trap," she admitted. "Outside Janet's sitting-room door. I'll forgive Morris if he rigged

247

it up. It was a beaut." The chuckle ended, the look of anger returned. That gave place to conquering weariness. "I think I'll lie down again. You've bent me neck or something, Leeper. But just you wait."

She refused assistance to rise from the chair, but the hospital training lost none of its power on Mrs. Leeper. She had the bedclothes straightened, and insisted on helping the patient into bed. Mary said, pointedly:

"To hell with the pair of you."

"Of course, Miss Mary," agreed Mrs. Leeper, and Bony left the Voice in charge.

Later, he opened the front door to Mawson and Lofty and Blaze. They arrived with the dawn. He told them where the body lay and issued particular instructions. Blaze he asked to remain in the hall and prevent Mrs. Leeper from going to the kitchen. Taking a lamp, he went up to Morris.

"Hullo, Morris, not in bed?" he asked, placing the lamp beside the toy engine.

The bearded man blinked at the light. He forced his eyes to accept it before turning to Bony.

"I was frightened. I found Janet. She was all quiet. Her head wouldn't stay right."

"I know, Morris."

"Is she dead, Bony?"

"'Fraid so. Who unbolted your door tonight?"

The blue eyes pleaded. One large hand stroked the yellow beard.

"I mustn't tell."

"Then I'll tell you. It was Janet."

"Yes. She told me she wanted me to go with her over the causeway."

"Why?"

"To run away from Mary. Mary was going to beat me because you gave me the lamp. She said Mary was coming up to beat me, and she said if she tried to I must break her neck like a carrot. We went to the passage and Janet ran away."

"What did you do then?" asked Bony.

"I tried to find her, and I made the booby trap for her by balancing a set of trays on top of a door I left open. Did you hear it? Wasn't it a lovely crash? I don't know who set it off. Mary could have, you know. Mary didn't find me. You will tell her not to come and beat me, won't you?"

"She will never do that, Morris. I'll not let her. When you went out that night with Janet, and went over the causeway, and met that man Janet knew, what happened?"

"I . . . I mustn't tell."

"Then I'll tell you. You beat him hard. And then you carried him into the water and held him down under it. Janet was with you all the time, and she told you what to do."

"Yes, Bony, she told me what to do."

"And when you came back to the house, your mother saw you and Janet. And Janet wouldn't let her speak to you. But your mother did speak to you, didn't she? She went round to your window to speak to you. And she asked you what you did when you went out that night with Janet, and you told her."

"Yes, Bony."

"Of course you did. Anyway, it doesn't matter now. I know everything."

"Are you pleased, Bony?"

"Yes. I am pleased you didn't have to break any promises."

"So am I. Janet always tells me I must never break a promise. Do you think now she is dead I might have another lamp like the one you gave me?"

"Yes, I think so. Do you remember that night you climbed out from your window after you and your mother had been talking, and you saw Janet lasso your mother?"

"Yes. But she didn't see me."

"What did you do?"

Morris chuckled.

"Janet didn't know about me climbing down from the window," he said. "I told her I saw her kill Mother and drag her away to the Folly, told her I saw her from that window." Morris pointed to the window from which he fished . . . the window but one from the porch.

"Weren't you sorry, Morris?"

"Oh yes. I told Janet she shouldn't have done it, but Janet said Mother had made up her mind to have me taken away to the place where they stick red-hot bodkins into people." He abruptly grasped Bony's arm. "You won't let them do that to me, will you? Now that Janet is dead?"

Bony placed his hand over the other gripping his arm.

"No, Morris," he said. "I'll never let anyone do that to you. Now I must go away, but I will come to see you again. By the way, did Janet play lassoes with you?"

"Oh yes, Bony."

"H'm! Well, I really must go now, Morris. I'll give you my other lamp to play with."

"Oh! Oh, thank you ever so much, Bony."

The new day reduced the power of Bony's spare torch, but not the joy in the heart of Morris Answerth.

Chapter Twenty-Seven

AN OLD HABIT

BLAZE was still in the hall when Bony descended. He was dressed in his working clothes, and to look at him was to think it mid-summer. His old face was like a long-stored apple, but his brown eyes were keen and anxious.

"End of the track, Inspector?" he asked.

"Yes, the end of the track," agreed Bony. "You know, in the days to come I'd like to think of you being in charge of this place, and keeping a general eye on Morris Answerth. I would like to see him playing with dogs, or a lamb or two, out in the sunshine. If you would stay on here, I would work to that objective."

"Suits me," Blaze said, quietly adding: "It's the sort of picture Mrs. Answerth would like to see, too."

Bony nodded, and turned to Mawson and the doctor, who appeared from the kitchen passage.

"You were correct, Inspector, about the odour," Dr. Lofty told him. "Neck broken. Almost shaken off the trunk. We transferred the body to an empty room."

"Then, you permitting, we will accompany you on your visit to Miss Answerth. There are a few points to be cleared up. Won't take long."

Mawson and Blaze stopped just inside the lounge doorway. The doctor went to his patient, and Bony stood in the background.

"Well, Miss Mary! How are you this morning?" asked the doctor brightly. The dark eyes blinked, and the daylight left much to be desired by the waiting Bonaparte.

"Not as good as I'm going to be, Lofty," replied the patient. "And I'm not paying for this visit, 'cos you didn't come to Venom House just to see me. That right Janet's dead?"

"It's true enough, Miss Answerth. That she was murdered cannot be denied. H'm! Didn't sleep well. Increase the tablets, Mrs. Leeper."

"Better leave a pot-full for Morris, Lofty. Having killed Janet, he'll want calming down for a day or two. Anyway, now that little bitch is dead, we'll have peace in this house at last, and me and Mrs. Leeper can look after him properly."

The doctor was drawn aside to permit Bony to sit at the foot of the bed.

"I am compelled, Miss Answerth, to charge you with the murder of your sister, and to warn you that anything you say may be taken down by Constable Mawson and used in evidence against you."

The woman attempted to sit up, groaned and pressed her hands to her neck.

"Is that so?" she sneered. "Well, I'm tellin' you I didn't kill Janet. And I'm tellin' you I would have made her sick for a month or more if I had met her in the dark like I met Leeper. Morris fixed her, because Janet let him out to murder me. You bring him down here, and I'll make him admit it."

"Perhaps you can explain . . ."

"I'm explainin' nothing, Inspector. Exceptin' that I know Janet had murder in her heart. I knew it when she came in here after I'd had me dinner, and she sneaked the box of matches from the mantel, took it while she soft-soaped me about me neck. It was her who tried to strangle me. She guessed that I knew it was her. So when she took the matches I knew she'd come back when I was asleep and bring Morris down to do her murder for her. You can't touch Morris, him being what he is, and Janet knew that."

"So you turned out your lamp as though it starved for oil, and waited in the dark?"

"Yes. Until I lost me patience and went upstairs to satisfy meself about Janet's little plan. Morris was out all right. So was Janet. Her bed was empty."

"And then you came back here and waited?"

"You know damn well I didn't. You know I met Leeper and she put one of her holts on me and I passed out. You know quite well that you and her came in and she undid me feet and wrists."

"H'm!" soothed Bony. "Let us try to make all clear. You won't mind?"

"Not from you, I'm beginning to like you."

Bony almost stood up to bow acknowledgment of the compliment.

"I'll begin from the beginning, Miss Answerth," he said. "From that moment when, in your wool shed, you worked it out that you had been robbed of wool equal to two bales."

"Ah!" Mary said. "Old Harston been tellin' you my business, eh?"

"Me and the Inspector worked it all out before we seen your figuring on the shed wall," interrupted Blaze, and the flashing eyes glared past Bony at the little cook.

"Having worked out the approximate amount of wool stolen," Bony proceeded, "you reached the natural conclusion that the presser, with perhaps an accomplice, engineered the theft. You tackled the presser about it,

253

and from him learned that Carlow, the butcher, received the wool and was to pay the thief, or thieves, half the proceeds.

"Instead of reporting this matter to Constable Mawson, you saw the handle you could turn to spite your sister. You were aware that Miss Janet devoted time and money to good works. You were aware that Miss Janet had greatly assisted Edward Carlow and his mother and brother, after you had compelled them to vacate the farm. And, Miss Answerth, you were aware that Miss Janet wanted Edward Carlow.

"The man for whom she cared, the man for whom she had done so much, robbed her . . . and you. And you twisted the handle of the dagger in her heart. You scoffed at her, and sneered, and when Carlow was found forcibly drowned, you knew who did it."

"You're not tellin' me that little doll Janet drowned a big hefty man like Carlow," objected Mary.

"Oh no. I am telling you, Miss Answerth, that your sister took your stepbrother over the causeway to meet Carlow, with whom she had arranged a meeting. As she was physically incapable of murdering Carlow, so was Morris mentally incapable of trying to make the crime look like accidental drowning. He had to be directed. Don't you agree?"

"Go on with your yarns, Inspector. You tell 'em good."

"When Janet and Morris returned over the causeway, they were met by Mrs. Answerth. Doubtless, Janet offered an explanation, but she knew, when the body was found by Blaze, that Mrs. Answerth was bound to connect Morris and herself with the tragedy. Till then, she had been putting her foot down against visits to Morris by his mother. From then on, she stopped the visits altogether.

"Your sister was unaware that Mrs. Answerth stole out at night to talk with Morris; as you were unaware that Morris sometimes slid down from his window to enjoy the night air. Miss Janet knew nothing of it till she heard you scolding Mrs. Answerth for being out of the house for the purpose of talking to Morris. All her care to prevent mother and son meeting after the murder of Carlow was for nothing. She went to Morris, and he confessed to her he had told everything to his mother.

"Your sister persuaded Mrs. Answerth to go outside with her later that night, and she strangled the old lady and dragged the body part-way over the causeway, that it might appear that Mrs. Answerth had slipped into deep water. Again, Morris was incapable of understanding the processes of putrefaction, which Janet anticipated would conceal at least the outward signs of strangulation.

"That you guessed she killed your stepmother, I have no exact proof, Miss Answerth. Or if you taunted her with that crime. I think that you did, which is why she attempted to kill you. It's a link in the chain. She was passionately fond of Morris, and her egotism demanded his complete subjugation to her will. She used him to kill Carlow, and she killed Carlow not only because he robbed her. The greater hurt was to her pride made to suffer by the realisation that Carlow had used her affection for him to further his ambitions.

"When your sister nearly succeeded in killing you, you decided to kill her and subsequently throw suspicion on Morris, because Morris could be led to confess to the killing of Carlow. Morris of the undeveloped mind was easy.

"It was Janet who aroused you the night before last by tapping on the outside of your window with a wall

broom manœuvred from the next window. It was
Morris you saw when you looked out, not an unknown
man wishing to talk about stolen cattle. That was your
story. You went down to investigate how and why Morris
was between the porch and his corner of the house.

"When you unlocked the front door, Morris was
stepping up to the porch. Hearing the door unlocked, he
stepped backward off the porch, continued to walk
backward for a dozen or so paces. He saw you come out,
and he saw Janet make the attempt to kill you. For
Janet, having roused you, followed you down the stairs,
was right behind you when you went out to the porch,
was standing on the step when you were off it, and thus
had the advantage of elevation to toss the noose over your
head. You were just in time to get your hand under the
noose, and Janet knew she was then physically incapable
of completing her design.

"As you have told others, so then did you decide you
would exact your own justice in your own time. Janet
suspected you knew it was she who had tried to kill you,
for she did not know Morris was able to climb down from
his window, and thus must have thought him in bed.

"Her only real chance to beat you, Miss Answerth, was
before you were well again. When she took your matches
you suspected she would hide all the matches in the house,
and you decided she would make the attempt again last
night. You turned down your lamp to pretend it needed
oil, in order to leave your room in the dark and go
hunting for Janet in the dark. You caught Janet in the
kitchen, and you snapped her neck like a carrot."

"You don't say?" sneered Mary. "I've heard that
expression before . . . from Morris . . . about snapping
necks like carrots. If I'd got me two hands on Janet last

night, I would have given her plenty to keep her in hospital for six months. I say I didn't break her neck like a carrot."

"And we say that you did. Would you like to know how we know that you killed your sister?"

"Not particularly," replied Mary, closing her eyes as though overwhelmed by weariness. "I'll tell you something for a change. For years I've been fed to the back teeth by the lunatics surrounding me . . . a mealy-mouthed lisping slut and a strong man who couldn't grow up. You mentioned good works. All she wanted was to be Lady Bountiful. Why, every time I went to Edison, people laughed at me behind me back. And me the only sane member of the lot of us Answerths, me who's worked like a slave saving this place from ruination, holding on to what great-grandfather thieved off the blacks and grandfather built up in his day.

"Yes, I know, Inspector. I know all of it. And when these lunatics started to murder each other, I said to meself, Mary, that's the way it's going to go. I never killed Janet, and you can't ever prove I did. With her out of the way, I'll make Venom House so's it stands for a thousand years. Now you can all get out and leave me in peace."

"Regretfully, Miss Answerth, we cannot leave you in peace," Bony said. "Having been charged with the murder of your sister, you will be conveyed to the lock-up at Edison as soon as Dr. Lofty gives permission. You will be away from Venom House for perhaps a long time, and meanwhile please think of Morris. I suggest that Mrs. Leeper could become his guardian now, and that Blaze could be promoted to manage the entire property."

Mary opened her eyes. She looked steadily at Bony.

"Tell me how you come to think I killed Janet," she said.

"You left your brand on her body, Miss Answerth."

"Left me brand on the little bitch. I wish I had."

"When you killed her, Miss Answerth, the odour of the salve applied to your neck and back was on your hands. The odour of oil of wintergreen is quite unmistakable. After Mrs. Leeper left you last night, she washed her hands in the kitchen. I heard her. About the shoulders and the head of your sister's body is the odour of wintergreen."

The tension waned. Mary said:

"That's a good idea about Morris being looked after by Mrs. Leeper, and the place being managed by Blaze."

It could be then that she understood the mind of this man who had proffered the 'good idea' and, understanding, was able to thrust aside the life-long aggressiveness to reveal the woman she might have been: the woman she might have been had not the aborigines pointed the bone at her forebears, cursing them and their children's children, slamming shut all avenues of escape for any Answerth down to the fourth generation.

She nodded as though agreeing with what she saw in Bony's mind, recognising and accepting the inevitable. It could have been to all those long-dead aborigines, as well as to Bony, that she admitted:

"You win."

"But without pleasure, Miss Answerth," Bony said. "I have won so often that I am not gratified by what has become a habit."